PLUM PUDDING
MURDER

Books by Joanne Fluke

CHOCOLATE CHIP COOKIE MURDER

STRAWBERRY SHORTCAKE MURDER

BLUEBERRY MUFFIN MURDER

LEMON MERINGUE PIE MURDER

FUDGE CUPCAKE MURDER

SUGAR COOKIE MURDER

PEACH COBBLER MURDER

CHERRY CHEESECAKE MURDER

KEY LIME PIE MURDER

CARROT CAKE MURDER

CREAM PUFF MURDER

PLUM PUDDING MURDER

Published by Kensington Publishing Corporation

PLUM PUDDING MURDER

JOANNE FLUKE

KENSINGTON BOOKS
http://www.kensingtonbooks.com

KENSINGTON BOOKS are published by

Kensington Publishing Corp.
119 West 40th Street
New York, NY 10018

All Kensington titles, imprints, and distributed lines are available at special quantity discounts for bulk purchases for sales promotion, premiums, fund-raising, educational, or institutional use.

Special book excerpts or customized printings can also be created to fit specific needs. For details, write or phone the office of the Kensington Special Sales Manager: Attn. Special Sales Department. Kensington Publishing Corp., 119 West 40th Street, New York, NY 10018. Phone: 1-800-221-2647.

Kensington and the K logo Reg. U.S. Pat. & TM Off.

ISBN-13: 978-0-7582-4152-8
ISBN-10: 0-7582-4152-6

First hardcover printing: October 2009

10 9 8 7 6 5 4 3 2 1

Printed in the United States of America

This book is for the lovely Thea Giulia

Acknowledgments

A big kiss for Ruel, who fixes all the boo-boos.
Hugs all around to the kids and the grandkids.

Congratulations to Dixie Lee, winner of the Kensington recipe contest, with her scrumptious German Apple Cake.

Thank you to: Mel & Kurt, Lyn & Bill, Lu & Sheba, Gina, Adrienne, Jay, Bob, Amanda, John B., Judy Q., Dr. Bob & Sue, Laura & Mark, Richard & Krista, Mark B., Lois & Neal, and my hometown friends in Swanville, MN.

Thank you to my multi-talented Editor-in-Chief,
John Scognamiglio,
for his infinite patience, excellent advice, and his unwavering trust in tasting every sample of Hannah's baked goods that I send to him.

Thanks also to Walter, Steve, Laurie, Doug, David, Maureen, Karen, Meryl, Colleen, Michaela, Kate, Adam, Jessica, Peter, Robin, Lori, Mike, Tami, Susie, and Barbara.

Thanks to Hiro Kimura for the delectable Plum Pudding on the cover.
(I love the Santa on the dessert server!)
And thank you to Lou Malcangi for designing such a delightful dust jacket.

Thanks also to all the other talented folks at Kensington who keep Hannah sleuthing and baking up a storm.

Thank you to Trudi Nash, a great friend and traveling companion!

And thanks to David for batching it while she's gone.

Thank you to Dr. Rahhal, Dr. and Mrs. Line, and Dr. Wallen.

Thanks to John at Placed4Success for Hannah's movie and
TV spots.
And thanks to Hans who saved me from buying a flat-screen
TV to use for target practice.

Thanks to Ken Wilson, the master of iced coffee.
And a big hug for Lois Brown, superb food stylist and baker.

Thanks to Jill Saxton for correcting my Minnesota mistakes,
baking bloopers, spelling slips, and grammatical goofs.
(You'll notice she doesn't correct alliteration.)

Many thanks to Terry Sommers for wading through the
Wisconsin snow to her grocery store for the ingredients to
test my recipes.

Thank you to Sally Hayes for so many yummy recipes. If I
click my heels together three times can I come to your
Kansas kitchen and bake with you?

Thank you to Jamie Wallace for keeping my Web site,
MurderSheBaked.com
up to date and looking great.

Hugs to everyone who sent favorite family recipes for
Hannah to try.
I'm going to increase the size of my "To Test" box . . . again.
And thanks so much for all the friendly letters and e-mails
about Hannah.
I'm delighted that you enjoy reading about her and trying
her recipes.

Chapter One

Lake Eden, Minnesota
Ten Shopping Days Until Christmas

There were nights like tonight, right after he'd bet a bundle on the losing team, when Larry Jaeger wondered why he'd ever come back to this dinky little town. When it came to money matters, people around here were clueless. Swindling them out of their savings was no contest at all. He preferred an even playing field where he could outwit the investors he thought of as his adversaries. It was a game, after all, and the game was boring if your opponents were pushovers.

In an effort to even the odds he'd taken more risks than usual, but not a single one of the locals were suspicious, not even Mayor Bascomb, who prided himself on his business savvy. This was like counting the leaves on a three-leaf clover, and that wasn't his idea of fun. The thrill came from taking off with the money right before someone was about to catch on. These people weren't about to catch on.

And then there was Courtney, his biggest investor, his partner, and his fiancée. She owned fifty percent of the Crazy Elf Christmas Tree Lot . . . on paper.

Courtney had insisted on taking a room at the Lake Eden Inn, rather than staying with him in the double-wide trailer they called Elf Headquarters. She was afraid that people would talk because they weren't married. She was right. They would talk. But that wouldn't bother him. His concern was that Courtney was living separately, and that gave her time to think. It was much easier to keep tabs on her when they were together twenty-four seven. She had some surprisingly good business instincts, unlike some of the other girlfriends he'd had. Courtney might just have the smarts to compare the business he'd fabricated for her on paper to what was actually happening right here in Lake Eden Park. If she did that, she might discover the inconsistencies that no one else had noticed.

The customers were long gone and the last employee had left the lot at least ten minutes ago. He was completely alone and once Hannah came to pick up her check, he'd be alone for the rest of the night.

It was time to close up shop. He stepped out the back door of the trailer and walked to the pole that held the breaker box. It was cold tonight, now that the elves had turned off the standing heaters, and he shivered even though he was wearing a heavy sweater.

There were three switches inside the weatherproof box. The top one controlled the electricity for the buildings, tree tents, rides, and tall candy cane lampposts that illuminated the park. The second switch powered the bare bulbs that were strung in a crisscross pattern overhead. They were the night security lights and they kept the park dimly illuminated when the main lights were out. The third breaker controlled the electricity for Elf Headquarters, and that was permanently set in the on position. He'd told the electrician to rig it so that no misguided employee could cut the power to his television set in the middle of an important game.

The music was blaring as usual and it seemed even louder now that it wasn't tempered by noisy crowds and the squeals of children riding the attractions. His trailer wasn't soundproof, but he'd learned to tune out the noise when he was inside. Now that the park was empty, the continuous loop of Christmas carols seemed ear-splitting.

Silent Night was playing as he clicked on the overhead security lights. He'd learned his lesson the first night he'd spent in the park. Once the main lights were doused, it was impossible to see the second switch. He'd picked his way gingerly back to the trailer to get a flashlight to illuminate the second switch so that he could engage it.

Larry reached for the top switch as the music went into the chorus. "Silent night, holy night. All is calm, all is . . ."

He threw the switch and smiled. "Not bright. Not bright at all," he said, heading back to the lights and warmth of Elf Headquarters.

A big swallow from the brandy snifter on the coffee table made short work of his shivers. A second snifter took care of his icy toes and hands, and then he played channel roulette with the remote in an effort to find something interesting. He bypassed cooking shows, nature programs, reenactments of great moments in history, several movies with actors he didn't recognize, a performance by a symphony orchestra with a conductor he didn't recognize, and reruns of ten-year-old game shows. He finally concluded that there was nothing he really wanted to watch on any of his two hundred plus satellite channels. The only thing that was slightly better than nothing at all was a replay of the championship college basketball tournament that had taken place last year.

A few sips from a third snifter of brandy made it easier to pretend that he hadn't seen the game before. He watched a three-pointer sink in without even rippling the net, and then he looked up as car lights flashed outside his window.

Someone was parking on the street and it was probably Hannah and the dentist. No one else would come here this late. The sign on the gate announced that they were closed, but he'd left it unlocked so that she could come in.

An envelope with her check and receipt was waiting on the table next to the door. He was nothing if not prepared. He picked up the platter she'd used for her plum pudding and glanced down at the remaining crumbs. She'd be pleased to hear that everyone had loved it and agreed that it would be a big hit at the Crazy Elf Cookie Shop.

When the knock came on the door, he was ready. He pulled it open, but when he saw who was standing there, he began to frown. "What are *you* doing here? You're the last person I expected to see!"

"I *will* be the last person you'll see." The words were clipped with anger. "It's what you deserve for what you've done."

"What do you mean?" His frown deepened and he stepped back in an effort to avoid a confrontation. It was clear that this was not a friendly social visit.

His uninvited guest stepped in, shut the door, and took another step forward, forcing him to back up even further. "What do you want?" he asked.

The answer to his question came in tangible form. When he saw the gun, he backed up several more steps and dropped the platter with a crash. His hands shot up in a futile effort to protect himself.

"No! You can't . . ." were the last words he spoke.

Chapter
Two

One Day Earlier

That horrid gingerbread man was poking her in the eye again! Hannah Swensen reared back to avoid the rounded tip of a well-spiced arm and the rickety step stool she kept at The Cookie Jar began to teeter on two legs. The instant before toppling was a certainty, she managed to grab a sturdy branch that was decorated with five colored lights, a chocolate chip cookie ornament, and a plastic sprig of holly. The branch held, the step stool stabilized, and what she'd feared would be a painful tumble to the floor below was averted.

"That's enough, I'm done," Hannah said to no one in particular since she was the sole occupant of her coffee shop and bakery. It was four-fifteen in the afternoon, and she'd taken advantage of the predictable lull that occurred this time of day. It was too late for most customers to come in for a mid-afternoon snack cookie and too early to pick up the boxes of cookies that had been ordered for evening parties and holiday buffets. Since her partner, Lisa Herman, had offered to make their daily cookie deliveries, Hannah had volunteered to finish decorating the Christmas tree in the front window of their shop.

It was time to admire her handiwork and have a cup of the coffee the *Lake Eden Journal* had called the best in the tri-county area. Hannah poured a cup and sat down at her favorite table at the back of the shop. As she sipped, she gazed out the front window at a scene that was straight from the front of a Christmas card. Lacy flakes of snow fell outside the glass, gently fluttering down to rest on the pristine white blanket that covered the sidewalk. The tree looked lovely, and Hannah gave a contented smile. It was the second week in December, and night came early in the North Star State. Thanks to the winter solstice, this was the time of the year when people drove to work in the dark, worked all day with only a glimpse of the sun from their office windows, and left work after sunset to drive back home in the dark.

A Minnesota winter could be long and claustrophobic, causing bouts of cabin fever that sent snowbirds, the people who packed up their RVs at the first sign of snow, on their annual migration to more hospitable places like Florida or California. Those who couldn't leave for the entire winter but needed a break from the unrelenting cold, purchased vacation packages and spent a rejuvenating week basking in the sun in Hawaii, or St. Thomas, or the Bahamas. They came back with suntans that were the envy of those who stayed behind in the land of snow shovels, ski masks, and chemical hand warmers.

The Lake Eden residents who stuck it out had months to perfect their survival skills. A Minnesota winter could start as early as October and last all the way through April. In the dead of winter, when the temperatures dropped to forty below, they dressed in layered clothing that added another twenty pounds to their silhouettes and hunkered down next to the heater vents, hoping that the furnace wouldn't go out.

When boredom set in as it inevitably did after the holidays, people created winter diversions to keep their minds off the endless black and white world outside their windows. The end of January brought the Lake Eden Winter Carnival with competitive winter games at the Lake Eden Inn and rides through town in old-fashioned one-horse sleighs. In February, there was a gala Valentine Night's Ball, preceded by a potluck dinner. March heralded a phenomenon called Crazy Days. Standing gas heaters were set up every few feet on Main Street and merchants displayed their wares on the sidewalk in front of their stores. It was a study in delusion, but everyone seemed to enjoy pretending that the banks of snow no longer existed and summer had arrived. In April there was the annual Easter Egg Hunt. If the weather was cold enough to freeze the hard-boiled eggs that were decorated by the Lake Eden Women's Club, the event was held in the community center.

Winter was hard, no doubt about that, but almost everyone agreed that December was a magical month. Any month with Christmas in it had to be enchanting. Lights twinkled in shop windows all along Main Street. The pink-flocked tree in the plate glass window of Doug Greerson's First Mercantile Bank glittered with garlands of gold tinsel artfully looped from branch to branch. Pink satin balls were interspersed with gold candy canes, and pink mini-lights twinkled merrily.

Gus York had decorated his barber pole with colored lights again this year, and it reflected against the freshly fallen snow. The picture window that featured two chrome and leather barber chairs was outlined with garlands of pine boughs, red satin bows, and flashing white mini-lights.

Not to be outdone by his neighbor, Al Percy of Lake Eden Realty featured a miniature home in his front window. It had been wired, and lights blazed in the dining room, where a Christmas dinner was being served while the Christmas tree glowed softly in the den. Miniature wreaths were on every door, and the roof was decorated with a miniature Santa in his sleigh.

The window at Trudi's Fabrics was a work of stitchery art. A red and green velvet quilt formed the background, and angels floated from nearly invisible fishing line hanging from the ceiling. Each angel wore a colorful robe, a sample of the Christmas fabrics that Trudi and Loretta featured in their store. Sparkling gold lights provided illumination as the angels floated over a miniature forest of potted baby spruce and blooming poinsettias.

Although Hannah couldn't see the front window of Hal and Rose's Café from her vantage point at The Cookie Jar, she knew Rose had put up her tree again this year. The shiny metal pine changed colors when a small spotlight shone through a disk of revolving colored gels. The metal trees had been very popular a few years before Hannah was born, and Hannah's grandfather and father had stocked them at Lake Eden Hardware. As far as Hannah was concerned, Christmas wouldn't be Christmas without Rose's tree on display.

"I'm back," a voice called out, breaking into Hannah's thoughts. It was Lisa, and she was back from her cookie deliveries. A few moments later the swinging restaurant-style door between the kitchen and the coffee shop opened and Lisa came in.

"The tree looks beautiful!" she exclaimed, walking closer to take a look. "I can't believe those shellacked cookie ornaments I made two years ago have lasted this long."

"Why wouldn't they? Shellac is a great preservative. Did you know that people used to believe it was made from the wings of an insect found in India?"

Lisa shook her head. "But it's not?"

"That's right. It's actually harvested from the secretions of the female insects and it's scraped from the bark of trees."

"Okay. I guess that's a little better."

"Not always. Sometimes they scoop up the insect along with the bark."

"Yuck! I wish you hadn't told me."

"Sorry about that. It *is* kind of unappetizing. Did you finish the deliveries?"

"They're all done, except for Mr. Jaeger. I'm going to drop those off on my way home." Lisa sat down next to Hannah and took a sip of the coffee she'd carried in with her. "I ran into Herb, and he drove me around. It's really cold out there, and his patrol car was nice and warm."

Hannah smiled. Lisa still had stars in her eyes when she talked about her husband of ten months. As Lisa's father and Herb's mother were fond of saying, they were perfect for each other.

"We got a chance to talk between deliveries," Lisa went on, "and Herb said Mayor Bascomb had to take Mrs. Bascomb to the emergency room at the hospital last night."

"That doesn't sound good." Hannah noticed that Lisa was still referring to her elders by their formal names, just as she'd done as a child. Old habits died hard in Lake Eden. "What's wrong with Stephanie, do you know?"

"Doc Knight diagnosed her with a bad case of the flu and he's keeping her in the hospital. He was really upset because she didn't show up to get her flu shot at the clinic, especially when he sent her a reminder and everything."

"Why didn't she get the shot?"

Lisa glanced around and leaned a bit closer even though there were no customers to overhear their conversation. "The reminder said that the shot was available for anyone over forty-five."

"And she didn't want to be seen at the clinic because that would be admitting she was over forty-five?"

"That's what Herb thinks, and he's almost always right."

"Vanity, thy name is Stephanie Bascomb," Hannah said, borrowing heavily from the Bard. "She's going to be all right, isn't she?"

"She should be. Doc's keeping her in the hospital for the rest of the week just to make sure she eats right and gets plenty of rest. And that's why I'm losing my husband until the weekend."

Hannah gave a little shake of her head. "What did you say?"

"I said that's why I'm losing Herb for the rest of the week. Since Mrs. Bascomb won't be home, the mayor's taking this opportunity to move his ice fishing house up to Mille Lacs Lake. He asked Herb to come along to help him. They're leaving tonight at midnight when there's less traffic, and once they put it out on the ice, they're going to stay and fish for a couple of days."

"I didn't know Herb liked ice fishing."

"He doesn't, not particularly, but it's the politic thing to do. Besides, Mayor Bascomb's ice fishing house is the fanciest one around. If he doesn't feel like fishing, he can watch television or play pool."

Hannah remembered her one and only tour of the mayor's ice fishing house. She'd driven across the ice to deliver coffee and cookies to the fishing contestants at Lake Eden's Winter Carnival. The mayor's ice fishing house had been luxurious, but the fancy lavish furnishings had been completely overshadowed by the grim discovery they'd made.

"I promised Herb I'd make him some Pork and Beans Bread before he left. It's his favorite and he thinks Mayor Bascomb will like it, too."

"Pork and Beans Bread?"

"It's Patsy's recipe. She got it last month when she went to California to visit a friend. They stopped in Paso Robles at a place called Vic's Café and ordered it off the menu."

"How did she get the recipe?"

Lisa gave a little laugh. "You know Patsy. She's not exactly shy."

"That's true." Hannah smiled. Patsy was Marge Beeseman's sister, and Lisa's new mother-in-law wasn't exactly shy either. "So Patsy asked for the recipe?"

"That's right in a roundabout way. Patsy talked to the owner, Jan, and explained that they were trying to make sure Dad gets enough complex carbohydrates. Lately all he's wanted is toast for breakfast, and Pork and Beans Bread toasts up really well. Patsy figured that two slices of that would be a lot more nutritious than two slices of commercial white bread."

"Do complex carbohydrates have an effect on your dad's Alzheimer's?"

"I have no idea, but Patsy's big on nutrients and she thinks a balanced diet will help. And before you even ask, I checked with Dad's doctor and she says eating Pork and Beans Bread toast can't hurt."

"The name's intriguing. Is it a type of bread that goes especially well with Pork and Beans?"

"No, it's bread that's *made* from pork and beans!" Lisa gave a little laugh. "You can't really taste them unless you know they're in there, but then you can. I'll make a double batch. That'll be four loaves. And I'll bring one in tomorrow morning for you to taste."

"I'll look forward to it. Did Herb tell you any other news I should know about?"

Lisa thought about that for a moment. "You already know about your mother, don't you?"

"What about Mother?"

"She signed up for a class at the college. Norman's mom, too. It's something to do with running a small business."

Hannah was surprised. Delores hadn't mentioned signing up for a business course. "Well, that's good I guess. But I wonder why she hasn't told me."

As if on cue, the front door opened and Delores Swensen came in. She brushed the snow from her cardinal red coat that went so well with her coloring and hung it on the rack by the door.

"Hello, dears," she said giving both of them a smile. "Am I too late for coffee?"

"It's never too late for coffee." Hannah jumped to her feet to pour a mug for her mother.

"How about a couple of cookies to go with that?" Lisa asked.

Delores considered it for a moment. "Thank you, dear. I have class tonight and I won't have time to run home and eat. Do you have anything with chocolate?"

"Do we have anything with *chocolate?*" Hannah laughed as she repeated her mother's question. "Almost everything we bake has chocolate!"

Lisa glanced over at the large glass jars they used to show-case their cookie selections for the day. "We have Chocolate Chip Crunch Cookies, Fudge-Aroons, one piece of Chocolate Almost Toast, and I think there's . . ." Lisa walked over to the counter for a closer look. "Yes. We've got two Chocolate-Covered Cherry Delights. One looks a little smushed on top, but it's still good."

"I'll have the cherries," Delores decided, sitting down at the table and turning to her daughter. "What are you doing tonight, dear?"

Hannah wanted to ask why her mother needed to know, but that wouldn't be polite. It was best to hedge a bit and see if Delores would volunteer the information. "I'm not sure yet."

"Then you don't have any firm plans?"

"Not really." Hedging hadn't worked and it was time to border on the impolite. "Did you have a particular reason for asking?"

Delores gave a little laugh. "I should have told you up front. But that was nicely done, dear. You weren't rude, but you avoided committing yourself."

"Thank you, Mother. And your reason for asking?"

"Carrie."

"Carrie wants to know my plans for tonight?"

"No, I do. But it's because of Carrie that I want to know." Delores stopped speaking as Lisa delivered her cookies and a fresh mug of coffee. "Thank you, Lisa."

"You're welcome." Lisa turned to Hannah. "I'll be in the kitchen if you need me. I want to mix up a batch of Blueberry Crunch Cookies for Grandma Knudson. Reverend Knudson told me she's a great believer in dark berries."

"Do you have any idea what Lisa was talking about?"

Hannah asked once her partner had disappeared behind the kitchen door.

"Yes, dear. Dark berries are all the rage now. Eating them is supposed to be beneficial to eye health."

Hannah gave a little shrug. "Is it true?"

"I don't know, but I like blueberries and blackberries, so there's no reason not to eat them. If it helps, that's wonderful. If it doesn't, what have I lost?"

"That's a good attitude," Hannah complimented her mother, "but let's get back to Carrie. What does she have to do with my plans for tonight?"

Delores took a sip of her coffee and sighed. "She canceled at the last minute again. We were supposed to go out to class together and this is the second one she's missed. I thought that if you didn't have other plans, you might go with me. I just hate to drive out to the college alone, especially at night in the winter."

Hannah was well and truly stuck and she knew it. It wasn't often her mother asked for help. "Okay, I'll go with you. What kind of class is it?"

"It's a business class called *Small Business Practices.*"

"That sounds interesting," Hannah said, but she meant just the opposite. It was possible she might learn something helpful from attending the session with her mother, but it could be a deadly dull way to spend an evening.

"The instructor, Miss Whiting, is very good. She has her masters in accounting and she's a CPA specializing in small business and corporate tax preparation. I'm learning a lot about keeping better books, and the difference between the paperwork I should save and the things I can throw away."

Hannah had the fleeting thought that since Lisa was now taking care of the financial end of their business, *she* should be the one to attend the class with Delores. Lisa would go if Hannah asked her, but that wouldn't be fair. This was Lisa's last night with her husband before Herb went ice fishing with

Mayor Bascomb. Thinking that way was quite selfless of her and Hannah felt good about it. But she also had an equally important selfish reason for not saddling her partner with the class. Hannah wanted Lisa to get home in time to bake the Pork and Beans Bread so that she could taste it in the morning.

"What's the problem with Carrie? Why can't she go with you?"

"I'm not sure."

"She didn't tell you?" Hannah was shocked. Delores and Carrie had been friends for years before they'd opened their antique business together. In the past, they'd discussed everything, including Delores's disastrous romance with Winthrop Harrington the Third.

"She just said something personal had come up and she was sorry, but she couldn't go to class with me. That's exactly the same thing she told me last week."

"Carrie didn't say what that *something personal* was?"

"No, she didn't."

"And you didn't ask her?"

"Really, Hannah!" Delores looked offended. "Carrie said it was personal. Asking her to elaborate would have been terribly impolite."

"I know, but did you?"

"Of course I did! She just repeated that it was personal and she'd tell me when she could. And then she hung up. It didn't faze me the first time it happened, but now I'm definitely concerned. It isn't like Carrie to be secretive. I just hope there's not any trouble."

"Trouble?"

"Yes. She could be ill and working a full day at Granny's Attic and then attending a night class is just too much of a drain on her health. Or . . . she could have turned into a closet drinker for some reason or other. There are people who can drink every night for years and no one ever suspects. And then there's the computer Norman got for her. What if she's addicted to one of those online poker places and she's lost all her retirement money?"

"None of those things sound like Carrie," Hannah commented.

"I know, but she's changed over the past few weeks. We used to talk, but she's just not open with me anymore."

Hannah heard the note of panic in her mother's voice, mixed with an undertone of pain that her oldest and best friend wouldn't confide in her. "Do you want me to try to find out what's going on?" she offered.

"Would you, dear? I'd be so grateful!" Delores looked very relieved. "You should probably start by talking to Norman. He may know something."

"Good idea," Hannah said. "Maybe I'll see him after class. What time do we get out?"

"Seven-thirty. It's only an hour."

"I'll call him and see if he can meet me at my place later. I'll bribe him with dessert."

Delores gave a little laugh. "I don't think you'll have to bribe him, dear. It seems to me that whenever you want him, Norman comes running. He's like your father in that respect. When we were dating, all I had to do was pick up the phone and he'd come over any hour of the day or night."

Hannah thought about that for a moment and realized that her mother was right. Unless Norman had a patient in his dental chair, he always seemed eager to see her.

"If Norman doesn't know anything, perhaps you could ask a few questions around town."

"I guess I could do that."

"Something else, dear . . . you could keep an eye out for Carrie's car when you're driving around town. If it's parked in some unusual place, it could give us a clue to what's going on."

"That's true."

"You could even drop in on her at night to see what she's doing firsthand. I'm sure you could talk Norman into going with you. All you'd have to do is think up some reason to pay her a surprise visit."

"Norman wouldn't really need an excuse to drop in on his own mother. I'm sure Carrie would love to see him. And maybe while they were talking, I could look around."

"That's an excellent idea. Thank you for your help, dear." Delores ate her last bite of cookie and drained her coffee mug. Then she stood up and gave Hannah a little pat on the back. "I'll drive out to your condo and pick you up at six. That gives us plenty of time to get to the college."

"You don't want me to drive?"

"No, dear. It's out of your way. It'll be better if I pick you up and drop you off at home after class."

"Whatever you say, Mother," Hannah replied obediently, watching her mother walk across the room, retrieve her coat, and hurry out the door. When the door closed behind her impeccably dressed, attractive mother, she let out a deep sigh that bordered on exasperation. She'd been maneuvered by an expert. Delores had elicited her help by claiming that she didn't like to drive to the college at night, yet she'd volunteered to drive a round trip from town to Hannah's condo, to the college, back to Hannah's condo, and all the way to town again.

Hannah was half amused and half annoyed as she got up to join Lisa in the kitchen. Delores really was a master manipulator. Not only had she talked her eldest daughter into attending a class that didn't interest her in the slightest, she'd also coerced Hannah to recruit one of her boyfriends to spy on his own mother!

Chapter Three

Hannah was struck by an odd sense of déjà vu as she walked with her mother down the sidewalk leading to Stewart Hall. She'd never attended Lake Eden Community College. It was still in the planning stages when she'd graduated from Jordan High and gone off to another school. But she noticed certain similarities between her hometown community college and the university she'd attended. The student parking lot was filled with what Cyril Murphy, the owner of Murphy's Garage, Shamrock Limos, and Murphy Motors, called *previously owned autos*. Most of the students' cars looked as if they'd been owned multiple times, and it was apparent that a large percentage of those owners had been accident-prone.

"This is for you," Delores said, handing Hannah a notebook. "I thought you might like to take notes since you're a small business owner, too."

"Thanks," Hannah said, tucking the notebook under her arm and following her mother.

As they crossed the quad that separated the buildings, they joined a steady stream of students hurrying to class clutching notebooks, books, and the occasional laptop computer. Even though the evening had turned cold and her mother had taken the precaution of plugging her sedan into the power strip that ran around the perimeter of the parking lot, most of these students were dashing along with their parkas unzipped and their heads bare. Some were even wearing tennis shoes rather than boots and Hannah remembered the same phenomenon occurring on the campus she'd attended. They were young. They were invincible. They were much too healthy to succumb to winter colds or other illnesses.

Delores slowed near the door to Stewart Hall to let a large group of students pass by. Hannah saw her mother eyeing them critically and as soon as they were gone, she turned to her mother. "What is it?"

"Not one single girl in that group had a hat or gloves. Don't they know what will happen to their skin and hair if they continue to expose it to this dry winter air? Or is it just that they don't care?"

"Both," Hannah took her mother's arm and escorted her into the warmth of the building. "Where's our class?"

"It's on the second floor. Follow me." Delores led the way to a stairwell and began to hurry up the steps. Hannah followed, but once she'd reached the landing between the first and second floors, she was sadly out of breath. She should have continued her exercise class at Heavenly Bodies Spa, but life had intruded with holiday orders for cookies coming in fast and furiously. She just didn't have the luxury of setting aside an hour and a half every day. At least that's what she told herself whenever the subject crossed her mind.

"Hurry, dear." Delores called out, turning around to look over her shoulder as she reached the door to the second floor. "We don't want to be late."

We don't want to be embarrassed either, Hannah thought, *and I'll be completely humiliated if I hurry into class breathing like a steam engine.*

"Hannah?" Delores called out.

"Just a second, Mother." Hannah knew she had to take a few seconds to catch her breath so she bent down to fiddle with the sole of her boot. "I think I stepped on a tack. Just go and wait for me in the hall. I'll pull it out and be right there."

It didn't take long for Hannah's breathing to return to normal. Perhaps some small benefit from her exercise class had stuck with her. She straightened up, climbed the rest of the stairs, and pushed open the door to the hallway. Her mother was waiting and Hannah had just about reached her when she caught sight of a vaguely familiar figure racing toward them from the other end of the hall.

The man glanced at his watch as he sped forward. It was clear he didn't notice Delores and Hannah standing there, and he struck Hannah's arm as he ran past, knocking her notebook from her hand and sending it flying across the hallway. He stopped and turned back, and then he retrieved her notebook and handed it back to her with an apologetic smile. "Sorry," he said. "I'm late for class, but that's no excuse. I should have been more careful. Are you all right?"

Hannah stared up at him and her breath caught in her throat. She must be imagining things. It couldn't be. She opened her mouth to assure him that she was fine, but no words came out.

"Don't worry. She's fine," Delores said, stepping into the breach. And then she turned to Hannah. "Aren't you, dear?"

It was like pulling teeth, but Hannah managed to croak out one word. "Fine," she said in a voice that didn't sound at all like hers.

"As long as you're okay, I'd better go," the man said. "My students are probably waiting for me."

"What do you teach?" Delores asked, picking up the conversational ball since Hannah was perfectly silent.

"Poetry, but I'm part of a team that's here from Macalester. We're putting together an intercollegiate event called the Christmas Follies."

"That sounds wonderful!" Delores exclaimed. "Will the show be open to the public?"

"Yes, and it's also being televised. It should be quite a production with talent from five different colleges." The man turned to Hannah. "Excuse me, but you look so familiar. Have we met before?"

As she looked up into the dark blue eyes she'd once described as *marvelous* and *soul-searching*, Hannah wanted to die. She prayed that the floor beneath her feet would disappear, dropping her all the way down to the basement so that she could hide in the darkest corner. It was achingly clear that he didn't remember. And he should!

"Hannah?" Delores prompted, and even without looking, Hannah knew her mother was regarding her curiously.

"Yes, we've met," Hannah said in a voice that was amazingly steady considering the circumstances. Then she took her mother's arm and pulled her down the hall, not looking back to see if he had continued on his way.

"Hannah!" Delores chided her in a whisper that seemed far too loud to Hannah. "You were rude to that nice young professor."

"Yes," Hannah admitted. There was no arguing with her mother's assessment.

"I don't understand."

"I know you don't, Mother."

Mother and daughter walked on until Delores stopped at a classroom door. "This is it," she said, glancing at her watch. "We have one minute before we're late. Who *was* that man, Hannah?"

"Someone I once thought I knew. Let's go in, Mother."

"Not quite yet." Delores grabbed Hannah's arm. "Why did you act as if you could hardly wait to get away from him?"

"You don't want to know."

"But I do! Was he the man you told me about, the reason you left college?"

Hannah drew a deep breath. A small part of her wanted to confide in her mother, but no good would be served by recounting the story of her failed and foolish romance. "I don't want to talk about it," she said firmly, opening the door and ushering her mother into the classroom.

* * *

Time had never passed so slowly. Some said that at the instant of a man's death, his whole life passed before his eyes. This was just the opposite. Hannah had never seen the minute hand move so slowly. After watching the clock for what seemed like three hours and was actually four minutes, Hannah took notes just for something to do as Miss Kimberly Whiting, CPA, droned on and on about profit and loss statements, the proper way to invoice, and the essentials of sales tax record-keeping. The information was dispensed fast and heavy with no break for questions until the dot of seven twenty-five when Miss Whiting stopped speaking and picked up the folder she'd placed on the podium.

"It's time for bad business practices," she said, and even those class members who'd been dozing sat up straight in their chairs. "Tonight's example concerns a large screen television dealership."

Hannah listened as their teacher went on to describe the four-man partnership. Three invested equal amounts of money and the fourth invested his time and expertise by actually running the business. There were handouts showing profit and loss statements, tax returns, copies of bank statements, and payroll rosters. Their assignment was to figure out how the dealership had managed to stay in business for more than five months despite selling television sets for less than cost.

As they filed out of class, Hannah found herself dreading the ride home. Delores was bound to ask more questions about Bradford Ramsey and she'd been perfectly honest when she'd said that she didn't want to talk about it.

They'd descended the staircase and were walking past the classrooms on the first floor when Hannah spotted someone she thought she knew. "Is that Dr. Love?" she asked her mother.

"Yes, but she's Dr. Schmidt out here," Delores said, poking her head in the open door and waving.

"Hello, Delores!" Dr. Love sounded very glad to see them.

"And Hannah. I haven't seen you since your mother's book launch party. How have you been?"

"Just fine, Dr. Schmidt."

"Call me Nancy." Dr. Love gave her a warm smile and then she turned to Delores. "I've been meaning to call you. I'm redecorating my office here on campus and I was wondering if you could find me an old-fashioned glass-door bookcase."

"This is your lucky day!" Delores said with a laugh. "My assistant, Luanne, just came back from an estate sale at the home of a prominent lawyer in St. Paul. She bought a pair of gorgeous bookcases in walnut with leaded glass doors on each shelf."

"The type of doors that pull up and then slide in?"

"That's right. Would you like to drop by to see them?"

"I would. They sound perfect. How about tomorrow around noon? I have to run out to the station at ten to do some voiceovers, but I should be through in a couple of hours."

"I'll have the coffee pot on for you," Delores said, turning to go. "Black with two sugars?"

"Perfect." Dr. Love turned to Hannah. "It was good to see you again, Hannah."

"Nice to see you, too," Hannah said, and then she followed her mother down the hall to the exit.

Once they stepped out of the building, the cold hit them so hard it took their breath away. While they were in class, an icy wind had begun to blow from the north. Both Hannah and her mother held their gloved hands over their mouths and noses as they walked directly into the wind and made their way to the parking lot. Most of the students had left immediately after class and Delores's car was the only one still plugged to the wall. Hannah was about to unplug it when she heard a voice call her name.

"Norman!" Hannah recognized him immediately, despite the bulky parka and fur hat he wore. She smiled at him and hoped her teeth wouldn't freeze in the bitterly cold wind. "What are *you* doing here?"

"I thought I'd save your mother a trip. This way she can go straight home and she won't have to swing by your place."

"That's sweet of you Norman, but I don't mind," Delores jumped into the conversation and Hannah knew she was thinking about her lost opportunity to find out more about Bradford Ramsey.

"Oh, but I have an ulterior motive," Norman said, unplugging Delores's car, wrapping the cord around her bumper, and opening the driver's door for her. "If I drive Hannah home, we'll get a little more time to talk."

Delores hesitated for a moment and then she slid in under the wheel. In the war between her curiosity about her daughter's old romance, and her concern about her best friend, Carrie had won.

"I'll see you tomorrow, dear," Delores said as she started her car and flicked on the lights. "I'll stop by for coffee before I open the shop."

A minute later, Hannah was in Norman's warm and toasty car. She unzipped her parka, took off her hat and her gloves, and reveled in the fact that she no longer had to fear frostbite.

"Did you eat?" Norman asked, pulling out onto the highway.

"Not yet. I had time to feed Moishe and that was about it."

"So Moishe comes first?" Norman's voice was warm and Hannah could see his smile in the lights of the dashboard. Norman loved her cat and the feeling was mutual.

"Moishe comes first," she confirmed it. "How about you? Did you eat?"

"No. I thought we'd stop for a bite if you wanted to go out."

Hannah thought about their favorite places, Bertanelli's Pizza, the Lake Eden Inn, and The Corner Tavern. It would be nice to go out to dinner, but what she really wanted to do was curl up on the couch with Norman and Moishe, and watch mindless television.

"Bertanelli's? The Corner Tavern? Sally's at the Inn?" Norman named the places Hannah had already thought of and dismissed.

"I'd rather go home and make something there," Hannah said, "if that's all right with you, that is."

"That's fine with me, but I don't want you to work. You've had a full day."

"It's okay. I've got some meatloaf I can heat up and I'll pop in a batch of Easy Cheesy Biscuits."

"Easy Cheesy Biscuits? I don't think I've tasted those."

"I *know* you haven't. I just got the recipe last weekend from an old classmate of mine at Jordan High. Prudence left Lake Eden right after school and moved to Niagara Falls."

"Do you have everything you need to make them? Or shall we run by The Quick Stop?"

"I have everything I need. I planned on baking them tonight anyway. Lisa loves cheese so I thought I'd take her a couple for breakfast."

The roads were clear and Norman zipped along in his well-maintained car. Hannah felt as if she were living in the lap of luxury as she listened to mellow jazz on the stereo and watched the night stream past her window. All too soon, they turned in at Hannah's condo complex and Hannah handed him her gate card to raise the wooden lever that let the residents in and out. This time the wooden barrier was intact and Hannah wondered if they'd solved the gate card problem at last. Even though residents were warned of the consequences, they still stuck the magnetic gate cards in their wallets next to other cards with information strips. When the gate cards ceased to work, some irate condo owners crashed right through the wooden arm. Perhaps she was exaggerating slightly, but Hannah believed that the one-by-four designed to keep non-residents out was broken more often than it was not.

"You can park in my extra spot," Hannah said, and Norman took the ramp to the underground garage. Her condo came with two parking spots, and Norman pulled in next to her cookie truck.

The first thing Hannah noticed when she got out of the car was the cold. Perhaps it was the fact that she'd just left a warm car, but it seemed even colder than it had at the college. "Better plug in your car," she said.

"Good idea."

Hannah watched as Norman unwound the power cord that was part of winterizing a car in Minnesota, right along with antifreeze, and the survival pack careful drivers kept in the trunk. The box containing blankets, extra parkas, gloves, an empty coffee can, a candle, and matches wasn't quite as necessary as it had been in the years before cell phones, but it was still possible to get stuck in a snowstorm with a non-working cell phone, and freeze to death in subzero temperatures.

When Norman was through, they walked across the floor of the garage and climbed the steps to ground level. When they left the shelter of the stairwell, a cold blast of wind hit Hannah's face and her eyes began to water. Norman grabbed her arm and rushed her up the covered staircase to her second-floor condo, taking the keys from her hand and opening the door.

A projectile with orange and white fur hurtled at them the moment the door opened, and Norman caught Moishe in his arms. Hannah's cat began to purr as Norman carried him inside and set him on his favorite perch on the back of the couch.

"Are you glad to see us, Big Guy?" Norman asked, and Moishe answered him with an even louder purr. "What do you say I throw your catnip mouse for you?"

This time Moishe gave a happy yowl and hopped off the couch to stare up at Norman while he located the mouse. With her cat occupied, Hannah shrugged out of her parka and went off to the kitchen to begin preparing dinner.

The Easy Cheesy Biscuits were first. Hannah preheated the oven, took out one of her medium-sized mixing bowls, and gathered the ingredients. She'd just completed the first step in her food processor, and she was about to dump the mixture into her bowl, when Norman came into the kitchen.

"Do you want some help?" he asked.

"Sure," Hannah answered, never one to turn down a genuine offer of assistance. "You can grate the cheese. I need a half cup of cheddar, a half cup of Asiago, and a half cup of Parmesan. You can use the food processor with the grating blade."

Norman eyed the food processor which still had a bit of flour clinging to the sides of the bowl. "I'd better wash it out."

"There's no need. I just used it to mix up the dry ingredients and butter for the biscuits. Since the cheese is going in the biscuit dough, it won't make a speck of difference."

Norman made short work of grating the cheeses and Hannah added the grated cheddar and Asiago to her bowl. She saved the grated parmesan for the biscuit tops and was just about to break the eggs into a glass to beat them when Norman spoke up.

"I can do that for you," he said.

"Okay. Just crack two into my glass and beat them up with a fork. I'll measure out the sour cream and the milk."

They worked in silence for several moments and then Norman handed the glass to her. "Are these okay?"

"They're fine," Hannah said, glancing down at the homogenous mixture of yolk and white. "Do you want to stir while I add everything else to the bowl?"

"Sure." Norman picked up the spoon.

Hannah added the eggs and he stirred them in. Then she scooped in the sour cream. When that was incorporated, she added the milk, dribbling it in slowly so that Norman could stir it in without splashing.

"Looks just like lumpy wallpaper paste," Norman said,

but Hannah saw the grin he tried to hide and knew he was kidding her.

"I prefer to compare it to cottage cheese," she countered. "At least that's edible."

"I'm not so sure about that. Mother made green Jell-O with cottage cheese and chives the last time I went to her house for dinner. And speaking of Mother, there's something I want to talk to you about. I was going to wait until after we'd eaten, but it's really bothering me."

"What is it?" Hannah asked, distracted enough to spray her baking sheet with Pam even though the recipe said it wasn't needed.

"I usually meet her on Thursday nights for dinner. One week she cooks and the next week I take her out. We've been doing it ever since I moved to Lake Eden."

"You're still doing it, aren't you?" Hannah asked, dipping a soup spoon into the batter and forming her first biscuit.

"I am, but I'm not so sure about Mother."

"What do you mean?" Hannah wet her fingers under the faucet and made one of the biscuits she'd dropped on the sheet a little rounder.

"I always thought Mother had a good time when we got together, but she's canceled on the last three Thursdays."

Hannah looked over and saw the concern on his face. "Didn't she give you a reason for cancelling?"

"Yes, but I don't think it was the *real* reason. The first time she said she was getting a bad cold, but when I talked to her the next day, she sounded just fine. The next week she said she was going to work late at Granny's Attic with Delores, but I drove by on my way home from the clinic and the lights were off in their shop."

Hannah wasn't sure what to say, but it certainly sounded as if Carrie had lied to Norman. Instead of commenting on that, she asked a question. "How about the third time?"

"That was last Thursday. When I called to confirm with her, she said that something came up and she couldn't make it. And when I asked about it, she wouldn't tell me anything. What do you think, Hannah? Am I making a mountain out of a molehill?"

"Not necessarily," Hannah said, sprinkling the last of the grated Parmesan cheese on her biscuits. She popped them into the oven, set the timer for fourteen minutes, and turned back to Norman. "Carrie did the same thing to Mother. That's the reason I went to class with her tonight. Our mothers signed up for the course together, but Carrie hasn't made it to a single class. Mother says she always backs out at the last minute."

"Is Delores concerned, too?"

"Yes. She told me that Carrie's always been very open with her, but things have changed lately. Mother's feelings are hurt because she thinks Carrie doesn't trust her enough to confide in her."

Norman was silent for a moment and then he shook his head. "I don't know if that makes me feel better, or worse."

"What do you mean?"

"On one hand, I feel better that it's not just me my mother is avoiding. On the other hand, I feel worse because if both Delores and I think there's a problem, then there probably is. I wonder if it would work to come right out and ask Mother what's wrong."

Hannah shrugged. "You can try it if you want to, but I doubt she'll tell you anything. Mother tried that and Carrie just said she'd tell her when the time was right."

"What does *that* mean?"

"I don't know." Hannah took the meatloaf out of the refrigerator and sliced it. She put the slices in the frying pan with a bit of butter, turned the burner on medium, and clamped on a cover. "I've got a bowl of Sally's Summer Salad. Do you want some?"

"Sure. I'll dish it up for both of us." Norman took the container Hannah handed to him and spooned the broccoli and cauliflower salad into two bowls. "I was just wondering . . . I know it's a lot to ask, but . . ." Norman stopped and swallowed hard. "It's just that I really need to know what's going on. It's not like Mother to cut me off from her life this way."

"That's true." Hannah flipped the slices of meatloaf and clamped the lid back on. Carrie was the type of mother who'd always wanted to manage her son's life and that meant being a nearly constant part of it. It was one of the reasons Norman had built the house Hannah had designed with him and moved five miles away. Norman had once told her he felt like a boy who had to report everything to his mother when he'd lived in the same house with Carrie.

"There goes the timer," Norman said, sprinkling some salted sunflower nuts on top of their salads. "Do you want me to take out the biscuits?"

"Yes, if they're golden brown on top. If they're not, give them another minute or two. And don't turn off the oven when you take out the biscuits. I'll turn it up to five hundred degrees before we carry our plates to the living room."

"Five hundred degrees is a really hot oven." Norman sounded quite proud of himself for knowing that. "Are you planning to bake something else?"

"I thought I'd mix up some Hot Fudge Sundae Cakes for dessert. They only bake seven minutes and they'll be ready by the time we have our second cup of coffee. You're going to love them."

"There's no doubt about that since they contain two of my favorite things."

"Hot fudge and cake?" Hannah guessed.

"That's right. But getting back to what we were talking about before . . . will you help me?"

"Of course I will." Hannah didn't even stop to consider that she'd broken one of rules she lived by. She'd promised to do something without finding out exactly what it was.

"Thanks, Hannah. I knew I could count on you."

Hannah gave him a smile and then she asked the impor-

tant question, hoping her promise wasn't one she'd live to re-
gret. "What do you want me to do?"

Norman looked very uncomfortable for a moment and
then he blurted it out. "I want you to help me spy on my
mother."

EASY CHEESY BISCUITS

Preheat oven to 425 degrees F., rack
in the middle position.

3 cups all purpose flour *(pack it down in the cup
when you measure it)*
2 teaspoons cream of tartar *(this is important)*
1 teaspoon baking powder
1 teaspoon baking soda
1 teaspoon sea salt *(regular table salt will also
work)*
½ cup salted softened butter *(1 stick, 4 ounces,
¼ pound)*

½ cup shredded strong cheddar cheese
½ cup shredded Asiago cheese*** *(or blue cheese,
Havarti, etc.)*
2 large eggs, beaten *(just whip them up in a glass
with a fork)*
1 cup sour cream *(8 ounces)*
½ cup milk****

½ cup grated Parmesan cheese for a topping *(use
real Parmesan cheese – it's so much better than
the type in the green foil can.)*

*** - *My family isn't fond of Asiago, so I leave out
the Asiago and make my biscuits with double cheddar.
They're absolutely delicious and I haven't met anyone
who doesn't like them! I have the sneaking suspicion you*

could use ANY cheese you like in these biscuits with the possible exception of triple creams like Brie and Saint Andre, or exceptionally strong flavored cheeses like Gorgonzola.

**** - *Prudence says that sometimes you'll need to add more or less milk, until everything combines together in a wet/dry like mixture that's about the consistency of cottage cheese. I've made these biscuits at least a dozen times and a half-cup milk has always worked perfectly for me.*

FIRST STEP

Use a medium-size mixing bowl to combine the flour, cream of tartar, baking powder, baking soda, and salt. Stir them all up together. Cut in the salted butter just as you would for piecrust dough.

Hannah's Note: If you have a food processor, you can use it for the first step. Cut ½ cup COLD salted butter into 8 chunks. Layer them with the dry ingredients in the bowl of the food processor. Process with the steel blade until the mixture has the texture of cornmeal. Transfer the mixture to a medium-sized mixing bowl and proceed to the second step.

SECOND STEP

Stir in the shredded cheddar cheese and the shredded Asiago cheese. Then add the beaten eggs and the sour cream in that order. Mix everything all up together.

Add the milk and stir until everything is thoroughly combined.

THIRD STEP

Drop the biscuits by soup spoonfuls onto an ungreased baking sheet, 12 large biscuits to a sheet. (*Prudence uses an ungreased baking sheet, Lisa bakes hers on a cookie sheet covered with parchment paper, and I spray my cookie sheet with Pam—everyone's biscuits turn out just fine.*)

Once the biscuits are on the baking sheet, you can wet your fingers and shape them if you like. (*I leave mine slightly irregular so everyone knows they're homemade.*)

Sprinkle shredded Parmesan cheese on the top of each biscuit.

Bake the biscuits at 425 degrees F. for 12 to14 minutes, or until they're golden brown on top.

Cool the biscuits for at least five minutes on the cookie sheet, and then remove them with a spatula. Serve them in a towel-lined basket so they stay warm.

Yield: Makes 12 large cheesy biscuits that everyone will love!

Hannah's Note: When I make these for Mother, she takes home one of the leftovers for breakfast. The next

morning, she splits it, toasts and butters it, and eats it with her scrambled eggs.

Lisa's Note: Herb loves to take these to work. I spread them with mayo and mustard and put a nice thick slice of ham in the middle. He says they make the best ham sandwich he's ever tasted.

Chapter Four

"This hot fudge sauce is incredible!" Norman spooned up the last of his ice cream and gave a satisfied sigh. "It's the kind of dessert I dream about."

"Me, too. Would you like another cake? The recipe makes six."

Norman considered it for a brief moment and then he nodded. "I think I can handle one more."

Hannah made a quick trip to the kitchen to upend another of the individual cakes on Norman's dessert plate. She pulled the top apart with two forks, a technique she'd learned from serving soufflés, let the fudge sauce pool in the center of the plate, and then dropped in a scoop of vanilla ice cream.

"You can have a little bit of my ice cream this time," she heard Norman say. The next sound she heard was a plaintive meow and it was clear he was talking to Moishe.

"This is good with coffee ice cream, too," she said as she carried the plate into the living room and handed it to Norman. "More coffee?"

"I'd love some. Your coffee is the best . . ." Norman stopped speaking as the doorbell rang. "Are you expecting anyone?"

"No, and I know it's not Mother."

"How do you know that?"

Hannah gestured toward Moishe. "His fur's not standing on end and it always does when Mother's at the door."

"So you don't know who it is?"

"No, I have no idea."

"Then you'd better let me get it."

Hannah bit back a grin as Norman went to the door and looked out the peephole. She lived in a fairly secure complex, burglaries and home invasions were unusual on nights this cold, and she was perfectly capable of grabbing the decorative hand-painted rolling pin that hung by the side of her door and wailing away at anyone who tried to enter her home without her permission.

"Who is it?" Norman called out after squinting through the peephole, and Hannah understood why he had to ask that question. Anyone who stood directly in front of her door was back lighted by the powerful security light on the outside post, plunging the visitor's features into deep shadows and rendering them totally unrecognizable.

"It's Mike!" a voice floated through the crack under the door. "Let me in, will you? It's cold out here."

Norman chuckled and turned to Hannah. "Shall I let him in?" he asked in an even louder voice that Mike would be sure to hear. "Or shall we keep all the Hot Fudge Sundae Cakes to ourselves?"

There was a moment of silence and then Mike asked, "Did you say Hot Fudge Sundae Cakes!?"

Hannah laughed. "Let him in, Norman. I'll go dish up another one for him."

As Hannah turned another helping onto one of the dessert plates Delores had given her for Christmas, she heard Norman greet Mike. Even though both of them were dating her, the two men were friends. Occasionally jealousy reared its head, but they got past it. As long as she steadfastly refused to choose one over the other, the three of them remained friends.

"Thanks for letting me in," Hannah heard Mike say from the living room.

"I had to let you in. You're the law."

"That's true. So what's this about Hot Fudge Sundae Cake?"

"It's like a hot fudge sundae inside of a cake," Norman explained. "You're going to love it."

At that moment Hannah came out of the kitchen with the dessert plate for Mike and two cups of coffee, one for Norman and the other for Mike. "Here you go," she said, setting the dessert plate and one coffee in front of Mike, and handing Norman his refill. "Go ahead and eat. It's better if it's hot."

Mike dipped his spoon in the pool of sauce and excavated a bit of cake and ice cream. He popped it in his mouth and gave a sound that resembled one of Moishe's happiest purrs. Then he plunged his spoon down for another bite.

"You like it?" Hannah asked him.

"You bet! Thanks, Hannah. I've been running all day and I didn't have a chance to eat."

"How about a meatloaf sandwich?" Hannah offered. "It's leftover meatloaf and I can heat it up like a hamburger on a cheesy biscuit."

Mike mumbled something that Hannah interpreted as assent and she went back to the kitchen to heat a slice of meatloaf in the microwave. She halved a biscuit, spread it with mayonnaise and dotted the bottom with a few slices of the bread and butter pickles that Lisa had given her. "Ketchup?" she called out.

"Yes, and mustard if you've got it," Mike replied.

As she put on the condiments, Hannah heard Mike's spoon scrape against the bottom of his dessert plate. She slid on the slice of meatloaf, topped it with the lid of the biscuit, carried in the plate, and exchanged it for Mike's dessert plate, which was scraped so clean she knew he was half-starved.

"Hi, Big Guy," Hannah heard him say to Moishe as she carried the dessert plate to the kitchen. "Sure you can have a bite. Hold on a second and I'll break off some meat for you."

Perhaps that was what she liked best about both men, Hannah mused as she rinsed off Mike's plate and slid it into the dishwasher. Norman and Mike were crazy about Moishe, and it was clear that Hannah's cat felt the same way about them. Perhaps she might have been able to choose between them if Moishe had loved one and hated the other, but that wasn't the case. And she was left, not at all unhappily, to date them both.

Hannah had just returned to her seat on the couch when the phone rang. She answered and began to frown as she heard her sister Andrea's panicked voice.

"You've just got to help me, Hannah! Bill's tied up at the station and there's no way I can do this alone!"

"There's no way you can do *what* alone?" Hannah asked, remembering her rule about not promising any favors until she found out what they were. Actually, Andrea was the reason for the rule. When Hannah was a senior in high school and Andrea was in eighth grade, her younger sister had elicited a promise from Hannah to help her out. To Hannah's chagrin, the "help" turned out to be attending a rock concert with Andrea and five of her classmates. Hannah had suffered through two and a half hours of screaming teenage girls, amplification so loud it threatened to deafen her, and alternative rock so atonal and nonmusical, she could have been listening to audiotapes of multicar crashes on the interstate.

"I have to get a Christmas tree by tomorrow morning. Tracey forgot to tell me until I tucked her in bed, but her teacher asked for a volunteer to choose the tree for their classroom, and Tracey volunteered me."

"Welcome to the world of parenting," Hannah said, chuckling slightly. "Relax, Andrea. I'll go with you pick out a Christmas tree for Tracey's classroom."

"Thanks, Hannah! I knew I could count on you."

"That's what big sisters are for. Shall I pick you up tomorrow?"

"Not tomorrow. It's got to be tonight." Andrea sounded very definite. "I have to deliver it when school starts tomorrow. The kids are going to have a tree trimming party and it needs time to spread out its branches."

"But where can you buy a Christmas tree at nine o'clock at night?"

"The Crazy Elf Christmas Tree Lot," Mike said, not even pretending he hadn't been listening to Hannah's end of the conversation.

"It's open until eleven tonight and that gives us plenty of time," Norman added.

"Us?" Hannah turned to him in surprise.

"Yes, us," Mike replied for both of them. "Norman and I'll go with you. Picking out a tree is men's work. You'd probably get some silly pink froufrou flocked thing that would embarrass Tracey in front of her class."

Hannah considered taking umbrage at Mike's slur on her judgment, but she was more amused than offended. It was a well-known fact that Andrea was fond of flocked trees, and Hannah had heard her admire the pink tree in Doug Greerson's bank window more than once this year. It would be considerably easier to keep Andrea from flocking if three out of four of them were non-flockers.

"Good," Hannah smiled at both of them. "I've been meaning to get out there. I don't put up a tree. My place is too small and I'm not here enough to enjoy it. But I hear Larry Jaeger did an incredible job creating a Christmas theme park and I really want to see it."

"He sells your cookies, doesn't he?" Norman asked.

"That's right. I'd like to talk to him about that, too. Somebody told me he's selling out near the end of the night. If that's true, he might want to increase his daily order."

Norman winked at Mike. "That business course she sat in on tonight at the community college must have given her ideas."

Hannah was about to deny it when a voice spoke directly in her ear. "Did I hear Mike and Norman?" Andrea asked, pulling her back into the telephone conversation.

"Yes, and they're both coming along to help. Let's meet in the parking lot at The Crazy Elf at ten o'clock. Is that okay?"

"That's perfect. It gives me time to go up to the attic and dig out our old Christmas tree stand. Tracey wasn't sure if they had one, or not."

"Okay, see you then," Hannah said. She hung up the phone and turned to Mike and Norman. "We should leave here in ten minutes. Does anyone want another cup of coffee for the road?"

Of course the answer was yes on all counts, and Hannah went into the kitchen to put on a fresh pot of coffee. Even though she'd had a long day and she was tired, she was looking forward to visiting Larry's Crazy Elf Christmas Tree Lot.

HOT FUDGE SUNDAE CAKES

Preheat oven to 500 degrees F., rack
in the middle position.

8 ounces salted butter (*2 sticks, ½ pound*)
8 ounces semi-sweet chocolate chips (*1 and ⅓ cup*)
    (*I used Ghirardelli*)
4 egg yolks (*save the whites in a covered bowl in the
    refrigerator to add to scrambled eggs*)
5 eggs
1 cup white (*granulated*) sugar
1 cup flour (*all purpose—pack it down when you
    measure it*)

Vanilla ice cream to finish the dish

Before you start, select the pans you want to use from
the following suggestions:

You can use large-size deep muffin cups to bake these
cakes, but if your muffin pan is solid and the cups don't lift
out, you'll have to remove each cake by using two soup
spoons as pincers to pry them out. Each batch will make 9
cakes if you use large muffin tins.

A popover pan is also a possibility, especially the kind
with removable cups, but you'll have to run a knife around
the inside of each cup and tip it over to remove the cake.
Each batch will make 6 cakes in large, deep popover cups.

You can also use individual soufflé cups, but again,
you'll have to use two soup spoons or run a knife around

the inside of the dish to remove the cakes from the soufflé cups. Each batch will make 8 small or 6 large soufflé dish cakes.

Hannah's Trick: I've found it's a lot easier to use the disposable foil pot pie tins you can buy at the grocery store. With those you can just flip them over on the dessert plate or bowl, press down on the foil bottoms with a potholder, and the cakes will flop right out. *(Yes, the pot pie tins are an extra expense, but removing the cakes will go much faster and the tins can be washed several times by hand or in the dishwasher before you'll have to throw them away.)*

Grease and flour the insides of the pans you've chosen. As an alternative to that messy procedure, you can spray them with nonstick BAKING spray *(the kind with flour added)*.

Place the butter and the chips in a medium-size microwave-safe bowl. Heat the contents for 90 seconds on HIGH. Take the bowl out of the microwave and try to stir the contents smooth. *(Chocolate chips sometimes maintain their shape even when they're melted.)* If you're able to stir the mixture smooth, set it on the counter and let it cool. If the chips aren't melted yet, microwave them in 20-second intervals on HIGH until they are.

When you're able to cup your hands around the bowl comfortably and you don't think the chocolate mixture is

so hot it'll cook the eggs you're about to add, separate 4 eggs into yolks and whites. Put the whites in the refrigerator to add to scrambled eggs the next morning, and whisk the yolks until they're thoroughly mixed. Then slowly add them to your bowl with the chocolate mixture, stirring all the while.

Add 5 more whole eggs to your mixture one at a time, stirring thoroughly after each addition.

Blend in the white sugar, stirring until it's thoroughly incorporated.

Mix in the flour and stir until the batter is smooth and free from lumps.

Transfer the batter to the pans you've selected, dividing it up between 9 large muffin tins, 6 large popover tins, 8 small soufflé dishes, 6 large soufflé dishes, or 6 disposable foil pot pie tins. Place the pans you used on a baking sheet and slip them in the oven.

Bake at 500 degrees F. for **EXACTLY** 7 minutes. Set the oven timer and don't open the oven door while they're baking. The success of this recipe depends on high even heat for a limited amount of time. Your want to bake the outside and leave the inside filled with hot molten chocolate.

When your timer rings, immediately take the cakes from the oven and place them on a wire rack. The damp center

of each cake will be barely visible and they may jiggle a bit when you move them to the cooling rack. Don't worry. That's the way they're supposed to be.

Give the cakes 2 minutes to set up slightly. Then upend them on dessert plates or bowls. Use two forks to pull apart the tops to expose the chocolate sauce in the center.

Use a small ice cream scoop to drop vanilla ice cream in the center of the rich molten chocolate.

Serve immediately to rave reviews.

Yield: 9 cakes in large muffin tins, 6 cakes in large removable popover tins, 8 cakes in small soufflé dishes, 6 cakes in large soufflé dishes, or 6 cakes in disposable foil pot pie tins.

If you have leftover cakes, they can be reheated in the microwave, but they won't be the same. They'll still be tasty, but the centers will turn into moist cake rather than hot fudge sauce.

Hannah's Note: If I want my dessert to be extra fancy, I make up some of the fruit sauce I use on potato pancakes and create little designs around the edge of large dessert plates while the Hot Fudge Sundae Cakes are baking. Mother prefers it that way. My sisters like it with their choice of ice cream. Andrea prefers chocolate, Michelle likes butterbrickle, and I think it tastes best with coffee ice cream.

Chapter
Five

When Norman pulled into the crowded parking lot, Hannah saw her sister standing in the center of a parking space right next to the entrance, waving her arms frantically. Andrea's green Volvo was parked next to the spot and it didn't take an expert on string theory to surmise that she was standing there to save the parking place for them.

The first thing Hannah heard when she emerged from Norman's car was a tinny version of *Hark the Herald Angels Sing* played at earsplitting volume. She glanced across the street at the houses nearby, and wondered whether any of the homeowners had filed nuisance complaints.

Hannah covered her ears and gave a little groan. And then she greeted her sister. "Hi, Andrea."

"Hi, Hannah." Andrea turned to Norman. "I'm really glad you came along. Three opinions are better than two."

"And four opinions are even better," Hannah told her. "Mike should be here any minute, and before he gets here I need to warn you about standing in the middle of parking spots to save them. That really wasn't smart, Andrea. What if someone had pulled in too fast? They could have plowed right into you."

"But nobody would do that! Everybody knows I'm the sheriff's wife!"

"True, but what if they didn't see you in time? It's not exactly daylight out here."

Andrea thought about that for a moment and Hannah could tell from her sister's set expression that she wasn't willing to give up the argument quite yet. "Norman saw me in plenty of time. He slowed down."

"Norman's a good driver. But what if someone else had been driving, someone who'd stopped at the Lake Eden Municipal Liquor Store to have a couple of hot toddies before coming here to buy a tree?"

"Well . . ." Andrea sighed. "You're right. I shouldn't have been standing there in the middle of the space." She turned to Norman. "Don't tell Bill, okay?"

Norman smiled. "Don't worry, I won't. I know what can happen to a messenger who delivers bad news."

"What's that?" Andrea asked.

"Sometimes they're killed. Sophocles' messenger in *Antigone* starts right off by saying, *Don't kill the messenger.*"

"That's awful!" Andrea was clearly appalled. "You can't just go around murdering people because you don't like the news they give you. Did the killers get life sentences? Or did this happen in a state with capital punishment?"

Hannah was used to her sister's hit or miss brush with literature and history and she hurried to explain. "This happened a long time ago in a different part of the world, and nobody really knows what happened. But the phrase stuck with us. Shakespeare used it in *Henry IV, Part 2*, and some people say that Oscar Wilde and Mark Twain used it, too."

"Mark Twain's real name was Samuel Clemens," Andrea announced, clearly proud of herself for remembering. She turned to look as a car entered the parking lot and gave a smile. "Oh, good! Here comes Mike. But there's no space left. I wonder where he's going to park."

"Anywhere he wants to," Hannah replied, watching as Mike turned on the flashing red lights on top of his cruiser and pulled up horizontally behind Norman's sedan and Andrea's Volvo.

Once Mike had joined them, Andrea gave them the note Tracey had brought home from her teacher. The tree should be between four and five feet tall, it should have short needles, and the branches should have space between them so that it would be easier for the children to hang ornaments.

"Blue Spruce," Mike said.

"Or Scotch Pine," Norman offered. "Let's go see what kind of trees the Crazy Elf has."

"I'm just glad you all came along with me," Andrea said, leading the way toward the entrance. "Bill always picks out our tree. He doesn't go to a tree lot. His parents have plenty of pines on the back forty and he drives out there to cut one down every year."

"Does Tracey go with him?" Norman asked her.

"For the last two years. Before that she was too little." Andrea turned back to Hannah. "You used to go with Dad when he picked out the tree, didn't you?"

"Yes, but we got ours from the Red Owl. Florence's father had them trucked in, and he stood them up outside the store like spears against the brick wall."

"They didn't thaw them out?" Norman asked.

"No, they were frozen solid. A delivery came in one time when I was there with Dad. The trees were stacked in a flat bed truck with a tarp tied over the back. The thing I remember best is how they were trussed up with twine like mummies. I asked Dad how he could tell what they'd look like when they thawed out, and he said there was a trick to it."

"What trick?" Andrea grabbed Hannah's arm. "You'd better tell us. Maybe the Crazy Elf's trees are frozen, too."

"Dad's trick didn't make any sense to me at the time. He said the tree should resemble a carrot and the height should be two times the circumference of the base. And when I asked him what that meant, he said you had to wrap a string around the bottom, cut it off with a knife, and then see if the string would reach halfway up to the top of the tree. I watched him do it."

"Wow!" Mike sounded impressed. "You must have had some beautiful trees."

"We did, except for one year. Dad and I brought home the tree and he put it in the stand. He took off the twine and then it was time for me to go up to bed. He told me that the tree would thaw out before I got up the next morning and it would be beautiful."

"Was it?" Andrea asked. "I don't remember this at all."

"You couldn't remember it. You were just a baby. And yes, it thawed overnight. But it must have been old because every single needle fell off while we were sleeping and it was perfectly bare when I came down the stairs in the morning."

"Dad must have been very disappointed." Andrea looked sympathetic. "What did he do?"

"He got somebody to fill in for him at the hardware store, and he went out to Grandma and Grandpa Swensen's farm to cut down another tree."

Andrea looked worried. "I hope that doesn't happen to Tracey's tree!" She turned around to face the three of them. "Does anybody know how to tell if a tree is fresh or not?"

"I do," Norman spoke up. "All you have to do is feel the needles. If they feel dry and break off in your hand, it's an old tree."

"There's an easier way," Mike said. "I flash my badge and demand to see the invoice for the last batch of trees. And then I demand to see a tree from that batch."

Norman clapped Mike on the shoulder. "That's better than my way. Let's go in and see what they've got."

As they walked into the park, Hannah noticed the rows of sleds lined up just inside the gate. They were painted bright green and each sled had room for a child. Behind the area where the child would be seated was a large red box that looked like the bed of a supermarket shopping cart. The box was obviously meant to store items to be purchased and it was large enough to hold quite a few.

"Clever," Norman said, also noticing the sleds.

"And how," Hannah replied. "I wonder what they do if a mother comes in with two kids."

"That's where I come in."

All four of them turned to look as a blond girl in a green elf costume spoke to them. "I'm Mary and I'll be your elf for tonight."

"Do you really say that to all the customers?" Hannah asked her.

"No, just to you. I'm kidding, Miss Swensen. I'm Tricia Barthel's younger sister, and I don't blame you for not recognizing me in this getup."

"It's better than the one I wore last Christmas at the Lake Eden Inn. At least your tights aren't too tight."

"Hi, Mary," Andrea smiled at the girl. "I'm looking for a tree for my daughter's classroom. It has to be between four and five feet tall with short needles and branches that make it easy for a child to hang ornaments."

"We've got just the thing. Follow me to the smaller tree tent and I'll show you a couple you'll like."

They all trooped after Mary to a tent near the edge of the lot. It wasn't a prime location and Hannah guessed that the larger, more expensive trees were housed in the closer tents. On the way they passed the Crazy Elf Toy Shop, the Crazy Elf Ornament Center, and the Crazy Elf Tree Stand Store. And all the while *We Wish You a Merry Christmas* was blaring out over the speakers.

Hannah moved closer to Mary the elf. "Doesn't the music drive you crazy?" she asked.

"It did at first, but now I'm so used to it, I don't even hear it. I guess if it stopped I'd notice, but it won't stop until eleven tonight."

"Haven't the neighbors complained about the noise?"

"No. I asked the elf manager how Mr. Jaeger got away

with making so much noise, and she told me that he gave everyone in the houses next to the park a free tree and a fifty-dollar gift certificate for the shops."

"Smart," Hannah said. Most people could use extra money around the holidays and a free tree with fifty dollars worth of ornaments or toys was a nice Christmas bonus for anyone.

"Here we are," Mary announced, leading the way into one of the large tents that were fashioned out of canvas with green and red stripes. "All of these trees have short needles."

The air inside smelled heavenly, like walking through a stand of pines, and Hannah took a deep breath and smiled. She was more than a little relieved to see that the tent was warmed by space heaters and all of the trees were thawed. At least she wouldn't have to put her father's trick to the test.

"The Blue Spruces are here," Mary pointed to a section that was roped off with blue tape. "I wouldn't recommend those. The needles might drop off in a warm classroom."

"Thanks for telling us," Andrea said, and Hannah could tell she was grateful. "What are those trees?" she asked, pointing to the largest section.

"Those are Scotch Pines." Mary led the way to the green-roped section. "A lot of teachers have been buying those. They're the most popular Christmas tree and needle retention is really good. They tend to stay on even when the tree is dry."

Hannah glanced at Andrea. She was almost positive she knew exactly what her sister was going to do. Andrea was a firm believer that an item's worth was directly proportional to its price.

"Well, I don't want to buy the cheapest," Andrea said, confirming Hannah's supposition. "How about those?" she asked, pointing to the smallest red-roped section. "They're gorgeous."

"Oh, those are the Noble Firs. They're much more expensive, but they're . . ." Mary moved a bit closer and lowered her voice even though there was no one else in the tent. "I probably shouldn't say anything, but they're the freshest trees we have and they won't drop their needles in a hot classroom. Not only that, their needles are more pliable." Mary plucked one off and rubbed it between her fingers. "When the needles get old, they're really sharp. I guess that's why they call them needles. These won't get sharp until the kids leave school for Christmas vacation."

"Then I'll take one," Andrea said, walking over to take a look. "But they're all mixed up in the section together. Is there a way to tell how tall they are without measuring?"

"I'll show you," Mary said, gesturing to Andrea. "Just follow me and I'll explain the color coding on the tags."

As Andrea and Mary walked deeper into the forest of trees in the red section, Norman moved closer to Hannah. "They're only on calling birds and already my head hurts."

For a moment Hannah was thoroughly mystified and then she realized that the *We Wish You a Merry Christmas* had ended and *The Twelve Days of Christmas* had taken its place. "Eight verses to go," she said. "I've probably got some aspirin in my purse. Do you want a couple?"

"No, thanks. I'll be fine just as soon as we get out of here."

"Hey, Hannah." Mike walked up to join them. "What do you say we try out the Yule Log?"

Hannah took one look at the Yule Log ride and shook her head. The "log" part was hollow and it held seats with harness-type safety belts to prevent falling as it swayed back and forth. The seats were divided into sets of pairs facing each other. At the apex of one end the rider was looking straight down at his partner, and at the apex of the other, their positions were reversed. The momentum gained on the downswings must have been fierce because the people who were riding were screaming every time they descended. Perhaps, when she was younger, she would have regarded his invitation as a challenge and gone on the ride just to prove she could. Now that she was older, she was wiser. "Thanks, but no thanks," she said.

"Then how about Santa's Magic Sleigh?"

"The Ferris wheel?"

"Yes, but each car is decorated like a sleigh and there's a

plastic reindeer in front. You can see the whole park from the top of the wheel," Mike gestured toward the designer Ferris wheel that was slowly revolving in the distance.

Hannah knew she could handle that ride, but there was another consideration. "Only if I can take the reins."

"But they don't really do anything. I mean, the reindeer doesn't move or anything and . . ."

"I know. I was just kidding you. Let's wait until Andrea picks out her tree and then we can all go."

"You two go ahead," Norman said. "I'll help Andrea with the tree. It won't be hard now that Mary's steered us to the right type."

"Are you sure?" Hannah asked, wondering if Norman was just being polite.

"I'm positive. And don't worry if you have to wait in line. You've got plenty of time. It's going to take a while for Andrea to choose, and then they have to net her tree and tie it on top of her car."

"All right then." Hannah turned to Mike. "Let's stop off at the Crazy Elf Cookie Shop on the way. I want to see if they really are running out of cookies."

Hannah and Mike walked down the path between the tents. It was labeled North Pole Avenue and at the end was a row of log cabins. Each one had a sign hanging over the door on a pole that jutted out from the cabin. The sign reminded Hannah of the pictures she'd seen of English pubs, but it was clear these log cabins didn't sell roast beef sandwiches and stout.

"Larry spent big bucks on those buildings," Mike said, gesturing toward the Crazy Elf Toy Shop.

"How do you know?"

"I priced them when I lived in The Cities. I wanted to put one in the backyard for the mower, and the snow blower, and things like that."

"How much were they?"

"It was a thousand for the smallest one, and that was a

couple of years back. These have got to be the largest. They're huge. And unless Larry got a real deal, they've got to run over five thousand apiece."

"Maybe he's renting," Hannah suggested.

"That would make sense since he'll be closing down right after Christmas. Either that, or he plans to put them up for sale."

"They're too big to put in a backyard." Hannah noticed that a steady stream of customers was filing into the log cabin on the end and she steered Mike that way. "Who would buy them?"

"I don't know. Someone with a hobby farm might like one. They could use it for a woodworking shop, or fancy storage, or anything like that. They're even big enough for farm machinery, or a couple of cars."

"Maybe," Hannah said, sounding doubtful. The cabins had doors that were much too small for car or farm machine storage. They'd have to be remodeled and that would cost.

Mike gave a chuckle. "Mayor Bascomb can take one and use it for a second ice fishing house. It's even bigger than the one he has."

"I wouldn't be a bit surprised if that happened," Hannah said, stopping at the cabin with the most foot traffic and the one sporting a Crazy Elf Cookie Shop sign.

"Let's go in and I'll buy you a cup of coffee," Mike said. "I'd buy you a cookie too, but they're out."

Hannah turned to him in amazement. "How can you tell from out here?"

"I've been watching and the only things the customers carry out are hot drink cups. If they had cookies, some of them would be carrying bags."

"I'm impressed!"

"You should be," Mike grinned down at her. "I guess that's why I'm the detective and you're not."

Hannah bit her tongue. There was no way she was going to ruin the evening and point out that she'd solved more than a dozen murder cases. If she did that, Mike would be sure to point out that she'd gotten herself into trouble a couple of times, and he'd been the one who had to bail her out. It was best to remain silent and not bring up the subject that was a sore point between them.

"After you," Mike said, opening the cabin door and holding it for Hannah.

"Thanks." Hannah stepped inside and blinked a couple of times. It was glitter and glitz, glitz and glitter. The inside of the cookie shop was decorated with thousands of miniature Christmas lights and they were all blinking on and off randomly. Wreaths hung behind the serving counter, a large stuffed bear with a plaid Christmas hat was positioned near the area where the line formed, and every time someone walked past, the bear wished them a merry Christmas. Glittering garlands of silver and blue foil were looped in every place possible, electric candles were perched on every windowsill, and two huge Christmas trees sat by the back wall, one in either corner.

"Look at those trees," Mike said, as if Hannah could possibly have missed them. They were at least fifteen feet tall and they were decorated with enough ornaments and lights for a half-dozen trees. The lovely angels on top had two-foot wingspans, and their gossamer wings were shimmering in the air currents as if trying to work up the speed for a takeoff.

Hannah and Mike passed the bear, who wished both of them a merry Christmas, and took their place at the end of the line. The procession of people waiting for sustenance was structured by red velvet ropes attached to giant candy canes on stands. Hannah noticed that Larry had taken his cue from amusement parks and purchased stands that could be arranged and rearranged to accommodate any size crowd.

The line moved swiftly and soon Hannah and Mike were almost at the front. "See?" he pointed to the empty display case. "No cookies."

"You're right. I wonder how long they've been out."

"Since six," replied the girl who'd moved over to wait on them. "Your cookies practically fly out the door, Miss Swensen."

"Krista?" Hannah asked. The girl in the elf costume looked a bit like Barbara Donnelly's granddaughter.

"It's me. Grandma dropped me off at work tonight and she said I don't look like myself."

"Your grandma's right. If you hadn't spoken to us I never would have recognized you."

"Maybe that's good. The customers aren't too happy when I tell them we're out of cookies. Can you talk Mr. Jaeger into ordering more?"

"I'll try. Is he here tonight?"

"He's here every night. If you keep on going past the toy shop and take a left at Rudolf Lane, you'll see a woodsy-looking trailer off to the right. It's all decorated with garlands of Christmas lights and there's a blue flocked tree out in front. That's Elf Headquarters. Just ring the bell and Mr. Jaeger will let you in. Now what can I get for you two?"

"I'll take a large Holly Jolly," Mike answered her and then he turned to Hannah. "How about you?"

"I don't know. What's a Holly Jolly?"

"It's hot chocolate mixed with coffee that's flavored with orange," Krista explained. "It's got whipped cream on top and it's really good, Miss Swensen."

"Then I'll have one, too."

In less than a minute Hannah and Mike were exiting the building armed with two carryout cups of Holly Jolly. Hannah took a sip of hers and was pleasantly surprised. "This is pretty good," she said.

"You're right. It's perfect for a cold night like this. The only way you could make it better is to put in a shot of brandy."

Hannah was surprised. Mike wasn't a big drinker. He'd have the occasional beer, or a glass of wine with a fancy dinner, but she'd never seen him drink brandy.

"Or you could go with an orange liqueur like Grand Marnier. That would bring out the orange in the coffee. Or you could use orange flavored vodka. They've got practically every flavor now."

He'd mentioned three kinds of liquor in as many seconds and Hannah thought she knew why. "You must have had a rough day," she guessed.

"Yeah. That's one of the reasons I dropped by, but I didn't want to say anything in front of Norman. It's just a hunch, that's all."

"*What's* just a hunch?"

"Norman's mother. I think she could be shoplifting."

"What?!"

"I told you, it's just a hunch. I've been thinking about it all day and it's the only explanation that makes sense."

Hannah planted her heels on the walkway and stopped. "Hold on a minute. What makes you think Carrie's shoplifting? And start from the beginning."

"Last night was the third time I followed her home from the mall. She was out there on Sunday night, and last week on Monday and Tuesday nights, too."

"You're following Carrie?" Hannah was amazed. Surely Carrie wasn't shoplifting! But shoplifting could be a disease . . . at least that was what she'd learned in psychology class. Some people who shoplifted did it because they couldn't afford some item they wanted. But other people who shoplifted really couldn't help themselves. They were addicted to the thrill and excitement. There were multistep programs to help addictive shoplifters that were modeled after the programs for alcoholics.

"I'm not following Carrie on purpose," Mike tried to explain. "It's just that she leaves the mall when it closes and so do I. Mall Security is shorthanded and I'm taking a couple of shifts until they find somebody to hire full-time."

"Lots of people like to shop at the mall until it closes. It's the only place where you can walk for miles in the winter without a coat and boots. What makes you think that Carrie's shoplifting?"

"I told you it's just a hunch, but every time I see her loading her trunk with packages, she looks guilty."

Hannah had to admit that Mike's hunches were usually right. But she still wasn't willing to believe that Norman's mother had a problem with shoplifting. "Those packages she loads in her trunk . . . can you tell what stores they're from?"

"Last night it was The Glass Slipper. It's an upscale shoe store. It was a really big bag, Hannah. She must have had six pairs of shoes in there."

"Did you check with The Glass Slipper to see if she bought anything?"

Mike gave her a look that would have withered the hardiest tree in the forest. "Of course I did! I'm not a rookie, you know."

"I know that. What did they tell you?"

"That she bought six pairs of shoes and put them on a credit card. The card was good. They checked."

"Then she *didn't* shoplift."

"Not from The Glass Slipper. She had some other packages in the trunk, but I didn't get close enough to notice the store names."

"Okay." Hannah drew a deep breath. "You don't know anything for sure, so let it go, at least until a store reports lost inventory. They do that, don't they?"

"Every Friday. You're right, Hannah. I can't jump to conclusions. I just didn't like the look on her face when she spotted me. It was like she was afraid I'd question her or something, and she's never looked at me like that before."

"I understand," Hannah said taking his arm and giving it a little squeeze. "Perhaps it was nothing. You must have been tired after working at the station all day and then putting in a shift at the mall."

"I was. But I wasn't imagining that look."

"Okay. Let's drop it for now and think about something really important."

"What's that?"

"Shall we ride Santa's Magic Sleigh first, or go talk to Larry about his cookie order?"

"Let's go talk to Larry," Mike decided. "I've got a couple of questions for him."

"What questions?"

"It's about the sign I saw on the checkout booth we passed on our way in."

"What sign?"

"The one that said, *We sell below cost and make it up on volume.*"

Hannah's mouth dropped open. "But . . . but . . ." she sputtered. "That's impossible!"

"I know it is. I want to find out if that's Larry's idea of a joke, or if he really believes it."

As she walked down the snowy path with Mike, Hannah just shook her head. Although she'd been dreading it, she now hoped her mother would invite her to small business class again. Larry Jaeger's sign was bad business whether it was a joke, or not. That meant she had something to contribute to the bad business practices segment of the class. The more she thought about it, the funnier it became and Hannah chuckled all the way to Elf Headquarters. She could hardly wait to tell Miss Whiting about this!

HOLLY JOLLY COFFEE

1 cup strong coffee, steaming hot
1 packet hot cocoa mix *(the kind that makes one cup)*
¼ teaspoon orange extract***

Mix everything up together and top with sweetened whipped cream.

*** - As Mike suggested you can substitute an ounce of brandy, an ounce of Grand Marnier, or an ounce of orange-flavored vodka.

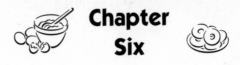

Chapter Six

"Who is it?" a male voice called out when Mike rang the bell.

"Mike Kingston and Hannah Swensen," Mike replied.

"Hold on. I'm coming."

A moment later, Larry Jaeger opened the door. It was clear he'd been sitting on the couch watching football, because there was a half-empty beer bottle on the coffee table, along with a bag of chips and a container of onion dip.

As Hannah moved closer to the giant flat screen television, she spotted familiar purple and gold uniforms. She glanced up at the rectangle at the top of the screen to see who the Vikings were playing, and read that the opponent was *LA*. No punctuation was present, and that meant the team could be Louisiana or Los Angeles. Rather than hazard a guess and risk exposing her pigskin naivety, Hannah settled for her favorite football ambiguity. "How about those Vikings," she commented, giving a little shrug.

"They're doing it again," Larry replied, leading them over to the chairs directly across from the couch. "They were ahead at the end of the half, but now they're blowing it. I'll just kill the sound so we can talk."

Hannah watched Larry as he hunted for the control. If she had to describe him in one word, that word would be "average." Everything about him was average, from his hair, a color midway between light and dark, his medium build, and his standard height. He was dressed in a pair of jeans, a plaid shirt, and a pair of pull-on deerskin boots.

Although Larry looked ordinary, Hannah knew he wasn't. You couldn't live in Lake Eden without hearing stories about the budding businessman who had devised unique ways of raising money. Larry had been a wheeler dealer even back in high school.

And now he was at it again. Larry's Christmas tree lot was packed with customers and it certainly looked to be a successful business. The sign Mike had noticed bothered her a bit, but perhaps Mr. Medium, as Hannah had come to think of him, possessed a weird sense of humor.

"I'm glad you're here, Hannah," Larry said in his medium-volume, medium-pitched voice. He hit the mute button, killing the sound, and turned to her. "I was planning on calling you in the morning. The girls at the cookie shop tell me we need to increase our order."

"That's great," Hannah said, giving him a smile. It seemed that Larry was on top of the cookie problem. "How many dozen extra would you like?"

"Let's see . . . we go through an average of six dozen an hour in the afternoons and it'll probably be more in the evenings. Let's say an extra thirty-six dozen. That ought to cover it."

It was a big order and Hannah was pleased. "We can do thirty-six dozen. Do you want any particular kind?"

"Actually, I do. I noticed we don't have anything with white chocolate."

Hannah thought fast. "I just tested a new recipe for White Chocolate Pumpkin Dreams and they were excellent. They're a soft cookie and they're very moist. Would you like to try those?"

"They sound fine. Could you deliver five dozen of those every day?" When Hannah nodded, he went on. "And we don't have a ginger cookie. Do you have anything like that?"

"I could give you five dozen Frosted Ginger Cookies."

"Sounds great. How about something with marshmallows? Kids love marshmallows."

"They certainly do," Hannah agreed, her sole point of reference being her niece Tracey. Tracey adored marshmallows and the last time she had come down to The Cookie Jar to spend the afternoon, they'd come up with a brownie that Tracey loved. "How about five pans of Fudge-Mallow Cookie Bars? You can get two dozen brownies from each pan. That'll be another ten dozen."

"Good!"

Larry was silent for several moments and Hannah wondered if he'd added wrong. "That's only twenty dozen extra," she reminded him.

"I know. I'm just considering something else. We get a big rush of customers right after the dinner hour. How about some kind of wonderful Christmas dessert, something so good it'll make them leave their own dinner tables and come to the Crazy Elf for dessert?"

"That's a good idea," Hannah said, and then she was silent. She wasn't about to suggest something like mincemeat pie or fruitcake at this point, not until Larry had given her a clue to what he considered wonderful.

"I'm thinking of something they wouldn't make at home. And something that's not available at local grocery stores. We might even need something that people around here haven't tasted before."

Hannah thought of several desserts that fit Larry's description, but she wasn't about to name them. They were overworked as it was at The Cookie Jar and there was no way they were going to bake cranberry tarts or miniature chocolate meringue pies. She'd wait for him to come up with something and then see if they had time to do it.

Larry thought for a moment and then he leaned forward in excitement. "How about plum pudding? They have it in England and I think it's a traditional Christmas dessert."

"It may be traditional, but nobody's going to order it twice,"

Mike said, entering the conversation for the first time. "I had it at a fancy restaurant in Minneapolis. It tasted like fruitcake, but what really got to me was there wasn't a single plum in it."

"No plums in plum pudding?" Larry asked, turning to Hannah for confirmation.

"Mike's right. The traditional recipe has citron and some other dried and candied fruit, but no plums."

"Then why do they call it plum pudding?"

Hannah shrugged. "Maybe it's because it's wrapped up in cloth and steamed. Somebody probably thought it came out shaped like a plum."

"Well, I guess plum pudding won't work." Larry looked disappointed.

"Don't give up quite yet," Hannah told him, her mind working a million miles a minute. She still had to come up with a spectacular dessert for Claire and Reverend Knudson's wedding dinner and she might be able to kill two birds with one stone. "I think I can create my own recipe for plum pudding and I'll make sure there are real plums inside. You probably don't want to flambé it if you're going to serve individual slices, though."

"Right," Larry agreed.

"Do the girls in the cookie shop have a microwave?"

"Yes."

"Good. I think it'll be better if it's heated. I'll try it and see."

Larry still looked slightly worried. "I hate fruitcake. It's not going to taste like fruitcake, is it?"

"Absolutely not. There won't be any citron or dried fruit in it except maybe a few golden raisins. Do you want me to try to bake a sample and bring it to you so you can taste it?"

"Yes."

Both men spoke at once and Hannah laughed. "I'll work on it at the The Cookie Jar tomorrow and bring you something with your afternoon cookie delivery. How's that?"

"That's great," Larry said.

Hannah turned to Mike. "And you can stop in around noon to try your sample. In the meantime, I'll give you extra sugar cookies, if that's okay."

"That's fine. Your sugar cookies are always a big hit." Larry stood up to walk them to the door, but Mike stayed in his chair.

"One more thing," Mike said. "I noticed you don't have any Christmas decorations in here."

"That's right. I get enough of all that every time I open the door. I don't know how Courtney can stand it."

"Courtney?"

"My fiancée. She heads up the sales staff in the toy shop and she has to listen to all those animated toys with the squeaky recorded voices every day."

"That must be tough," Mike said.

"It is. She complains about it all the time, but she won't shut them off. She says it's good for business." Larry stood up and gestured toward the door. "Sorry to cut this short, but I have a business meeting in five minutes and it's important."

Mike and Hannah rose from their seats. They followed Larry toward the door and once they'd reached it, Mike stopped and turned back to Larry. "I noticed your sign by the checkout booth, the one about selling below cost and making it up on volume. You were kidding, weren't you?"

"Of course I was kidding! You can't sell below cost and make a profit regardless of the number of units you deal. Everybody knows that."

"Then why do you have the sign?" Hannah asked, hoping for an addition to her story for Miss Whiting.

"When I was still in junior high a guy on a TV commercial said that he was selling below cost and making it up on volume. I think it was some spokesman for a mattresses store. I thought it was funny and I signed up for a shop class so I could make up a professional-looking sign. That's the original out by the checkout booth. It's turned into a tradition for

L. J. Enterprises. That sign has hung by the door in every business I've ever started."

It was a clear winter night and the stars were sparkling as if they were made of multifaceted ice crystals. The moon was up, a silvery ball overhead casting blue shadows on the snow below them. The music was pleasant at this altitude. The melodies floated up to embrace them for brief moments and then dispersed in the dark frigid air.

"Are you cold?" Mike asked, and not waiting for her answer, slipped an arm around her shoulders.

Not at all was the answer on the tip of Hannah's tongue, but Mike's embrace felt wonderful and rather than speak, she smiled.

"There's the cookie shop." Mike leaned out the side of their sleigh to see. "And there's the flocking tent. I'm really glad Andrea didn't go for one of those."

"So am I!" Hannah's reply was heartfelt. A flocked tree was fine for the lobby of a hotel, or the front window of the First Mercantile Bank, but school kids should experience a real tree that wasn't sprayed all over with plastic and adhesive and whatever else the Crazy Elf used for flocking material.

"They really swing up high on that Yule Log." Mike leaned out the side of their sleigh to take a better look. "I think there's one point where you stop and you're perfectly suspended before you go on the downswing again."

Hannah thought about being suspended with Mike's arm around her. That would be nice, but only if they could just stay there and not go on the downswing again.

"There's Larry's headquarters," Mike pointed from his side of the sleigh. "See it?"

Hannah glanced down in time to see a man entering Larry's trailer. He must be arriving for the business meeting Larry had told them about. As the man passed through the doorway, Hannah realized that he looked a bit like Earl Flensburg. Of course that was about as likely as snow in July. The Winnetka County tow truck and snowplow driver wasn't the type to attend a business meeting, especially a one-on-one meeting with a high-powered executive like Larry Jaeger.

"It's funny, isn't it, how there wasn't a single Christmas thing inside?" Mike asked.

For a moment Hannah was puzzled and then she realized that Mike was referring to Larry Jaeger's trailer. "Not really. If you were around something every waking minute, you'd probably want to get away to something completely different."

"Careful, Hannah," Mike said, giving her the devilish grin that always made her toes tingle. "I think you just gave me the guy's argument for infidelity."

And naturally you recognized it, Hannah thought, but of course she didn't say it. "I prefer to think of it as an argument for going camping after a hard week at work," she countered, "or the reason someone who lives in Minnesota likes to vacation in Hawaii."

"You've got a point. I wouldn't mind a little fun in the sun in the dead of winter. Say, Hannah . . . I've got two weeks of vacation coming at the end of January. I was thinking about flying to St. Thomas and I . . . isn't that Andrea?" Mike leaned out even farther and waved his arm. "It's her, all right. Andrea's down there waiting for us."

Saved by the sister, Hannah thought, not quite sure if she was grateful or disappointed that Mike hadn't finished what had sounded like an invitation to come along on his winter vacation.

The sleigh began to descend and their time for privacy was over. Hannah leaned out to smile at her sister as they came to rest and an attendant rushed over to help them out.

"Did you have fun?" Andrea asked when they were both on the ground.

"It was nice," Hannah answered.

"Nice," Mike teased her. "I thought it was more than nice."

"Okay, it was fun." Hannah turned to Andrea. "You can go on this one with Tracey. It won't make her sick. You could even take Grandma McCann and Bethany if you want to. But watch out for the Yule Log."

"I know. I walked past it on the way over here, and the Yule Log is definitely out." Andrea led them toward the entrance. "We're all through shopping and Norman's out in the parking lot helping them tie on the trees."

"I'll go help him," Mike said, striding forward and leaving the two Swensen sisters alone.

"You said *trees*," Hannah reminded her. "Did you get more than one tree?"

"Did I say trees? I didn't mean to. I just hope mine doesn't scratch the roof of my Volvo."

"Yours?" Hannah asked. "Does that mean there's a tree that isn't yours?"

"Of course there is. My tree is mine. It's the one I bought for Tracey's class. It's mine as opposed to somebody else's. My tree is mine. Their tree is theirs. I didn't mean anyone else's tree in particular. I just meant somebody else's tree in general. This is a tree lot and there are other people here. Some of those people are buying trees, right?"

Hannah turned to stare at her sister, who immediately averted her eyes. Andrea was dissembling and that meant something was up. She moved a little closer to her sister and asked the question. "Do you want to tell me now? Or do you want to tell me later?"

"Later," Andrea said with a sigh. "I promised I wouldn't say anything and I already blew it. Don't ask me anymore questions, okay?"

"Okay." Hannah capitulated. Andrea looked completely chagrinned. "Just tell me if you happened to go into the toy shop. I'm curious."

"Yes, I did." Andrea looked very relieved. "I was looking for a toddler's globe for Bethany, but they didn't have one."

"What's a toddler's globe?"

"It's a globe filled with soft squishy padding. Toddlers can grab it, and roll it, and squeeze it, and throw it. It's a really great early learning tool. They can learn about the world, and the oceans, and the continents, and the countries before they even go to school."

"Right," Hannah said. It was a sweet idea and Bethie would love a globe ball, but it would be hopelessly out of date by the time she could read the names. Proof of that pudding was at the Olympics. Every year new countries were formed, old countries were dissolved, and other countries were renamed. The parade of nations was never the same from one Olympics to the next.

"It was just a thought and I found something else for her," Andrea said, approaching the gate to the parking lot.

"What?"

"They had these darling crocheted animals. The clerk said they were handmade by someone in Lake Eden, and I bought an elephant for Bethie. Then I noticed a lion and I got that for Tracey. She's into big jungle cats this year."

"Were they expensive?"

"Yes, but they were really well made and they're washable. I don't think twenty dollars is too much to pay for a hand-crafted stuffed animal, do you?"

"No, especially not if you're supporting a local cottage industry. That's important." Hannah remembered what Larry had told her and turned to look at her sister. "Did you happen to notice the woman who was running the toy shop? Her name is Courtney and she's Larry Jaeger's fiancée."

Andrea thought for a moment. "She was probably the short brunette wearing the red velvet jumper and white lace blouse. She had on a Santa hat and all the rest of the cashiers were high school girls dressed like elves."

The two sisters walked down the row until they came to Andrea's car. Norman and Mike had loaded the tree on top and tied it down securely. Hannah turned to look at Norman's car and she saw that he also had a tree tied to the top. "You got a tree?" she asked him.

"No, *you* got a tree."

"Me!?" Hannah looked up at the huge Scotch Pine and then she turned back to Norman. "This is really nice of you, Norman. But cats and Christmas trees don't get along."

"Have you ever tried it?"

"Well . . . no, but I've heard it doesn't work out. Cats do things like climb up the branches, bat all the ornaments to the floor, and swallow the tinsel."

"You won't know that for sure unless you try it," Andrea pointed out. "Barbara Donnelly has a cat and she always gets a Christmas tree."

"That's right," Mike said. "Barbara told me that her cat never even notices her tree. I think you should try it. Moishe's a nice cat. He's always been a good boy and he probably won't bother your tree at all."

Hannah turned to stare at Mike in disbelief. He'd just described the cat who'd run laps in her bathtub at two in the morning as a *nice cat*. This same *good boy* had torn all of the stuffing out of her couch pillows, emptied his litter box on the laundry room floor, chewed a hole in the side of her kitchen broom closet, and dragged her underwear out of the laundry basket to scatter over the living room rug as a display for any company she might bring home with her. Moishe was a funny cat, a great companion, and a well-loved roommate. But not by any stretch of the imagination could he be accurately described as a *nice cat*, or a *good boy*.

"Just try the tree overnight," Norman suggested in an attempt to overcome her lack of enthusiasm. "I'll set it up for you and everything. I just hate to think of you without a Christmas tree. It smells good, and it's pretty, and it'll make your whole condo feel like Christmas."

"Well . . ." Hannah hesitated. She'd really missed having a Christmas tree.

"I tell you what," Norman went into his closing argument. "If it doesn't work out, I'll come and take it away."

"How can I refuse an offer like that?" Hannah stepped closer to hug him. Buying a Christmas tree for her was a sweet thing to do. "But I want you to have a heart-to-heart talk with Moishe tonight, right after you set it up."

"What do you want me to say?"

"Just tell him that my tree isn't really a tree."

"What?"

"I mean . . . it's a tree, but it's not a regular outside tree. It's an inside tree and it's a decoration for Christmas."

"Do you think Moishe can tell the difference?"

"I think so, especially if you give him an example. You might want to explain that his kitty kondo is entertainment for kitties, and the Christmas tree is entertainment for people." Hannah stopped and shook her head. "On second thought . . . never mind."

"But why?" Andrea asked her. "I thought that sounded perfectly reasonable."

"It did and it is. It's just that the distinction won't work on Moishe."

"Why not?" This time it was Mike who asked the question.

"Because Moishe doesn't recognize the difference between people things and cat things. He thinks he's a four-legged person in a fur suit. He has no idea that he's a cat."

WHITE CHOCOLATE PUMPKIN DREAMS

Preheat oven to 350 degrees F., rack
in the middle position.

**This recipe is from Michelle's roommate, Susan, and it's
a real winner!**

1 cup softened salted butter (*2 sticks, 8 ounces,*
½ pound)
½ cup white (*granulated*) sugar
½ cup brown sugar (*pack it down in your cup when*
you measure it)
1 large egg, beaten (*just whip it up in a glass with a*
fork)
1 teaspoon baking powder
1 teaspoon baking soda
¼ teaspoon salt
½ teaspoon nutmeg (*freshly ground is best*)
1 teaspoon cinnamon
½ teaspoon cardamom (*or an extra half-teaspoon of*
cinnamon, but cardamom's really a lot better)
1 cup canned pumpkin*** (*I used Libby's*)
2 cups flour (*pack it down in the cup when you*
measure it)
2 cups (*12-ounce package*) white chocolate chips
1 cup chopped pecans (*measure after chopping*)

*** - *Make sure your pumpkin has NO spices added. Some canned pumpkin is already spiced for use in pumpkin pies. You could probably use it if it's snowing outside and your car won't start and it's more than a mile to the store, but just remember that it's somebody else's mixture of spices, not yours.*

You can either spray your cookie sheets with Pam or another nonstick cooking spray, or line them with parchment paper. Either way will work fine.

Mix the white sugar with the brown sugar. Stir until the mixture is a uniform color.

Add the sticks of softened butter and beat until the mixture is light and fluffy.

Add the beaten egg and mix it in thoroughly.

Stir in the baking powder, baking soda, and salt. Mix them in thoroughly.

Mix in the nutmeg, cinnamon, and cardamom. *(Susan uses pumpkin pie spice instead of the freshly ground nutmeg, cinnamon, and cardamom.)*

Measure out one cup of pumpkin and add it to your bowl. Stir it in until the mixture is smooth.

Add the flour in half-cup increments, stirring the batter smooth after each addition.

Add the white chocolate chips. Mix them in and then add the chopped pecans. Stir everything in thoroughly.

Use a teaspoon to scoop out some dough and drop it on your cookie sheet. These cookies will be small, but they spread out when they bake. Place the cookie dough balls 3 to a horizontal row, 4 rows to a cookie sheet.

Bake the White Chocolate Pumpkin Dreams at 350 degrees F. for 12 to 14 minutes, or until they're firm. *(Mine took 13 minutes.)*

Remove the cookie sheets from the oven and let the cookies set up for 2 minutes. Then use a metal spatula to remove the cookies from the cookie sheets and transfer them to a wire rack to cool completely.

When all the cookies are baked and cooled, it's time to frost them. The following is a wonderful brown sugar frosting that will go well with White Chocolate Pumpkin Dreams.

Susan's Frosting:

½ cup brown sugar *(pack it down in the cup when you measure it)*
3 Tablespoons salted butter***
¼ cup milk *(I used half and half)*
1 to 1 ½ cups powdered *(confectioner's)* sugar *(no need to sift unless you have big lumps)*

*** - That's 1½ ounces or a little less than half a stick—don't worry if you're not super accurate. A little more butter won't hurt.

Combine the brown sugar and butter in a saucepan and bring it to a boil on the stove over medium-high heat.

Boil the mixture for 1 minute or until it's slightly thickened.

Pull the saucepan off the heat and cool the mixture for 10 minutes.

Add the milk *(or half and half)* and beat the mixture until smooth.

Add the powdered sugar by half-cup increments, stirring after each addition. Keep adding the powdered sugar until the mixture reaches spreading consistency.

Frost the cookies. If you'd like to dress them up a bit, place a half pecan on top of each cookie before the frosting hardens.

Hannah's Note: I just want to point out that since these cookies are made with pumpkin and pumpkin is a variety of squash, the kids may try to convince you that eating several White Chocolate Pumpkin Dreams takes the place of a serving of vegetables.

Lisa's Note: Sometimes I don't have the time to make this frosting, especially when Dad and Herb are standing

right there, waiting for the White Chocolate Pumpkin Dreams to come out of the oven. They won't wait for me to cook frosting, so I just sprinkle the cookies with powdered sugar and serve them that way.

Yield: approximately 6 dozen yummy cookies, depending on cookie size.

Chapter Seven

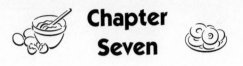

Mike was waiting for them when they pulled into the garage and Hannah noted with some amusement that he'd parked in her second spot right behind her cookie truck. It was another example of the rivalry that still existed between the two men. Mike had probably thought that if Norman had to move his car to the guest parking lot once they'd unloaded the tree and carried it upstairs, he probably wouldn't stay. But what Mike hadn't known when he'd taken the prime parking place was that Hannah's neighbors, Marguerite and Clara Hollenbeck, had offered the use of their second spot whenever Hannah needed it.

"You can park behind Marguerite and Clara's car," Hannah told Norman.

"Perfect." Norman pulled into the adjacent spot. "It'll be easier to unload the tree from here. Your spot is right next to the post."

As they got out of the car, Hannah turned to look. Norman was right. If he'd parked in her second spot, the one behind her cookie truck that currently held Mike's cruiser, they would have had to work around one of the big concrete pillars that held up the garage.

"I'll take it from here," Mike said, walking over to the driver's side of Norman's car.

Norman walked around the back of the car and stood by the passenger door. "I'll get it on this side," he said.

Hannah watched as the two men worked in tandem. Norman loosened the rope from his side and threw it over the top of the car to Mike, who untied it and tossed it back. They did this a half-dozen times before the rope was off and her tree was free.

"Your side or mine?" Norman asked.

"Yours. There's more room over there. We'll pull it off and stand it up. Then you take the top and I'll take the base, and we'll carry it up the stairs."

"Wait a second," Norman gestured to Hannah. "There's a tree stand in the backseat on the floor. Will you get it out and loosen the screws? We'll put your tree in the stand down here and then we'll carry it upstairs. You won't have as many needles on your rug that way."

"Thanks!" Hannah said, opening the back door to retrieve the tree stand. As her mother and sisters were so fond of telling her, Norman was a real find. Most men wouldn't have given her living room rug a second thought, but he was always planning ahead to make her life easier.

The tree stand was a challenge as they soon discovered. There were four long screws protruding into the center ring that could be cranked in or out to tighten the base of the tree in the stand. At the present, they were in all the way and it took longer than Hannah thought it would to loosen them. Both Norman and Mike knelt down to help and the three of them turned the cranks until their wrists were sore.

"Is that in far enough?" Hannah asked, pointing to her screw.

Norman looked over at what she'd done and nodded. "It looks good to me. Just let me work on this last screw for a minute and I'll see how much room we've got."

"When you're through, we can try to put the tree in." Mike straightened up and rubbed the small of his back. "I don't like this tree stand."

Norman looked up from his crouched position on the garage floor. "Neither do I, but this was the best they had. The problem was, I didn't know if Hannah had one and I didn't want to spoil the surprise by asking."

"It's a good thing you got it," Hannah told him. "I have the one down at the shop, but that's it."

"You'd think that with cell phones that do practically everything except pack your lunch, somebody could come up with a better design." Mike looked down at the tree stand. "This one's been around since I was a kid."

"There was another kind, but I thought it looked even worse," Norman told them. "It has a sharp spike on the bottom and you're supposed to lay the tree on its side and drive the spike into the base with a hammer."

Mike looked confused. "How are you supposed to do that?" he asked. "If you try to pound in the spike, the tree will just scoot across the floor. And even if you hold it with one hand, you need both hands to pound in the spike."

"You're right." Norman said. "You need one hand to hold the spike at the center of the trunk. And you need the other hand for the hammer."

"Then it must take two people to use that kind of tree stand," Hannah suggested.

"I think it would take three people," Norman corrected her. "Have you ever tried to hold a board steady while someone else hammers a nail into it?"

"I have," Mike told him. "My brother and I used to put up fencing around my mother's vegetable garden to keep out the rabbits. Other people used chain link, but our mother wanted a green picket fence with two inches between the pickets. I was the youngest so I used to be on the outside holding the picket while my older brother drove the nail to hold the strip of wood that attached them. Every blow knocked me back, even though I braced myself. And when I tried to anticipate and jump forward to meet the hammer blow, my timing was off and that didn't work either."

Once Norman had decided that the center ring was large enough for the tree trunk, Hannah held the stand in place while the men took the tree down from the top of Norman's car and attempted to insert the trunk into the ring.

"It won't go down," Mike stated the obvious. "It's catching on those branches at the bottom."

"Then we'll have to cut them off." Norman turned to Hannah. "Do you have a pruning saw?"

Hannah shook her head. "I don't have any gardening tools. All that's done by the grounds crew and it's part of my monthly maintenance assessment."

"You've got to have some kind of a saw," Mike said. "Most homeowners do. We can use anything."

"Like what?" Hannah asked him.

"Hand saw, crosscut saw, coping saw, keyhole saw, or even a hacksaw," Norman told her. "We'll take anything at this point."

Hannah was at a loss. She knew what all those saws were. She'd worked summers in her father's hardware store. But she didn't own any of them. "How about a Ginsu knife?" she asked. "I got it from a TV commercial, and it said it could cut through frozen vegetables. Maybe it would cut through a tree branch?"

Mike rolled his eyes. "Never mind," he said. "I'll make a call and get a pair of bolt cutters. That should work on the bottom branches."

While they waited for Lonnie Murphy to arrive with the bolt cutters, Hannah opened the storage area over her carport and took out the box of her grandmother's ornaments. She'd never used them, and this was the perfect time. None of her sisters had wanted them. Andrea had ornaments from Bill's family, Michelle was still living at home and didn't need them, and Hannah had become the beneficiary by default.

"What's that?" Mike asked, watching Hannah retrieve the box.

"Christmas ornaments. They belonged to my grandparents."

"Are they glass?" Norman asked her.

Hannah tried to remember. She recalled delicate blown glass baskets filled with purple glass grapes. There were also glass strawberries with curved stems that made their own hangers, and huge silver and gold balls that had seemed as big as balloons to her as a child. The only ornaments that weren't glass were the ones that her Great-Grandma Else had made. They were handcrafted birds that perched on the tree branches.

"I think most of them are glass," she said.

"If you use any of the glass ones, put them on branches near the top," Norman told her.

"Because of Moishe?"

"Right. I made the mistake of putting a glass ball on a branch near the bottom of my tree. Cuddles thought it was a toy."

"Did it break?"

"No, but it could have. Now the only things I have hanging from the bottom two branches are plastic ornaments."

"I thought you said Cuddles didn't bother your tree," Hannah reminded him.

"She doesn't, not anymore. That ball just intrigued her, I guess. It was really shiny and it probably acted as a mirror. And Cuddles loves to bat at her reflection in the mirror."

Hannah thought about putting the box of ornaments back in her storage area, but she really wanted to see her family's Christmas keepsakes again. She'd compromise by using the ones that wouldn't break and hanging only one of each glass ornament on the upper branches where Moishe couldn't reach them.

"Here comes Lonnie," Mike said as a police cruiser came down the ramp of the parking lot. He gave a wave and Lonnie pulled up to them.

Lonnie rolled down his window. "You need these?" he asked, handing the bolt cutters out the window to Mike.

"I don't need them. *You* need them." Mike stepped back so that Lonnie could get out of the cruiser. "Trim the bottom branches off the Christmas tree so it'll fit in the tree stand."

"And this is the police emergency the dispatcher called me about?" Lonnie asked, grinning at his boss.

"Yes, it is. Your supervisor was down on the floor of Hannah's garage and his knees were getting sore. Your knees are younger. You do it."

They watched as Lonnie made short work of trimming the lower branches of the tree. Then Mike held it in place while Norman, Lonnie, and Hannah tightened the screws to hold it securely.

"All done," Lonnie said, getting to his feet.

"Not quite," Mike told him. "Now you're going to help us carry it up the stairs to Hannah's condo. I'll take the top, you take the bottom, and Norman will take that box of ornaments."

"And Hannah will take the bag in the trunk," Norman added, clicking his remote to open it. "I picked up some mini-lights and a few ornaments."

A few moments later the procession moved up the outside staircase to Hannah's condo. Mike was in the lead with the tip of the tree, Lonnie followed behind him, Norman was next carrying the big box of Swensen family ornaments, and Hannah brought up the rear with a plastic red and green bag that said CRAZY ELF on both sides in four-inch high block letters.

Mike reached the landing first. He moved back as far as he could so Lonnie could join him and they set the tree down in front of the door. "Can you unlock it, or shall we move the tree back?" he asked Hannah.

"I think I can get it." Hannah reached between two branches and inserted her key in the lock.

"How about Moishe?" Mike asked. "If he tries to jump out in your arms, he's going to think the forest has come to visit."

Hannah laughed. "He'll be fine as long as it's not Birnam Wood and his name isn't Macbeth."

But Moishe was nowhere to be seen when Hannah opened the door and the men carried in the tree. He must have heard the commotion and decided that discretion was the better part of valor, or in his case, wriggling under or behind something was better than remaining in the open.

"I'll find him," Norman said, setting the box of ornaments on the floor and heading straight for the kitchen. "Here he is," he called out.

Hannah got to the doorway just in time to see her cat jumping down into Norman's arms from the top of the refrigerator. Norman carried him out to the living room couch, put him down in his favorite spot, and gave him a scratch behind the ears. "Don't worry," Norman told him. "It's just a Christmas tree."

Moishe looked over at the tree, which was now sitting in the corner of the living room, and laid his ears back flat against his head. Hannah knew what that meant. Her cat did not approve of a tree in his living room. He gave a little growl deep in his throat to confirm it and welcomed the stately Scotch Pine with a malignant stare.

"Coffee?" Hannah asked the assembled group of men. Even though she really didn't feel like making a pot, it was the proper question for a good Minnesota hostess to ask.

"I could use another cup," Mike said.

"Me, too," Norman chimed in quickly.

"Count me in," Lonnie told her. "I'll water your tree while you make it. All I need is a plastic pitcher."

"Wait a second," Hannah said. "I want to put something under that tree stand in case it leaks."

Norman look puzzled. "But it shouldn't leak. It's brand new."

"I know, but I don't want to take the chance. Phil and Sue's living room is right below mine and they just got new carpeting. I'll just be a second."

For once in her life, the large, square, plastic box was right where she remembered. Hannah got it down from the top shelf of the guest room closet and carried it out to the living room. "This yarn box should be about the right size. I'll get a bag for the yarn and needles."

"I didn't know you crocheted," Norman called after her.

"I don't." Hannah came back with the garbage bag and proceeded to dump in the yarn.

"Then you must knit," Norman tried another alternative.

"I don't do that either."

"If you don't knit or crochet, why do you have a box full of yarn and needles?" Mike asked.

"Because someone left it in the last apartment I rented when I was in college and none of the neighbors had a forwarding address. It was too good to throw away, so I just moved it along with the rest of my things."

While they were talking, Lonnie had lifted the tree, shoved the empty box under it with his foot, and set the tree stand inside the box. "It's a perfect fit," he said. "What are you going to do with all that yarn?"

"Give it to the thrift store, I guess. I know a couple of people who quilt, but I don't know anyone who knits or crochets."

"*I* do." Lonnie began to smile.

"Who?"

"My sister-in-law. Jessica learned how to crochet these really cute stuffed animals for the kids. Larry Jaeger saw one of her lions when they brought the kids out to the Crazy Elf to buy their tree and he told Jessica he'll take as many as she could turn out. He pays her ten dollars for each one and he sells them in the toy shop."

Hannah realized that Jessica's crocheted toys were probably the ones Andrea had bought for Bethie and Tracey. If Andrea had paid twenty dollars each and Larry had bought them for ten dollars apiece from Jessica, the toy shop was making a hundred percent profit.

"Take the yarn with you when you go," Hannah told Lonnie. "Jessica's more than welcome to it."

While Hannah put on the coffee, Lonnie found a pitcher and filled the tree stand with water. Hannah glanced around her kitchen, trying to think of something to serve along with the coffee and her gaze fell on the package of soda crackers sitting on the counter. That was a good base. What else did she have?

One glance into the refrigerator and she had her answer. She'd made a triple batch of Nancy Henderson's Christmas Cheese Rounds and they were wrapped in plastic wrap in the cheese drawer. Cheese and crackers would do nicely, especially since it was spur of the moment. But Norman and Mike had eaten Easy Cheesy Biscuits only a few hours ago. Was there such a thing as too much cheese?

Hannah considered it for a brief moment and then dismissed it. Minnesota was a dairy state. Anyone who lived here couldn't get too much cheese, butter, milk, and cream. Besides, she wanted to try one of Nancy's cheese treats. They were unusual and one of the ingredients was sure to cause raised eyebrows.

Hannah opened a jar of the jalapeno jelly that Florence had special-ordered for her at the Red Owl. She placed the cheese ball in the center of a serving plate, heated a few spoonfuls of jelly in the microwave until she could stir it smooth, and spooned it over the top of the cheese round. As she added a small serving knife to the plate, she decided that there was no way she'd mention what kind of jelly she'd used before they tasted it.

It was a simple matter to put some crackers into a napkin-lined basket and she carried it to the table, along with the cheese ball. "Try my homemade cheese ball," she said. "Coffee's coming right up."

Of course they tried it. And as she poured coffee and placed the mugs on a tray, she listened to the conversation taking place while they munched.

"Do you taste some kind of spice?" Norman asked.

"I don't know," Lonnie replied. "Maybe it's onions?"

"It doesn't *taste* like onions," Mike offered his opinion. "It tastes more like . . . peppers or something like that."

"Whatever it is, it's good!" Lonnie said. "What do you think, Norman?"

"I think it's in the sauce or whatever that is on top. And I like it a lot."

Hannah came through the doorway with the coffee and plunked it down on the table. "Jalapenos," she said. And then she watched their expressions change to surprise.

"But it's not *that* hot," Mike said. "Believe me I've had jalapenos before and they're a lot hotter than this."

"That's because this is jalapeno jelly, not straight jalapenos from the can."

"Maybe the sugar takes away some of the heat," Norman guessed, reaching for another cracker and loading it up with cheese and jelly. "This is really good, Hannah. I've never tasted anything like it before."

"I have," Mike said, giving Hannah a knowing look. "Somebody I know made Jalapeno Brownies as a special surprise for me."

Hannah itched to correct him. The brownies hadn't been a special surprise. They'd been an attempt to get even when he'd said that another woman's brownies were the best he'd ever tasted. Unfortunately, her brownie punishment had backfired. Mike had loved his fiery treats.

"Eat up boys, and then it's time to go," Hannah said. "It's already after eleven and I have to get up at four in the morning."

"But how about decorating the tree?" Norman asked her. "Don't you want us to help you with it?"

"Yes, but not tonight." Hannah gave him a smile to show that she appreciated his offer of help. "I'm just too tired to do any more tonight. I'll call you in the morning and we'll set something up."

Five minutes later the cups, the cheese plate, and the serving knife were in the dishwasher, and Hannah had reset the coffee pot for the morning. It didn't take her long to brush her teeth, wash her face, and put on the oversized sweat suit she wore to bed when it was sub-zero weather. She was about to climb into bed when she realized that Moishe wasn't in his accustomed spot on the pillow next to hers.

"Moishe?" she called out, but there were no soft kitty footfalls in the hallway. Moishe was still in the living room and that was when Hannah remembered that neither Mike nor Norman had pulled Moishe aside for that cautionary talk about the Christmas tree.

It's always up to the mother, Hannah thought, and then she grinned at her phrasing. She wasn't Moishe's mother. She'd need four legs and a tail to qualify for that position. But there were times, like now, when she felt she should exercise some maternal authority.

He was on the back of the couch looking perfectly inscrutable when Hannah retraced her steps to the living room. He was facing the tree and Hannah had the feeling that she should be extremely persuasive.

"How's my kitty boy?" she asked, sitting down on the couch and reaching up to pet him. "Do you like *my* Christmas tree?"

There was a beat of silence, and then another. After ten seconds or so, Hannah figured that Moishe was not going to respond.

"We'll decorate it tomorrow night and you'll see how pretty it is," she told him. "You'll like it, Moishe. I know you will. It's the holidays and we're celebrating."

More silence, stretching out for even longer this time. Hannah continued to pet and reassure her feline roommate. "Since it's Christmas, I think I should get you some new catnap mice. What do you think of that?"

There was another second of silence and then she heard a very soft meow. "Two mice?" she asked. "Or three mice?"

"Rowwwww," Moishe responded, moving over to lick her hand.

"Three mice it is then," Hannah repeated, scratching him

on his favorite spot under the chin. "Come on, Moishe. It's late and I'm tired. Let's go to bed."

This time Moishe followed her to the bedroom and jumped up on his pillow. Hannah climbed in, pulled the covers up to her chin, and reached out to touch his soft fur. This was nice. This was peaceful. The sound of her pet's even purring was wonderfully relaxing.

In no time at all, Hannah began to doze off to her pet's soft purring. It had been a lovely evening, the scent of pine filled the condo, her cat was purring softly beside her, and all was right with the world . . . except Bradford Ramsey. He was the only fly in the ointment. Why did he have to come back into her life now and spoil her perfect world?

CHRISTMAS CHEESE ROUNDS

For each cheese round you will need:

1 cup finely shredded cheddar cheese *(measure after shredding, but pack it down in the measuring cup—I prefer a sharp cheddar.)*
1 cup finely chopped pecans *(measure after chopping)*
8-ounce package softened cream cheese *(the brick kind, not the whipped kind in the crock)*
½ cup finely chopped green onions *(you can use up to an inch of the stem)*
1 small jar jalapeno jelly *(I used Knott's)*

Combine all the ingredients except the jalapeno jelly. Pack them into a small round mold, or form a ball and flatten it to resemble a hockey puck *(or a baby Brie if you're not from Minnesota and into winter sports.)*

Chill the cheese round for at least 2 hours. *(Overnight or even over several days is fine, too.)*

When you're ready to serve, place the cheese round on a pretty serving plate. Heat the jalapeno jelly in the microwave for a few seconds until you can stir it smooth. Then spoon approximately ¼ cup over the top of the cheese round, letting it drip down the sides and puddle on the plate. Accompany it with a basket of crackers or cocktail bread, and enjoy.

Yield: One cheese round that should serve as an appetizer for 6 to 8 people.

Chapter Eight

The alarm clock went off much too early to suit Hannah. All she wanted to do was duck back under the covers and hide from the day that was about to begin. Why couldn't she just find a nice nine to five job? Other people had jobs that paid benefits, and overtime, and periodic raises, and a bonus at Christmas, and . . .

Hannah's busy mind skidded to a halt. Christmas. It smelled like Christmas in her bedroom. The lovely pine scent from the Christmas tree that Norman had bought for her was perfuming her whole condo with the scent of a winter forest. Why hadn't she ever had a Christmas tree before? The scent was wonderful and it would be so nice to sit on the living room couch and gaze at lovely ornaments glowing in the reflections from soft twinkling lights nestled among the branches. She could sip hot chocolate, snuggle up warm and cozy with Norman, or Mike, or even Moishe.

Hannah's thoughts took another quick three-sixty. She was almost positive that Moishe had been in bed when the alarm went off. Her arm was still slightly numb from twenty-three pounds of purring feline using it as a pillow.

She reached out to flick on the light. Moishe had been here, but he wasn't here now. There was no cat in the bed, no furry pal on the windowsill hoping to catch a glimpse of a rabbit running across the snowy rose garden, no feline roommate perched on top of her dresser, purring loudly in an invitation to get up and feed him. Moishe wasn't in her bedroom at all.

There was a crash in the distance. It wasn't a loud crash, but it was worthy of notice. It seemed to take a long while to happen, like a tree toppling in the forest. Branches crackled, something swished, and a moment later, there was a hollow thud. And then there was water splashing out and then dripping . . . dripping . . . dripping . . . in her living room!

Moishe. Her Christmas tree. What was surely no more than a nanosecond after the thought occurred to her, Hannah was up and running. She sped down the hallway, flicking on lights as she went, and came to a skidding halt as she reached the tree, the one that had been in the corner of her living room and was now prone on her rug, the tree stand tipped up on two legs over an impossibly large lake of water that was spreading out over her carpet.

Hannah hissed out a word she would never have used around her nieces. All her precautions had been for naught. Her tree was down and the plastic pan had caught only a small amount of the water that had been in the tree stand. Her precaution hadn't worked. There was a rapidly spreading lake of water on her rug.

A groan worthy of a rudely awakened hibernating bruin emerged from Hannah's throat. As she stood there watching in dismay, the rest of the water saturated the fibers of her rug, seeped through the pad under her carpet, dripped past the joists that separated her apartment from her downstairs neighbors, and soaked the insulation and drywall that rested immediately above Phil and Sue Plotnik's living room ceiling.

Hannah ran to the laundry room for a stack of towels and spread them out over the puddle. She patted them down, hoping she could soak up some of the moisture, and then she made her unsteady way to the kitchen for a wake-up dose of caffeine. Coffee would help and perhaps all this was a bad dream.

As she opened the cupboard and stared at the array of coffee mugs that awaited her, Hannah tried to convince herself that she was still fast asleep and merely dreaming that she was in her kitchen, choosing a coffee mug for the morning. She got out her favorite, the one that bore the words, *That's the Way the Cookie Crumbles*, and carried it over to the coffee pot. It was amazing how realistic a dream could be. She could almost feel the weight of the mug in her hand and hear the clink as she set it down on the counter to pour herself a cup of liquid caffeine.

Hannah stood there and took the first scalding sip. And at that instant, she knew that this was *not* a dream. Moishe really *had* tipped over the tree, it had probably soaked through the floor and ruined Sue and Phil's new carpet, and her name was mud with her downstairs neighbors. She knew this for a fact because she'd just scalded her tongue and it hurt like blazes.

Hannah was waiting for her first attempt at plum pudding to come out of the oven when Lisa came in the backdoor.

"Hi, Hannah. It's sure is cold out there!"

Lisa was smiling a smile that stretched all the way back to a tooth number that Hannah didn't know, but Norman would probably agree that it was a molar. "You look happy," Hannah said.

"I am. Herb and Mayor Bascomb decided not to stay over to fish. They're coming back this afternoon."

"That's good."

"It's better than good. It's great. I brought you a loaf of Pork and Beans Bread. Do you want to try a slice? It's really good toasted and buttered."

"I'd love to try it. I'm hungry this morning."

It didn't take long for Lisa to slice the bread, pop it in the toaster, and butter it. She brought it to Hannah, along with a fresh mug of coffee. "Now pretend you don't know what's in it and see if you'd be able to tell by just tasting."

"Pretend I don't know? That's a little like un-eating a cookie, isn't it?"

"I guess," Lisa gave a little shrug. "I probably shouldn't have told you in the first place. Then I could have asked you to guess."

"That's okay. We'll try it out on the first person who comes through the door and see if they can guess."

"Good idea. But I want to know what *you* think."

Hannah took a bite and was amazed at the nutty, spicy flavor. It reminded her a bit of banana or date bread, but the texture was less cakelike. Lisa's bread was delicious and if she hadn't known it was made with pork and beans, she was almost certain she wouldn't have guessed.

"What do you think?" Lisa asked, clearly eager for Hannah's opinion.

"Delicious. I want the recipe."

"You've got it." Lisa opened her purse and drew out a recipe card. "I knew you'd want it so I copied for you early this morning."

Hannah turned to study her young partner's face. There were dark circles under Lisa's eyes. "How early?"

"It was about one o'clock I think. Once Herb left, I couldn't get to sleep. The house was so empty with him gone. It's not that I'm afraid of being by myself. It's just that I'm lonely." Lisa stopped talking and turned to Hannah. "How do you deal with that anyway?"

If that question had come from anyone else, Hannah might have taken offense. But Lisa was waiting for an answer, and she looked as if she really wanted to know. "I have Moishe," Hannah said, not mentioning that there were times, like this morning, when she wasn't sure if that was a curse or a blessing.

"Of course you do!" Lisa looked as if someone had handed her a wonderful present. "I never thought of that! You're never alone, not really. Herb and I need to get a dog."

Hannah was silent for a moment. She really shouldn't interfere. Lisa and Herb had their own lives and it wasn't up to her to offer advice. But aside from all that, she simply had to give her opinion. "Good idea!" she said. "Bill's dad just had puppies, and . . ."

Lisa cracked up and that made Hannah realize what she'd just said. "Okay. That didn't come out right. Bill's dad has a dog named Flopsy and she had puppies two months ago."

"Flopsy?" Lisa looked confused. "Isn't that the name of a bunny in *Peter Rabbit*?"

"Yes, but this Flopsy isn't a rabbit. She's a yellow lab. Bill's mother named her Flopsy because her ears flop all over the place when she runs."

"Oh. That makes sense, I guess. But yellow labs are pretty big. Does that mean that Flopsy's puppies will be big when they grow up?"

"Not necessarily. Bill's dad thinks the father is his neighbor's Jack Russell terrier."

"Like the one that was on *Frasier*?"

Hannah nodded and waited for the next question. It was bound to come. Lisa had been raised around farmers.

"But . . . a terrier like that is pretty small. And a yellow lab is big. How . . . ?"

"Don't ask me, but it happened," Hannah told her. "Andrea asked Dr. Bob, and he said he thought a staircase must have been involved."

Lisa sank down on one of the stools at the stainless steel worktable and chortled a bit. When she was through, she wiped her eyes and asked, "Dr. Hagaman didn't go into any details?"

"No. I think he figured that Andrea was a married woman and she could use her imagination. They've already found homes for all the puppies except one, and he's yours if you want him. He's really cute. Andrea showed me some pictures."

"Can I see them?"

"Yes. I'll call Andrea and tell her to bring them in. Bill went out there and snapped a few photos. I'm pretty sure he thought Tracey was ready for a puppy, but Andrea's still holding out."

"That could be lucky for us. Herb really wants a dog." Lisa thought about it for a moment and then she smiled. "Do you think Andrea could come by this morning?"

"I'm almost certain she can. She should be about ready to drive to Tracey's classroom with the tree she picked out last night. Do you want me to ask her to stop on the way back?"

"That would be perfect." Lisa turned toward the ovens. "What smells so good?"

"Plum pudding. I promised Larry Jaeger I'd take him a sample when I deliver his cookies this afternoon." Hannah waited for the question and when it didn't come, she added, "He increased his order, by the way."

"That's wonderful! You're a good salesman, Hannah." Lisa turned back from the kitchen coffeepot where she was pouring herself a cup. "Does your plum pudding have plums in it? The English one doesn't, you know."

"I know. Mine is different from the English pudding. I actually used purple plums."

"Oh, good! I tasted the other kind and I didn't like it. Marge bought some in a can last year and it was even worse than canned fruitcake." Lisa gave a little shudder at the memory. "What cookies does Larry want for his extras?"

"Ginger cookies," Hannah named one of the cookies that Larry had requested. "I thought we'd use Lois Brown's Frosted Ginger Cookie recipe. And until Larry decides if he wants the plum pudding, we'll fill in with more Old Fashioned Sugar Cookies."

"Do you have the recipe printed out for the ginger cookies?"

"Right here." Hannah handed her a sheet of paper.

"I'll get the ingredients," Lisa said, and headed off to the pantry. She opened the door and was about to enter when she turned back. "Do you know there's only ten shopping days left until Christmas?"

"No."

"I heard it on KCOW radio this morning. Do you have all your shopping done?"

"I do. I took Mother's advice and did it before Thanksgiving."

"That's great. I'm through, too." Lisa disappeared inside the pantry, but she stuck her head out again. "Do you think you could call Andrea now? The more I think about it, the more I want that puppy. Herb's been talking about getting a dog to make rounds with him, and he's really good with animals."

"If he runs true to his heritage, this pup should be easy to train," Hannah said. "Jack Russells are smart little dogs, and yellow labs are loyal and want to please their owners."

"That's true. Of course Herb can't take the puppy to work until he's trained, and I wouldn't want to leave him home alone. Do you think I could bring him down here on a leash in the kitchen until he's settled in?"

"That's fine with me," Hannah said, without a second thought for the health board or the city regulations. There were ways around those and she would find them. "If you decide to adopt the little guy, I'll support you all the way."

"Oh, he's so cute!" Lisa smiled down at the pictures Andrea had spread out on the kitchen counter. "I know I should wait for Herb to get back, but I'm almost positive he'll want him."

"Do you want to call and talk to him about it?" Andrea asked.

"I'd like to, but he didn't take his cell phone with him. He thought I might need it while he was gone."

"That's not a problem." Andrea pulled out her cell phone and hit a number. "I'll call Bill. He'll have Mayor Bascomb's cell phone number."

There were times when the electronic age was wonderful. Hannah admired the efficient way Andrea obtained the mayor's number and dialed it for Lisa. In less than a minute, Herb was on the phone talking to his wife. Of course Andrea had plenty of good reasons for wanting Lisa to take the puppy. Muddy footprints all over the sparkling white tile in her kitchen, a doggy entrance to the backyard that would have to be cut into the new designer door she'd just ordered for the kitchen, and accidents on her ice-blue living room rug were only three of those reasons.

"Then you really don't mind?" Lisa asked, and the answer she received caused a huge smile to spread over her pretty face. She listened for a moment and then she blushed. "I miss you too, honey. What time do you think you'll get here?"

Andrea nudged Hannah and they grinned at the way things were going. Hannah was happy that Lisa was getting a nice companion for the times that Herb worked late. Andrea was happy that she wouldn't have dog walking duty in the dead of winter.

"Okay. I'll see you before we close then. Hannah made plum pudding and I'll save you a piece." There was silence for a moment and then Lisa laughed. "Not *that* plum pudding. Hers has real plums in it and it smells divine. I'll wait until you get here and have a slice with you."

Andrea had just put her phone in the outside pocket of her purse when the front door opened and Delores came in. "Hello, dears!" she said, hanging her white leather, fleece-lined coat on the rack.

"Hello, Mother," Hannah and Andrea responded, almost in unison.

"Hi, Mrs. Swensen," Lisa chimed in.

"You don't have to call me Mrs. Swensen. Delores will do just fine. And if that makes you uncomfortable, you can call me Mother, too." Delores gave Lisa a smile. "Now what cookies do you recommend for a tired old woman this morning?"

"We just made a dozen batches of Frosted Ginger Cookies," Lisa told her. "How about a couple of those?"

"Perfect."

Hannah was disturbed by the phrase *a tired old woman*, especially since it had come from the mother who would rather endure torture than admit she was over fifty. "What's wrong, Mother?" she asked, the moment that Lisa had left for the kitchen to fetch the ginger cookies.

Delores walked over to take a seat next to Hannah. "Guess who didn't show up for work this morning?"

"Carrie?" Hannah guessed, knowing that her mother was worried about her partner.

"No. Carrie's there now, or I wouldn't have left. Luanne didn't show up."

"Is Susie sick?" Hannah took a guess at the only reason she could think of that would cause Luanne to miss work.

"I don't know. She didn't call in and she doesn't answer her phone. Do you think I should call Nettie?" Delores named the former sheriff's wife, who would surely have been Luanne's mother-in-law if her son, Susie's father, had lived.

"No. Let me see if I can find out what's wrong," Hannah responded quickly. She knew how much Luanne valued her job at Granny's Attic, and also how much she valued her privacy. Something must be terribly wrong if she'd been scheduled to work and hadn't shown up.

"Thank you. You might know today would be the day she'd miss work. I really need her help!"

"Is there anything I can do?" Hannah offered.

"I don't think so, dear . . . not unless you've figured out our homework assignment for Miss Whiting."

Hannah shook her head. She hadn't even looked at the sheaf of papers since she'd carried them to The Cookie Jar. She intended ask someone knowledgeable, like Stan, their tax man, or Doug Greerson, the local banker, but she just hadn't gotten around to it.

"I thought Luanne might have some ideas," Delores went on to explain. "She's been taking night classes in accounting."

"Really!" This was the first Hannah had heard of it.

"When she's ready, she's going to take over the books for Granny's Attic." Delores stopped speaking and frowned. "You won't forget to check on her, will you, dear?"

"I won't forget."

Delores took a bite of the cookie that Lisa had brought to her. "Very nice," she commented. "I especially like the lemon icing." And then, in the seamless way some mothers switch subjects with their offspring, she said, "So tell me . . . how are you coming along with your inquiries?"

Hannah managed to silence Andrea with a glance that indicated she'd explain later. "Just fine, Mother."

"Very good, dear." Delores turned to Andrea. "And how are you, dear?"

"I'm fine, Mother. Lisa and Herb are going to adopt one of Flopsy's puppies. They're going out this weekend to get the little guy. That means they all have homes."

Delores gave a little laugh. "And that means you're off the hook . . . for now, that is. I really don't think you've thought this puppy business through, dear. There'll be other puppies, you know. Tracey and Bill won't give up, and when Bethie gets old enough, she'll join them. You'll have to give in and get a puppy eventually. I did."

"But I remember Bruno. He was perfectly trained and he never had accidents, or barked, or chewed things."

Delores laughed. "That's true, but the question is, how did he get so well trained?"

"Hannah did it?"

"Not Hannah. She was in school all day."

"Dad?"

"He was at work in the hardware store."

Andrea's eyes opened wide in surprise. "*You* trained Bruno?"

"Of course I did. I was the only one home all day. Get used to it, dear. You're the mother. Tracey and Bill will promise you that you won't have to lift a finger, but you'll be the one to take walks around the block with a puppy that doesn't know how to sit, heel, or do his business in the bushes."

PORK AND BEANS BREAD

Preheat oven to 350 degrees F., rack
in the middle position.

15-ounce can of pork and beans *(I used VanCamp's)*
4 eggs, beaten *(just whip them up in a glass with a
fork)*
1 cup vegetable oil *(not canola, not olive—use vegetable oil)*
1 teaspoon vanilla extract
2 cups white *(granulated)* sugar
1 teaspoon baking soda
½ teaspoon baking powder
½ teaspoon salt
1 and ½ teaspoons ground cinnamon
1 cup chopped pecans or walnuts *(measure after
chopping—I used pecans)*
3 cups all-purpose flour *(pack it down in the cup
when you measure it)*

Prepare your pans. Spray two 9-inch by 5-inch by 3-inch-
deep loaf pans with Pam or another nonstick cooking spray.

Don't drain the pork and beans. Pour them into a food
processor or a blender, juice and all, and process them
until they're pureed smooth with no lumps.

Place the beaten eggs in a large mixing bowl. Stir in the
pureed pork and beans and mix them in well.

Add the vegetable oil and the vanilla extract. Mix well.

Add the sugar and mix it in. Then mix in the baking soda, baking powder, salt and cinnamon. Stir until everything is incorporated.

Stir in the chopped nuts.

Add the flour in one-cup increments, stirring after each addition.

Spoon half of the batter into one loaf pan and the other half of the batter into the second loaf pan.

Bake at 350 degrees F. for 50 to 60 minutes. Test the bread with a long food pick inserted in the center. If it comes out sticky, the bread needs to bake a bit more. If it comes out dry, remove the pans from the oven and place them on a wire rack to cool for 20 minutes.

Run the sharp blade of a knife around inside of all four sides of the pan to loosen the bread, and then tip it out onto the wire rack.

Cool the bread completely, and then wrap it in plastic wrap. At this point the bread can be frozen in a freezer bag for up to 3 months.

Hannah and Lisa's Note: If you don't tell anyone the name of this bread, they probably won't ever guess it's made with pork and beans.

FROSTED GINGER COOKIES

Preheat oven to 350 degrees F., rack
in the middle position.

¾ cup softened butter *(1 and ½ sticks)*
1 cup white *(granulated)* sugar
1 large beaten egg *(just whip it up in a glass with a
    fork)*
3 Tablespoons molasses***
1 teaspoon baking soda
½ teaspoon salt
1 and ½ teaspoons ground ginger
1 teaspoon ground cinnamon
½ teaspoon ground cloves *(see Hannah's note)*
½ teaspoon ground nutmeg
2 cups flour *(pack it down when you measure it)*

¼ to ½ cup white *(granulated)* sugar for rolling
    dough balls

*** - If you spray your Tablespoon measure with Pam
or other nonstick cooking spray, the molasses will slide
right out without sticking.

The Glaze (after baking):
  1 cup powered *(confectioner's)* sugar
  1 teaspoon lemon juice

Hannah's Note: If you plan to give any of these cookies
to Delores, please leave out the cloves. She doesn't like
cloves.

In a medium-sized mixing bowl, combine the butter and the sugar. Beat the mixture until it's light and fluffy.

Mix in the beaten egg. Add the molasses and stir until the mixture is a uniform color.

Add the baking soda and the salt, and stir well.

Sprinkle in the ground ginger, ground cinnamon, ground cloves, and ground nutmeg. Stir until they're thoroughly mixed in.

Stir in one cup of flour, mix it all up, and then mix in the second cup of flour.

Measure out ¼ cup of white sugar and place it in a shallow bowl. You'll use this bowl to coat dough balls with sugar. When the sugar gets low, add more as needed.

Break off pieces of dough and roll them into one-inch balls. Roll the dough balls in the sugar and place them on a cookie sheet that has been greased or sprayed with Pam *(or another nonstick cooking spray.)* Place the dough balls in four rows with three in each row to make 12 per cookie sheet. Press them down just slightly so they won't roll off on the way to the oven.

Bake the ginger cookies at 350 degrees F. for 10 minutes. Cool for 2 minutes on the cookie sheet and then transfer them to a wire rack to cool completely.

When the cookies are cool, make the glaze.

Combine the powdered sugar with the lemon juice. If it's too thick to drizzle, stir in a bit more lemon juice. If it's too thin, add a bit more powered sugar. When it's just right, drizzle the tops of the cooled cookies with the glaze.

Let the glaze dry before you store the cookies in a cookie jar. The glaze should be dry in 20 to 30 minutes.

Yield: 6 to 7 dozen nicely spiced cookies, depending on cookie size.

Chapter
Nine

In the hour and a half that remained of the morning, Hannah tried Luanne's number a half dozen times. Something was wrong. She was sure of it. Luanne was one of the most conscientious people she knew. In the entire time she'd worked at Granny's Attic, she'd never been late. It was simply unthinkable that she wouldn't show up at all!

Hannah dialed Luanne's number one last time and listened to the empty ringing. This just wasn't right. After she delivered Larry's order of cookies and gave him a taste of her plum pudding, she planned to drop by the duplex where Luanne, her mother, and Susie lived. If Luanne wasn't home, she'd knock on Nettie Grant's door, armed with a gift of cookies, and make some careful inquiries about Luanne's whereabouts.

Even though she hadn't yet been able to solve the mystery surrounding Luanne's absence, the day was definitely improving. It improved even more when the bell on the door jingled and Norman walked in. She'd already decided not tell him about Mike's suspicions. There was no proof that Carrie was shoplifting and it would just worry him. It was entirely possible that Mike was seeing criminals on every corner, especially if he'd been putting in a full day at the sheriff's station and then working another shift for the mall security company.

"Hi, Hannah." Norman took a seat at the counter. "How's your Christmas tree?"

"Don't ask," Hannah said, pouring him a cup of coffee and presenting him with a slice of plum pudding she'd warmed in the microwave behind the counter.

"What's this?" Norman asked.

"Plum pudding."

"But it's got *plums* in it. Plum pudding doesn't have any plums."

"This plum pudding does. If it's good and Larry uses it at the Crazy Elf, I'll have to think of a new name, something that tells people it's not English plum pudding."

"Call it Minnesota Plum Pudding," Lisa said, coming up to the counter to gaze at Norman's slice. "That's what you called your peach cobbler when it was different than the southern one."

"Minnesota Plum Pudding is a good name," Hannah agreed, her knife poised to cut another slice. "How about you, Lisa?"

"I want to, but I can't. I promised Herb I'd wait and have a slice with him."

"Then I'll just give you a tiny bit as a taste. You can have a regular slice when Herb gets here."

"Okay," Lisa said immediately, and Hannah knew she'd been looking for a convenient excuse not to wait.

Once the Minnesota Plum Pudding, which was really more of a cake, was served, Hannah waited while Lisa and Norman tasted it. When they both reached for another forkful before they'd even swallowed the first, she knew she had a hit on her hands.

"This is wonderful!" Norman declared.

"Yes, it is." Lisa finished her tiny slice and looked longingly at the rest of the pudding. "It's so good, I'd better get out of here before I hurdle over the counter and eat the whole thing. I'm going to the kitchen to bake two pans of Lovely Lemon Cookie Bars. Sally Percy needs them for a tree trimming party she's having tonight."

Once Lisa had left for the kitchen, Norman turned to Hannah. "Why did you say I shouldn't ask about your Christmas tree?"

"Because Moishe decided it would be fun to climb it at four this morning."

"Uh-oh. Did the Big Guy knock it down?"

"Oh, yes. And the water spilled out on the rug. The only good thing is that it didn't soak through to Phil and Sue's apartment. I checked with Sue and everything's fine."

"That's good." Norman took another bite of his Minnesota Plum Pudding. "This really is great, Hannah." He took time for another bite and then he turned to her again. "I think I've got the solution to your tree problem. I'll put on some guide wires this afternoon to hold your tree in place."

"But don't you have to work?"

"Only for part of the afternoon. My last appointment's at three and that's just a cleaning. I'll be out of the clinic by four at the latest, and that gives me plenty of time to fix your tree before you get home from work. I think I'd better decorate it first though. Otherwise it'll be too hard to duck in and out around the wires."

"Right," Hannah said, picturing a spider web of wires holding her Christmas tree in the corner so that Moishe couldn't get near it. "It's going to look pretty ugly, isn't it?"

"Not at all. I'll only need two wires to hold it and those will be hidden in the corner."

"Okay, but . . ." Hannah gave a little sigh. She knew she was being selfish, but she didn't want someone else, even if that someone was Norman, to decorate her Christmas tree.

"What?"

"I was looking forward to unpacking the family ornaments and choosing which ones to use. If you do it, I won't get to hang up my favorite things."

"True. How about if I put on the lights and that's it? Then we can decorate it tonight."

"That's perfect." Hannah gave a relieved smile. Perhaps

she should have a tree trimming party. That might be fun. She'd invite Norman, of course. And it would be nice to invite her mother. Delores might enjoy seeing the old decorations again. And perhaps Carrie might like to join her, and . . .

"What?" Norman asked, watching the play of expressions across Hannah's face.

"I'm thinking about inviting you and the mothers to help me trim the tree. That way we can see if your mother gives an excuse and turns down the invitation."

"That's a good idea! Why don't you call my mother first? Then, if she says she can't make it, you don't have to upset Moishe by inviting *your* mother."

"Genius!" Hannah gave him a fond pat on the shoulder. Delores was not one of Moishe's favorite people and Hannah's mother had a drawer full of shredded hosiery to prove it.

Norman listened while Hannah made the call. When she hung up, he asked, "What excuse did she give?"

"She said she'd love to come over, but she promised to fill in for one of the women at bridge club."

Norman began to frown. "That's crazy. My mother doesn't know how to play bridge. It's a family joke. She's so horrible at cards, no one ever suggested playing anything."

"Maybe she just didn't feel like decorating my tree." Hannah thought for a moment and then she turned to Norman again. "Why don't you call and invite her to something she likes to do? Then we can see if she gives you the same excuse?"

"Good idea." Norman pulled out his cell phone and dialed. A moment later he had his mother on the line. "How about dinner at the Inn tonight? Sally's making your favorite Pasta Porcini."

Hannah watched as Norman's eyebrows shot up. "Sure, Mother. I understand." He chatted for a moment longer, said goodbye, and clicked off his phone.

"Well?" Hannah asked after Norman had slipped his cell phone in his pocket.

"She can't make it. How about going out to dinner with

me, Hannah? Sally really *is* making Pasta Porcini. I was planning to invite you to dinner so I called out there to check on the specials. And after dinner, we can we can trim your tree, just the two of us."

"That sounds good to me," Hannah told him, partially because Norman still looked upset and partially because she loved Sally's pasta dishes. "Did your mother tell you she was filling in at bridge club?"

"No. She told me she'd really like to go out to dinner with me, but she promised to go to the movies with a friend."

"Not bridge?"

Norman shook his head. "Not bridge. Something's definitely up, Hannah. My mother lied to both of us and she's never done anything like that before."

Hannah had just picked up Norman's dishes and wiped down the counter when Mike walked in the door. "I came to taste that plum pudding of yours," he announced, taking a seat at the counter. "I just ran into Norman on the street and he said it was great."

"You didn't mention anything about his mother, did you?" Hannah asked, pouring a cup of coffee for him.

"Of course not. Besides, it looks like she actually bought all that stuff at the mall."

"How do you know that?" Hannah heated a slice of plum pudding in the microwave and served it to Mike.

"I checked with a couple of stores this morning. Some of them keep electronic inventories and nothing was missing from their stock." Mike took a bite of his Minnesota Plum Pudding and gave her the thumbs-up sign. "Excellent!" he said.

"I'm glad you like it."

"Larry's crazy if he doesn't want to sell this." Mike took another bite. "The upshot is, I still don't know for sure."

"But I thought you liked it!"

"I do. I wasn't talking about your plum pudding. I was talking about Carrie."

"Oh. What about Carrie?"

"I still don't know if she's shoplifting or not. It's possible items are missing from the stores that don't keep electronic inventories. And I won't find out about that until Friday."

An image of Norman's mother in handcuffs fllashed through Hannah's mind. "What are you going to do if Carrie really *is* shoplifting?"

"That's a tough call." Mike sighed deeply. "Norman's a friend, and I like Carrie, too."

"But you'd go by the book?" Hannah guessed.

"Yes. *Strictly* by the book. That means I can't arrest her unless I catch her red-handed, or she's captured on surveillance tape."

"But you haven't caught her either way . . . right?"

"That's right, so I can give her the benefit of the doubt. If any inventory is missing and she's implicated, I'll talk to her privately and tell her that if she wants to make restitution, I'll arrange for her to do it anonymously. Of course I'll want her to promise not to do it again. And if she's got some kind of psychological problem, I'll give her a list of places she can go to get help."

"You're a good man, Mike." Hannah walked around the counter to give him a little hug.

Mike turned to grin at her. "Thanks. Does that mean I get a second helping of plum pudding?"

MINNESOTA PLUM PUDDING

Do not preheat oven yet.
This plum pudding must settle for
30 minutes before baking.

1 twenty-ounce *(approximate weight)* loaf of sliced
"store boughten" white bread***
2 fifteen-ounce cans purple plums *(I used Oregon
brand)*
2 cups golden raisins *(I used Sun Maid brand)*
1 and ½ cups white *(granulated)* sugar
2 teaspoons cinnamon
1 cup melted butter *(2 sticks, ½ pound)*

7 eggs
2 cups heavy *(whipping)* cream
Sprinkling of freshly grated nutmeg

*** - A sandwich loaf is best because it's easier to cut
off the crusts. I used Oroweat white sandwich bread. There
are usually 22 slices, but you won't use the end pieces.

Generously butter and flour the inside of a Bundt pan.

Hannah's 1st Note: You can make this task easier by buttering it, *(don't forget to butter the middle part,)* dumping
in a quarter cup flour, and sealing the open top of the pan
with plastic wrap. Then you can shake it every which way
to Sunday and your flour won't fall out on the floor. *(It won't
hurt if you hold it over the sink just in case, though.)*

You can make this task even easier by using the kind of nonstick baking spray with flour in it. *(I used Pam Baking Spray and it worked just fine.)*

Divide your loaf of bread into thirds. *(I used 7 slices, 7 slices, and 6 slices.)* Stack several slices of the first third on a cutting board and cut off the crusts. Then cut the slices into 4 triangles. *(Just make an "X" with your knife and you'll have it.)* Repeat until the entire first third of your loaf is in triangles with no crusts.

Arrange the bread triangles in the bottom of your Bundt pan covering as much of the bottom as you can.

Open the two cans of plums and drain them in a strainer. *(My cans had 10 plums apiece.)*

Slice open half *(that's probably ten)* of the plums and remove the pits. Then place the half plums cut side down on top of the bread triangles.

Measure out one cup of golden raisins and spread them out on top of the plums in the pan.

Sprinkle one half cup of sugar on top of the bread, plums, and raisins in your pan.

Sprinkle the sugar with 1 teaspoon cinnamon.

Melt one stick of butter *(½ cup)* in the microwave for 45 seconds on HIGH. Pour it over the bread, plums, and raisins in your Bundt pan.

Repeat the whole thing with the second part of the bread, removing the crusts, cutting it into triangles, and placing them on top of the first layer in your Bundt pan. Pit the remaining plums, cut them in half, and place them on the bread triangles. Add another cup of golden raisins, sprinkle on ½ cup sugar, and top it with one teaspoon of cinnamon. Melt the second stick of butter and pour it over the top.

Remove the crusts from the last third of your bread, cut it in triangles and place them on top of the ingredients in the Bundt pan. Press them down a little with your impeccably clean hands. Sprinkle the top with ½ cup sugar.

Get out a mixing bowl large enough to hold 7 eggs and 2 cups of heavy cream. Crack the eggs into the bowl and whip them up with a wire whisk *(or with a hand mixer.)* Be careful not to over beat the eggs. You're making custard, not sponge cake.

Add the cream and mix it in.

Place your Bundt pan on a cookie sheet with sides, or another shallow pan that can hold any spills. Pour the custard mixture slowly over the top of your pan. It will need time to soak into the bread so don't hurry. If it threatens to spill over the top or run down the fluted tube in the middle, just wait a minute or two and when the level goes down, add more custard mixture. You may not be able to add it all to

the pan. That depends on how much the kind of bread you bought will soak up. Don't overfill.

Hannah's 2nd Note: I was able to use all of my custard mixture. The Oroweat white sandwich bread soaked it all up.

Once you've added all the custard mixture that you can, grate a little nutmeg over the top and let your creation sit and settle for 30 minutes.

When 30 minutes are up, preheat the oven to 350 degrees F., rack in the middle position.

When your oven comes up to temperature, place your Bundt pan AND the pan you're using for spills in the oven. Bake at 350 degrees F. for 70 minutes.

Let your Minnesota Plum Pudding cool for 20 minutes and then turn it out on a pretty platter. If you're not going to serve it that day, let it cool completely, cover it with plastic wrap, and refrigerate. It will keep in the refrigerator for 3 to 5 days.

Let refrigerated Minnesota Plum Pudding come up to room temperature before serving. Dust it with powdered sugar, place a spring of plastic holly or another pretty non-toxic Christmas decoration in the center, and carry it to your table for a wonderful finale to your holiday celebration.

Hannah's 3rd Note: This pudding is best served slightly warm and drizzled with Hard Sauce (contains liquor), or Soft Sauce (contains no liquor). Recipes for the Sauces are below:

Hard Sauce:
   ½ cup softened butter (**1 stick, ¼ pound**)
   2 cups powdered *(confectioner's)* sugar *(there's no need to sift unless it's got lumps)*
   2 Tablespoons *(1/8 cup)* brandy, whiskey, or rum

Beat the butter until it's fluffy.

Continue to beat as you add 1 cup of the powdered sugar and 1 Tablespoon of the liquor.

Add the final cup of powdered sugar and the final Tablespoon of liquor and beat the mixture until smooth.

Check for consistency. This Hard Sauce should be fairly thick, but still pourable. If it's too thin, beat in more powdered sugar. If it's too thick, add a bit more liquor.

Store the Hard Sauce in a tightly-covered container in your refrigerator until thirty minutes or so before using it on your Minnesota Plum Pudding.

Soft Sauce:
   ½ cup softened butter (**1 stick, ¼ pound**)
   2 cups powdered *(confectioner's)* sugar *(there's no need to sift unless it's got hard lumps)*
   2 Tablespoons *(⅛ cup)* milk

Beat the butter until it's fluffy.

Continue to beat as you add 1 cup of the powdered sugar and 1 Tablespoon of milk.

Add the final cup of powdered sugar and the final Tablespoon of milk and beat the mixture until smooth.

Check for consistency. This Soft Sauce should be fairly thick but still pourable. If it's too thin, beat in more powdered sugar. If it's too thick, add a bit more milk.

Store the Soft Sauce in a tightly-covered container in your refrigerator. Take it out thirty minutes or so before you're ready to serve it.

Hannah's 4th Note: Edna Ferguson, Lake Eden's expert on shortcuts, says to tell you that if you don't want to go to the bother of making Hard Sauce or Soft Sauce, just open a can of vanilla pudding and thin it with some liquor for the Hard Sauce. Make the Soft Sauce the same way, but thin it with a little milk. (You can also use instant vanilla pudding made according to the package directions and then thinned with either liquor or milk.)

Lisa's Note: If you don't feel like making a sauce you can use heavy cream poured over a heated slice of pudding. You can also top individual slices with dollops of sweetened whipped cream, or scoops of vanilla ice cream. Herb says it's good if you cut a leftover slice of Minnesota Plum Pudding for breakfast and don't top it with anything at all.

Chapter Ten

"So why doesn't Mayor Bascomb want to stay at Mille Lacs Lake and fish?" Hannah asked, as she stood side by side at the counter with Lisa, packing up the cookies for the girls at the Crazy Elf Cookie Shop.

"He told Herb he was worried and he thought he'd better come back in case he had to pull the plug."

Hannah turned to look at her partner in alarm. "What happened?! I thought you said Stephanie wasn't that sick!"

"Oh, she's not. Mrs. Bascomb's fine. Mayor Bascomb was talking about the Crazy Elf Christmas Tree Lot. He says they're losing money every day, and he's going to demand that Larry show him the books. If things don't look good, he's going to get out before he loses his shirt."

Hannah had trouble believing that Mayor Bascomb would lose money on his investment. Last night the Christmas tree lot had been packed with people. "It was crowded last night. And every time I've driven past, it's been mobbed with families buying trees."

"That's exactly what Herb thought, but Mayor Bascomb explained it to him. If trees are *all* they're buying, the mayor's in trouble because Larry's selling them at cost. That's what's known as a *loss leader*. The whole idea behind it is that people come in for the bargain Christmas trees, but while the kids are riding on the Crazy Elf Christmas Train and going through the Crazy Elf Fun House, their parents buy trees stands, decorations, and toys from the Crazy Elf Toy Shop."

Hannah remembered that the only line she'd seen last night was the one in front of the cookie shop. Mayor Bascomb could be right. "But the parents aren't buying tree stands, decorations, and toys?"

"That's what the mayor's afraid of. He told Herb that Larry should have known better, especially since he was raised right here. Lake Eden people don't fall for loss leaders. Why buy a new tree stand when you've got a perfectly good one down in the basement?"

"And why buy decorations when you packed them up last year and saved them?" Hannah added her question to the mix.

"You got it. Toys are probably cheaper at CostMart. Everybody in town knows that. And there's no reason to buy a wreath when you can make one from the bottom branches your husband cuts off to get your tree in the stand. Mayor Bascomb suspects that the only part of the whole operation that's showing a profit is the refreshment stand. And that's because Larry gets the cookies from us!"

"Don't break your arm patting yourself on the back," Hannah repeated the warning her father had given her when she'd brought home a perfect report card.

"I won't, but you know our cookies are the best." Lisa set a canister of flour on the table and went back to the pantry. "Of course all this about Larry is hearsay."

"Yes, but it could be true. I'll try to check it out when I deliver his cookies."

"How will you do that?"

"Larry's fiancée works in the Crazy Elf Toy Shop. I'll stop in and see how many customers are waiting in line. And if it's not crowded, I'll ask her some questions."

"Good idea," Lisa said, putting together another of their distinctive dessert boxes for Hannah. "It's possible that

Mayor Bascomb is painting things a little blacker than they really are, especially when it comes to finances. Herb says he does that sometimes. He thinks it's because the mayor doesn't want any of us ordinary Lake Edenites to know how much money he has."

"Herb could be right," Hannah said, remembering how Mayor Bascomb had sympathized publicly with a group of homeowners who were concerned about making their mortgage payments, and how he'd claimed that he was in the same boat. It hadn't gone well for the mayor when an investigative reporter for the *Lake Eden Journal* had discovered that he owned his home outright and had no mortgage payment to make.

"I sure hope Mr. Jaeger likes your plum pudding." Lisa lifted the plum pudding Hannah had made and placed it in the center of the dessert box. "Baking these would be a break from baking cookies all the time."

"Are you getting bored with cookies?" Hannah turned to look at her partner in alarm.

"No. Every kind of cookie we make is different, so it doesn't get boring. It's just that plum pudding would be really different. And I just love unmolding cakes from Bundt pans. They make plain, old, ordinary cakes beautiful."

"You're right. Did you know the Bundt pan was invented by a Minnesotan?"

"Really?" Lisa sounded shocked.

"His name was H. David Dahlquist and he was from Edina. He's the man who founded Nordic Ware."

"I got a Nordic Ware Bundt pan for a wedding present. When did they make the first ones?"

"In the early nineteen-fifties. Mr. Dahlquist modified a German design and named them Bundt pans."

"They must have been a huge success. Everybody's got one now."

Hannah shook her head. "But they didn't back then.

Nordic Ware didn't sell very many until nineteen sixty-six, when a Texas woman won second place in the Pillsbury Bake-Off for her Tunnel of Fudge cake. It was baked in a Bundt pan and the recipe was so tempting, everybody wanted to try it."

"So everybody bought Bundt pans."

"That's right. And now we use them for all sorts of things."

"Including Andrea's Jell-O molds," Lisa added. "Is she making one for Christmas?"

"Yes. She got a new one from our family friend, Sally Hayes." Hannah glanced up at the clock and sighed. "I'd better load up and get going. I want to be back here by three at the latest so we can try out your Aunt Helen's Christmas Lace Cookies."

"You're going to love them, Hannah. Aunt Helen used to bring a box to the house every time she visited. When we saw her coming up the walkway with a box in her arms, we all used to cheer. Those cookies were so good! They're crunchy and chewy at the same time, if you know what I mean."

"I don't, but I can hardly wait to find out." Hannah grabbed a stack of boxes and headed out to her cookie truck. The Christmas Lace Cookies sounded wonderful and if they were as good as Lisa said, they'd use them for their next holiday cookie catering job.

After the fifth knock, Hannah stepped back and massaged her aching knuckles. She'd started by ringing the doorbell, but no one had answered her ring. She'd even leaned on it for a good thirty seconds, but that hadn't worked either. After that she'd knocked, louder and more violently, but not even her last volley of knuckle-damaging thumps had caused Luanne to respond. Hannah was about to go to her alternate plan, the one that involved Nettie Grant and the cookies she'd use to camouflage the real purpose for the visit and sweeten her questions she planned to ask about Luanne's whereabouts, when she heard footsteps approaching the door from inside.

"Who is it?" a voice called out.

It was Luanne. Hannah recognized her voice. "It's Hannah Swensen. I need to see you."

There was the sound of a lock disengaging and the door was pulled open from inside. The sight that greeted Hannah wasn't pretty. Luanne stood there swaying slightly, blinking groggily in the beam of sunlight that streamed in from the open door.

"Hannah," she said, moving back to let her enter. "What time is it?"

"One-thirty."

Luanne looked stunned. "In the *afternoon*?" she asked.

"Yes." Hannah set the bag of cookies down on a coffee table filled with books and papers, and decided to get straight to the point. "What's going on, Luanne? Mother was worried about you when you didn't show up for work this morning."

"This morning? But . . . but . . ." Luanne took a deep breath and let it out with a sigh. "I must have fallen asleep after Nettie came to get Susie. I told myself I was just going to shut my eyes for ten minutes, but I was so tired, I was afraid I wouldn't wake up. I set the alarm so that wouldn't happen and I wouldn't oversleep. But . . . I must have slept straight through the alarm!"

"And the phone when we all called you. And the doorbell when I rang it five times." Hannah was aware of a faint electronic beeping coming from the back of the duplex. She recognized the sound as a twin to her own alarm clock at home. "You'd better go shut off your alarm clock, Luanne. It's still going off. I can hear it. Did you get to bed late last night?"

"Late? I didn't get to bed at all!" Luanne gestured toward the pile of papers on the table. "I must have gone over it a hundred times, but it just won't come out right."

Hannah glanced down at the papers. They were filled with columns of figures that meant nothing to her. "*What* won't come out right?"

"The books for the Crazy Elf Christmas Tree Lot. Nothing balances. I just don't know what to do, Hannah. I added, and re-added, and double-checked every number, but the accounts won't balance. The only thing that makes sense is that I'm missing something."

"Like what?" Hannah asked, wondering why Luanne was doing the books for the Crazy Elf Christmas Tree Lot.

"Like . . . I don't know. Maybe there's a bunch of receipts that I don't have, or some income that's not listed on the sheets Courtney gave me." Luanne stopped to wipe the tears from her eyes.

Or maybe there's something fishy going on with Larry, the Crazy Elf, Hannah thought. *Mayor Bascomb's concerned and he's pretty sharp when it comes to investments. There might be something really wrong with the books.*

"All I know is that if I can't get the accounts to balance, I won't get paid. And if I don't get paid, I can't buy the dollhouse I promised Susie for Christmas!" Luanne buried her face in her hands. "I don't know how I did it, but I must have made a mistake. I looked and I looked all last night and I couldn't find it. I just don't know what to do."

"I do."

"You *do?*"

"Absolutely." Hannah picked up the bag of cookies and handed it to Luanne. "Have a cookie. A little chocolate will make you feel much better about everything."

Luanne opened the bag and took out a cookie. And for the first time since Hannah had come in the door, she smiled. "Chocolate chip. They're my favorites."

"Good. These aren't just any chocolate chip cookies. These are Valerie's Chocolate Chip Pretzel Cookies."

"Chocolate chip *pretzel?*"

"That's right. Take a bite and tell me how you like them."

Luanne took a bite and munched. Then she looked up with another smile, even bigger this time. "They're really good. I like these a lot better than the plain chocolate chip cookies."

"So do I. And they came about because I made a mistake."

"How did you do that?"

"Valerie was a friend of mine in college and I wanted to bake her something special for her birthday. I called her mother and asked her what kind of cookies were Valerie's favorites, and her mother told me they were chocolate chip and Pizzelles."

"I've heard of Pizzelles. They're Italian, aren't they?"

"That's right. And it takes a special kind of tiny waffle-like iron to bake them. But I was in a hurry, and I thought her mother said Chocolate Chip Pretzel Cookies. I wasn't sure what those were, but I figured I could make them so I crushed up some pretzels and added them to chocolate chip cookie dough instead of chopped nuts."

"Did Valerie like them?"

"She was crazy about them. And her mother thought it was the funniest thing she'd ever heard. So making mistakes isn't always a bad thing, Luanne."

"Well . . . not in your case. But . . ."

"And maybe the mistake isn't yours," Hannah interrupted her with a possible explanation. "Eat a couple of cookies. Then go wash your face, brush your teeth, and get dressed in fresh clothes. When you come back out, I want you to gather up all your paperwork and ride with me to the Crazy Elf Christmas Tree Lot."

"But . . . why?"

"Because I have to deliver cookies and you have to go talk to Courtney. I'm willing to bet she forgot to give you some important piece of information that'll balance those books."

"But what about my job at Granny's Attic? I'm already over five hours late!"

"I'll call and explain while you're getting ready to go. They'll be so glad you're all right, they won't mind at all if it takes you another half hour or so to get there."

CHOCOLATE CHIP PRETZEL COOKIES

Preheat oven to 350 degrees F., rack
in the middle position.

1 cup softened butter *(2 sticks, ½ pound)****
2 cups white *(granulated)* sugar
3 Tablespoons molasses
2 teaspoons vanilla
1 teaspoon baking soda
2 beaten eggs *(just whip them up in a glass with a fork)*
2 cups crushed salted thin stick pretzels *(measure AFTER crushing) (I used Synder's)*
2 and ½ cups all-purpose flour *(pack it down in the cup when you measure it)*
1 and ½ cups semi-sweet *(the regular kind)* chocolate chips

*** - *The butter should be at room temperature unless you live in an igloo.*

Hannah's 1ˢᵗ Note: If you can't find thin stick pretzels in your store, you can use the mini regular pretzels. Just make sure that any pretzels you use are SALTED.

Hannah's 2ⁿᵈ Note: This dough gets really stiff—you might be better off using an electric mixer if you have one.

Mix the softened butter with the sugar and the molasses. Beat until the mixture is light and fluffy, and the molasses is completely mixed in.

Add the vanilla and baking soda. Mix them in well.

Break the eggs into a glass and whip them up with a fork. Add them to your bowl and mix until they're thoroughly incorporated.

Put your pretzels in a zip lock plastic bag. Seal it carefully *(you don't want crumbs all over your counter)* and place it on a flat surface. Get out your rolling pin and run it over the bag, crushing the pretzels inside. Do this until there are no large pieces and the largest is a quarter-inch long.

Measure out two cups of crushed pretzels and mix them into the dough in your bowl.

Add one cup of flour and mix it in. Then add the second cup and mix thoroughly. Add the final half cup of flour and mix that in.

Measure out a cup and a half of chocolate chips and add them to your cookie dough. If you're using an electric mixer, mix them in at the slowest speed. You can also put the mixer away, and stir in the chips by hand.

Drop by rounded teaspoons onto greased *(or sprayed with Pam or another nonstick cooking spray)* cookie sheets. You can also line your cookie sheets with parchment paper, if you prefer. Place 12 cookies on each standard sized sheet.

Hannah's Note: I used a 2-teaspoon cookie disher to scoop out this dough at The Cookie Jar. It's faster than doing it with a spoon.

Bake the cookies at 350 degrees F. for 10 to 12 minutes or until nicely browned. *(Mine took 11 minutes.)*

Let the cookies cool for two minutes and then remove them from the baking sheets. Transfer them to a wire rack to finish cooling.

Yield: Approximately 5 dozen chewy, fairly soft chocolaty cookies that are sure to please everyone.

This recipe can be doubled if you wish.

Hannah's Note: These cookies travel well. If you want to send them to a friend, just stack them, roll them up like coins in foil, and cushion the cookie rolls between layers of Styrofoam peanuts, or bubble wrap.

Chapter
Eleven

A cold wind wrapped itself around Hannah's neck and she turned up her collar. The thermometer mounted outside the kitchen window of The Cookie Jar had hovered around the minus ten mark when she'd left to deliver her cookies. From the way her cheeks stung from the cold, she was willing to bet that it had fallen another couple of degrees since then. Not to mention wind chill. She didn't even want to think about wind chill. Anyone who'd grown up in cold country knew that it was the apparent temperature felt on exposed skin due to the wind. The degree depended on both air temperature and wind speed, and Hannah was willing to bet that an actual ten below on the thermometer easily translated to twenty below when it came to the exposed skin of her neck!

Hannah had just left Luanne at Elf Headquarters, and she was headed to the Crazy Elf Cookie Shop to deliver her wares. They'd stopped at the toy shop so Luanne could talk to Courtney and tell her the bad news about the trial balance, but the elf who was manning the register had told them that Courtney had an appointment to have her hair done and she wouldn't be back for at least thirty minutes, perhaps longer. Rather than leave Luanne there to wait for Courtney, Hannah had asked her to walk along to Larry's trailer.

Once they'd stepped inside Elf Headquarters, Hannah had presented Larry with a whole Minnesota Plum Pudding, and a mixed bag of Frosted Ginger Cookies, White Chocolate Pumpkin Dreams, and several squares of Fudge-Mallow Cookie Bars. Then she'd introduced him to Luanne, explaining that Luanne was doing some work for Courtney.

Of course Larry had wanted to know about the work Luanne was doing, and Luanne had explained about the trial balance and how she couldn't seem to get it to come out right. Larry had offered to take a look to see if he could spot her error, and Hannah had left after arranging to meet Luanne at the cookie truck when both of them were ready to leave.

A few hardy souls, bundled up in parkas and knitted caps pulled down low over their ears, were on the paths, but the tree lot was largely deserted. Hannah wasn't surprised. It was cold and turning colder. Her fingers felt numb inside the leather gloves she wore and she thrust them into her pockets. Her nose was numb too, and it felt like a stubby icicle sticking out from the middle of her face, but there wasn't much she could do about that. She increased her pace, fairly flying down the path, and arrived at the Crazy Elf Cookie Shop breathless.

It was warm inside! Hannah took a deep gulp of heated air and headed for the front of the shop. She said *Merry Christmas* to the bear before he could say it to her, and she heard a startled gasp of laughter from the direction of the counter.

"Hi, Hannah!" Krista Donnelly greeted her as she reached the front of the line that wasn't. "Did you bring us more cookies?"

"I did, but you might not need them. It's cold out there this afternoon and I don't think anybody's going to venture out."

"It won't be cold for long. The boys just went out to light the gas heaters. We'll be turning on the lights in twenty minutes or so, and that's when the crowds start to come in."

"Can you spare someone to help me unload my cookie truck?"

Krista gestured toward two boys who were unpacking cases

of supplies behind the counter. "Go out to Miss Swensen's truck and bring in the cookies."

"It's open," Hannah told them, "and you can leave it that way. After you carry the cookies inside, there's nothing to steal."

Once the boys had left and Krista had settled her at a stool with a hot cup of coffee, Hannah leaned close to ask some questions. "Do you know Larry's fiancée?"

"Courtney?" When Hannah gave a nod, Krista went on. "She's the head elf."

"I thought Larry was the head elf."

"No, Larry's the *crazy* elf. Courtney's the head elf who keeps him on track."

"What does that mean?"

Krista glanced around, but the only customers in the cookie shop were sitting at a table in the far corner, well out of earshot. She turned back to Hannah and said, "Courtney's really serious about making a go of the business. That doesn't mean that Larry isn't, but she's all business all the time, and he knows how to have fun."

"Example?" Hannah asked her.

"Right after we close down for the night, Larry takes us all on the Yule Log. Courtney stands there and watches, but you just know she thinks Larry ought to shut off the electricity and save money."

"I see." Hannah drew the obvious conclusion. "So the elves don't like her very much?"

"They think she's okay, but they'd like her a lot better if she'd let Larry do some of the things he talks about at the elf meetings."

"What things?"

"Like the free Christmas tree he was going to give to every elf. Courtney thought that was too expensive so she talked him into charging us half price. It's still a good deal, but not as good as if we'd gotten it for free."

"That's true."

"And then there was the big party for the elves and their families that Larry was going to hold on Christmas Day. He was going to hire a caterer and everything, but Courtney convinced him that they couldn't afford it."

Hannah's mind flew through the possibilities. It was obvious that Courtney wanted Larry to curtail expenses. Perhaps she was thinking of their future together and she was worried she was marrying a spendthrift. Or perhaps she had a vested interest in the success of the Crazy Elf Christmas Tree Lot. "Do you know if Courtney owns a share of the business?"

"She owns fifty percent. Her husband started a whole chain of tire stores and when he died, he left Courtney all his money. That's how she met Larry. Larry was waiting in his lawyer's office to sign some papers and she came in for the reading of her husband's will. They hit it off and started dating, and then they got engaged and she invested her money with him, and that's how everything started."

"Larry told you all this?"

"No, Courtney did. She's friendly and all. It's just that she's serious about business. I can't really blame her. It's her husband's money and all, and he probably worked hard for it."

"But you and the rest of the elves wish she'd loosen up a little?"

Krista gave a little shrug. "I guess. But when we're talking about something that doesn't have anything to do with business or money, she's a lot of fun."

The door opened and the two boys came in, their arms laden with cookie boxes. "Where do you want these, Krista?" one of them asked.

"Just stack them on the counter for now," Krista answered, moving to the end of the counter to make room. "Are there more?"

"One more load." The boys headed back out and Krista began to put the cookies away in the display case. She was almost through when the door opened again and a family of six came in. Another group of four followed, and Hannah knew that her time for a private conversation with Krista was over.

"I'll see you later." Hannah gave a wave as she got up and headed for the door. She was going to stop in at the Crazy Elf Toy Shop to see if she agreed with Krista's assessment of Courtney.

When Hannah stepped outside, she was prepared to face the arctic winter again. But to her surprise, the wind had died down and it was appreciably warmer. Part of that warmth could not be credited to the cessation of wind chill. While she'd been talking with Krista, the boys had lit the stationary gas heaters that were placed along the walkways, and it was really quite comfortable as long as one kept to the designated path.

Twilight was approaching and the sky was a lovely shade of delft blue that reminded Hannah of walks home from grade school in winters past. Lavender blue shadows crept across the patches of white snow, and the warm yellow light that spilled out through the windows of the Crazy Elf Toy Shop cast golden rectangles that were turned into trapezoids by the uneven icy surface.

Hannah pushed open the door expecting to hear a cacophony of electronic toy voices, but all she heard were traditional Christmas carols played at an unexpectedly low volume.

"Hello there," a non-recorded, obviously human voice greeted her from the front counter and Hannah looked up at the woman standing there. She was wearing a green velvet full-shirted jumper over a white lace blouse with puffy sleeves. There was a green velvet Santa hat on her head and she was the sole occupant of the toy shop. She was wearing a similar outfit to the one that Andrea had described. The only difference was that today it was green velvet and last night it had been red velvet.

"Courtney?" Hannah asked, almost sure that this must be Larry's fiancée.

"Yes. And you're . . ."

"Hannah Swensen. I bake the . . ."

"Cookies for the Crazy Elf Cookie Shop!" Courtney broke in to finish the sentence. "I'm glad to meet you, Hannah. Your cookies are delicious. Larry told me about the plum pudding and I'm looking forward to trying that, too."

"Thank you." Hannah walked over and picked up one of the crocheted animals that Andrea had bought for Bethie and Tracey. For one nanosecond she considered buying it as a toy for Moishe, but she figured it would last all of thirty seconds before the yarn was unraveled and the stuffing was in fluffy little pieces on her living room rug.

"These are really cute," she said, holding it up so that Courtney could see,

"They're darling. A local woman makes them for us."

"Twenty dollars is a lot for a stuffed animal." Hannah felt a bit like a traitor to the Murphy family as she made her comment, but she wanted to find out what Courtney would say.

"I know, but you always pay more for handmade. These aren't produced in a big factory somewhere overseas and sewn together by workers who make less than a dollar a day."

"That's true. Are these made by Jessica Murphy?"

"That's right!" Courtney smiled. "She's simply wonderful at it. Larry contracted with her to produce them for us."

"The markup is a hundred percent, isn't it?"

"A *hundred* percent?" Courtney looked astonished. "Good heavens, no! It's only twenty percent. Larry buys them for sixteen dollars apiece and we sell them for twenty. Wherever did you get the idea that the markup was a hundred percent?"

Hannah was embarrassed. She shouldn't have brought up the subject. "Jessica's brother-in-law told me she gets ten dollars apiece."

"Well, he's wrong. I know Larry pays sixteen for each one. He gives me all the paperwork for the toy shop and I file it right here in back of the counter." Courtney looked disturbed for a moment and then her expression cleared. "Maybe Jessica's brother-in-law misunderstood what she told him. Or maybe she didn't want him to know how much money she was making."

"That's possible," Hannah said, and she was saved from further embarrassment when the bell on the door tinkled and Luanne walked in. There was a smile on her face and Hannah surmised that her conference with Larry had gone well.

"Hello, Luanne," Courtney greeted her.

"Hi, Courtney." Luanne came up to hand Courtney a large envelope with the paperwork. "Everything you gave me is in here, along with my work. I'm really sorry, but I couldn't get the profit and loss statement to come out right, and the trial balance was a disaster."

"That's all right," Courtney said, smiling at Luanne. She didn't seem a bit surprised by Luanne's confession and Hannah wondered about that. "I hope you didn't work too long on it."

"She worked all night," Hannah said, knowing that Luanne would never mention it.

"Oh, no! I'm so sorry, Luanne. I never meant for you to spend over an hour or two on it." Courtney opened the register and took out some bills. "I promised you forty dollars, but I'm going to give you fifty. And you can have that dollhouse for your daughter at our cost."

"Oh, thank you! But you don't have to pay me. Mr. Jaeger already did."

"*Larry* paid you?"

"Yes. Since you weren't here when we stopped in earlier, I went along with Hannah when she delivered her plum pudding and sample cookies to Mr. Jaeger. She mentioned that I was doing some work for you and he asked me about it. I said that I must have made a mistake because the trial balance wouldn't come out right, and he offered to help me find my mistake."

"Did Larry find it?" Courtney asked her.

"No. He said my work was correct as far as it went. And

then he told me not to worry, that it wasn't my fault because there was some information I didn't have and that's why the columns wouldn't balance." Luanne looked a bit uncomfortable. "I really didn't understand a lot of what he said. I think that's because I've only had one bookkeeping class. But I'm sure it would have made sense to somebody who's a real accountant."

"Did he ask you why I wanted you to go over the paperwork?"

"No. I thought you'd told him about it because he didn't seem surprised at all. We talked for about five minutes and he told me to contact him after I graduated and maybe he'd have extra work for me. And then he told me to bring all the paperwork back to you and tell you that he'd already paid me."

Courtney put the money back in the register and Hannah noticed that her hands were shaking. "I hope he paid you plenty."

"Oh, he did. And that's why I can pay retail for Susie's dollhouse. I really appreciate this work you gave me, Courtney. And I'm sorry if I was out of line talking to Larry about it."

"Relax. You didn't do anything wrong," Courtney told her. "Now I want you to take that dollhouse floor sample and put it under the tree for your daughter. We discount the floor samples anyway and you can consider it a little extra gift for trying so hard to balance the books for me."

"Really?" Luanne looked as if she were about to argue and Hannah knew how she felt about taking anything she didn't think she deserved.

"Go ahead," Courtney told her. "You ought to have more than money for working so hard and so long."

"I'll help you carry it," Hannah said, taking matters into her own hands before Luanne could think of some other reason to object. Somehow she had to teach that girl not to look a gift horse in the mouth. Perhaps Luanne was oblivious, but it was obvious to Hannah that Courtney had never expected Luanne to be able to balance the books. She'd just wanted a second opinion. And now that she had it and Larry knew she was checking up on him, there might be a fireworks show later tonight that had nothing to do with pyrotechnics.

FUDGE-MALLOW COOKIE BARS

Preheat oven to 350 degrees F., rack
in the middle position.

¾ cup all-purpose flour *(pack it down in the cup
when you measure it)*
¾ cup white *(granulated)* sugar
½ teaspoon salt
½ cup softened butter *(1 stick, ¼ pound)*
2 eggs
2 one-ounce squares unsweetened chocolate *(I used
Baker's)*
1 teaspoon vanilla extract
½ cup chopped nuts *(I used walnuts, but pecans are
fine, too)*
10.5 ounce package miniature marshmallows *(you'll
use ¾ of a package—I used Kraft Jet Puffed)*
2 cups semi-sweet chocolate chips *(I used
Ghirardelli)*

**Hannah's Note: This is a lot easier with an electric
mixer, but you can also make these cookie bars by hand.**

Melt your chocolate first so that it has time to cool. Unwrap the 2 squares of unsweetened chocolate and place them
in a microwave-safe bowl. Heat them for 1 minute on HIGH.
Let them sit in the microwave for another minute and then
take them out and stir them to make sure they're melted.
*(If they're not, heat them again in 15 second intervals
until they are.)* Set the bowl with the chocolate on the
counter to cool while you mix up the rest of the recipe.

Combine the flour, sugar and salt in the bowl of a mixer. Beat them together on slow speed until they're combined.

Add the softened butter and beat well until the mixture is light and fluffy.

Add the eggs and beat well.

Check your chocolate to make sure it's not so hot it'll cook the eggs. If it's cool enough, add it to your bowl. If it's not, have a cup of coffee and wait until it is. Mix in the chocolate thoroughly.

Add the vanilla and the half cup of chopped nuts. Mix thoroughly.

Grease *(or spray with Pam or another nonstick cooking spray)* a 9-inch by 13-inch cake pan. Pour in the batter and smooth the top as evenly as you can with a rubber spatula.

Bake at 350 degrees F. for 20 minutes.

Take the pan from the oven and immediately pour the miniature marshmallows in a single layer over the top. This should take about ¾ of a 10.5-ounce bag. Work quickly to spread them out as evenly as you can.

Cover the pan with foil crimped down tightly over the sides, or with a spare cookie sheet for 20 minutes. You want the miniature marshmallows to melt on the bottom and attach themselves nicely to the hot chocolate fudge bars.

When 20 minutes have passed, melt 2 cups of semi-sweet chocolate chips in the microwave on HIGH for 2 minutes. Stir the chips smooth and spread the melted chocolate over the marshmallows as evenly as you can. Set the pan on a wire rack to cool.

When the bars are cool and the chocolate on top has hardened, cut them into brownie-sized pieces and serve. If you want to hasten the hardening of the chocolate, slip the pan into the refrigerator for thirty minutes or so, and then take it out to cut the bars.

Arrange the bars on a pretty platter and serve for a luscious treat. You can store any leftovers in a tightly-covered container, but Lisa and I bet there won't be any!

Yield: Each pan makes approximately 24 bars.

Lisa says Herb loves these because they remind him of the chocolate-covered marshmallow cookies he used to eat as a child. He confessed he traded them with his friends, giving them the homemade cookies Marge made and put in the lunchbox for the "store boughten" marshmallow cookies. Lisa says that if you know Marge Beeseman, please don't tell her that her son did this!

Chapter Twelve

Hannah heard Lisa's delighted laugh as she took the last pan of Christmas Lace Cookies out of the oven. Herb must be back from his trip with Mayor Bascomb. She waited a minute until the cookies were set, and then she pulled the parchment paper and cookies from the pan and slipped them onto the baker's rack. She filled a plate with cooled cookies and went out through the swinging restaurant-type door that separated their kitchen from the coffee shop to see who had arrived.

"Hello, dear."

Delores was the first to greet her. Hannah gave her a smile that included all four of the guests seated at the table at the back of the shop. There was her mother, Herb, Mayor Bascomb, and a familiar-looking woman that Hannah couldn't quite place.

"Look who's here, dear," Delores continued. "It's Miss Whiting from class."

Of course! Hannah recognized her now, but the out-of-context phenomenon had confused her at first. She'd seen Miss Whiting last night in a completely different setting. Then she'd been wearing a tailored suit of navy blue wool with a cream-colored silk blouse, and she'd been standing in front of the blackboard in her mother's small business class. In today's setting, the community college teacher seemed much younger, but perhaps that was because she was dressed in jeans and a fluffy pink sweater with her hair pulled back in a ponytail.

"Hi, Miss Whiting," Hannah greeted her. "Did you come to check on our homework?"

Miss Whiting laughed and shook her head. "I stopped in at Granny's Attic to pick up a Christmas gift. I had no idea I'd run into one of my students. And then your mother brought me here to try a slice of your plum pudding."

"How do you like it?"

"It's excellent. Lisa mentioned that you'll be selling it at the Crazy Elf Christmas Tree Lot."

Hannah turned to look at Lisa, who nodded. "Krista called while you were in the kitchen and she put in an order for five Minnesota Plum Puddings every day."

"That's great. I was hoping they'd like it." Hannah set the plate down on the table. "Have one of our new Christmas Lace Cookies. We're testing them today."

Never one to refuse a free cookie, Mayor Bascomb reached for one. He took a bite and looked a bit surprised. "These are good and they're much more substantial than they look."

"They're great," Herb said, turning to smile at Lisa. He'd obviously missed his bride of less than a year, and the loving expression on his face gave Hannah a little wistful twinge. If she had accepted Norman's proposal, he'd probably look at her like that. As a matter of fact, she was *sure* Norman would look at her like that. Norman was true blue, and he'd be the sort of husband who would never risk his marriage by having an affair with another woman.

On the other hand, if she'd accepted Mike's offer of marriage he'd probably . . . Hannah's daydream evaporated in a flash of painful reality. If she'd married Mike and he went out of town for the night, she couldn't be sure he wouldn't stray. It might be a repeat of his nights with Ronni Ward and Shawna Lee Quinn. If she were Mrs. Mike Kingston, she'd always wonder what he was up to when she wasn't with him. Part of the problem was that Mike was sinfully handsome and women tended to throw themselves at him. *Yes, but he doesn't have to catch them when they do,* Hannah reminded herself.

"What the matter, dear?" Delores asked, catching her eldest daughter's unhappy expression.

"Not a thing. I was just thinking about all the things I have to do before Christmas."

"I hope one of those things is making more of these cookies," Herb commented.

Miss Whiting nodded. "These are excellent cookies. They're chewy and crunchy at the same time."

"Exactly right." Mayor Bascomb reached out for another. "I think Stephanie would love these and I suppose I should take her something when I go visit her tonight."

It was a blatant bid for a box of free cookies and Hannah almost laughed. But she didn't. The mayor wasn't happy with anyone who laughed at him and it was politic to stay on his good side. "I'll put some in a box for her."

"Are you going to sell these at the Christmas tree lot?" Delores asked.

"I'm not sure," Hannah said, but the fact her mother had mentioned the Christmas tree lot reminded her of Larry's sign and she turned to Miss Whiting. "I've got an example of a bad business practice for you."

"Oh, good. Let's hear it. I'm always on the lookout for new examples."

"There's a sign at the entrance to the Crazy Elf Christmas Tree Lot that reads, *We sell below cost and make it up on volume.*"

"What?!" Miss Whiting looked shocked to the core.

"I know it's impossible to do that, but the sign is hanging right there. We asked Larry if it was some kind of a joke and he said it was."

"Larry?"

"That's his name. Larry Jaeger. His company is L. J. Enterprises. He said he heard somebody advertising mattresses on television when he was in high school, and that was the company slogan. He thought it was so funny, he made up a sign and he's hung it in the front of every business he's ever owned."

"I see."

"I guess it *is* kind of funny, but I still think it's a bad business practice. What if people take it seriously?"

"That's a valid point." Miss Whiting stood up. "I'm sorry, but I have to leave. I have an appointment with one of my students and I don't want to be late."

"What was that about homework?" the mayor asked, after Miss Whiting had left.

"It's for my class in small business practices," Delores told him. "Carrie couldn't make it and Hannah went to class with me. Miss Whiting gave us the paperwork from a company that had bad business practices and we're supposed to identify the bad practice."

"What's the name of the company?" Herb looked curious.

"We don't know," Hannah answered him. "It's blocked out on the paperwork."

"Probably for legal reasons," Mayor Bascomb gave his opinion. "Let's see that paperwork. Maybe I can help you with your homework."

"You?!" Delores looked shocked. "You were always terrible at arithmetic."

"I was?"

"Yes, you were. I spent a whole summer trying to teach you your sevens."

"Sevens?" Herb looked puzzled.

"His times tables. Multiplication. You know. He had the fives down just fine, and he knew his eights and nines. But the sevens stumped him every time. Isn't that right, Ricky Ticky?"

Hannah hid a grin. Her mother had been Mayor Bascomb's summer babysitter when he was in grade school. To this day, she was the only one who used his first name, which was Richard, and the nickname she'd given him, Ricky Ticky.

"It's true," Mayor Bascomb conceded the point, "but that's something only my old babysitter would know."

Delores bristled at the phrase, "old babysitter," and Hannah chalked one up for the mayor.

"I did fine when I got to high school," Mayor Bascomb continued. "That's when I found out that you don't need to know your sevens anymore. All you need is a calculator and there are calculators all over the place. My cell phone even has one. Now let me take a look at the homework and we'll see if I've lost my touch for business."

Hannah dashed to the kitchen to get her homework from Miss Whiting's class and handed it over to the mayor. "Here it is," she said.

Mayor Bascomb paged through the sheaf of papers, giving everything a once over. Then he went back and examined several sheets more closely. "Here it is," he said, looking smug as he tapped his finger against one of the columns of figures. "Not bad for somebody who doesn't know their sevens, right Delores?"

"Not bad at all . . . *if* you're correct." Delores qualified it. "What did you notice?"

Mayor Bascomb pushed the paper over to Delores. "Take a look for yourself. I want to see if you can find it."

"It's a record of receipts for supplies," Delores said, glancing down at the paper. "They're added correctly. I already checked the math. What's wrong with it?"

"Take a look at how it's paid."

Hannah slid over next to her mother and they leaned forward to examine the paperwork together. "It's paid by cash," Delores said, looking up at the mayor. "What's wrong with that?"

"A legitimate businessman wants more than a cash receipt. He pays by check so that he can use both the receipt and the cancelled check to verify business expenses."

There was a gasp behind her and Hannah turned to see

Lisa standing there with the coffee carafe. She'd been about to refill the mayor's cup when he'd made the comment about verifying expenses."

"What's wrong?" Hannah asked her.

"I don't know. Maybe nothing. But Larry always pays us in cash and he never has the receipt filled out all the way. He just asks me to sign it and he says he'll fill in the amount later."

Mayor Bascomb's eyes narrowed and Hannah could tell he disapproved of the way Larry did business. "Is that bad?" she asked him.

"It's not good." Mayor Bascomb turned to Lisa. "A less than honest businessman could fill in an amount that didn't match what he paid you. And you wouldn't be able to prove otherwise since the transaction was completely in cash. You should never sign a receipt that's not complete," he warned, "especially if you're being paid in cash."

"Then I won't do it again!" Lisa promised, looking properly chastised. "I had no idea I shouldn't do that."

Mayor Bascomb smiled. "It's probably perfectly okay. It's just that most people don't do business that way and it's unusual when they do. There's always the possibility that they're not keeping accurate records . . . for one reason or another."

"Thanks for telling me," Lisa said, and then she turned to Hannah. "Did Larry have you sign a blank receipt this afternoon when he paid you for the cookies?"

"He didn't pay me for the cookies. I just assumed he sent us a check or something like that. I guess I should have asked . . . but I didn't. And I didn't ask anybody to sign for the delivery I made, either."

"Better call Larry and tell him you're coming back out to pick up a check," Mayor Bascomb advised. "If you don't, you won't have a record of how many cookies you delivered. That's not the way to do business."

"I'll call Larry right now," Lisa offered, heading for the phone behind the counter. A moment later, she covered the receiver with her hand and motioned to Hannah. "He's tied up right now, but he wants us to pick up a check after the lot closes. That's at nine tonight."

"I'll do it," Hannah told her. It was only fair. She was the one who'd forgotten to get a receipt for the cookies and ask for payment.

Lisa said something to Larry and then she covered the receiver again. "He says he'll leave the gate open and you should come straight to Elf Headquarters."

"That's fine. Tell him I'll be there. I'm going out to dinner with Norman, and I'll call him when we're through to let him know we're on the way."

CHRISTMAS LACE COOKIES

Preheat oven to 350 degrees F., rack
in the middle position.

1 and ½ cups rolled oats *(uncooked dry oatmeal—*
use the old-fashioned kind that takes 5 minutes
to cook, not the quick 1-minute variety)
½ cup melted butter *(1 stick, ¼ pound)*
¾ cup white *(granulated)* sugar
1 teaspoon baking powder
1 teaspoon flour
½ teaspoon salt
1 and ½ teaspoons vanilla extract
1 beaten egg *(just whip it up in a glass with a fork)*
½ cup chocolate chips

Measure out the oatmeal in a medium-sized bowl. Melt
the butter and pour it over the oatmeal. Stir until it's thoroughly mixed.

In a small bowl, combine the sugar, baking powder, flour,
and salt. Mix well.

Add the sugar mixture to the oatmeal mixture and blend
thoroughly.

Mix in the vanilla and the beaten egg. Stir well.

Add the chocolate chips and stir the mixture until it is
well combined.

Line cookie sheets with foil, shiny side up. Spray the foil
lightly with Pam or another nonstick cooking spray.

Drop the cookie dough by rounded teaspoon onto the foil, leaving space for spreading. Don't crowd these cookies together, no more than 6 or 8 per sheet.

Hannah's 1st Note: I used a 2-teaspoon cookie scoop to form these cookies. It was just the right size.

Bake at 350 degrees F. for 12 minutes. Remove them from the oven and cool them on the cookie sheet for 5 minutes. Pull the foil off the sheet and over to a waiting wire rack. Let the cookies cool completely.

When the Christmas Lace Cookies are cool, peel them carefully from the foil and store them in a cool, dry place.

If you want to dress up these cookies for special company, wait until they're cool and then drizzle them with melted chocolate chips mixed with coffee. Start with ½ cup of chips mixed with 6 Tablespoons coffee and microwave for 30 seconds on HIGH. Stir it until smooth. If the mixture is too thick to drizzle, add additional coffee and microwave in 20-second intervals on HIGH until it is.

Hannah's 2nd Note: These cookies look delicate, but they travel well if you pack them correctly. Start with a layer of Styrofoam peanuts (or bubble wrap) at the bottom of your box. Cover that with a layer of wax paper. Put down a single layer of Christmas Lace Cookies. Cover that with another layer of wax paper and cover with another single layer of peanuts (or bubble wrap.) Keep on layering

peanuts (or bubble wrap), wax paper, Christmas Lace Cookies, wax paper, and peanuts (or bubble wrap) until your box is full. Top off with a layer of peanuts (or several layers of bubble wrap), seal and send to your lucky recipient.

Yield: One batch of Christmas Lace Cookies makes about 2 and ½ dozen cookies. This recipe can be doubled, tripled, or even quadrupled if you wish.

Chapter Thirteen

"I can't believe how good this was!" Hannah said, forking up the last bite of Sally's Triple Threat Chocolate Cheesecake Pie.

"Mm-hmm," Norman answered, finishing his slice of pie at the same time. "More coffee?"

"Yes, thanks. I need coffee to cut all that yummy chocolate." Hannah waited for Norman to fill her cup from the small silver pot that their waitress had brought. She took a sip and then she gestured toward the elevated booths that lined the far wall. "It's a good thing Mother isn't here."

"Why's that?"

"She'd be making her fourth trip to the ladies room and she'd be going the long way around so she could pass that booth with the curtains drawn. And if just walking by didn't satisfy her curiosity, she'd drop her purse, kneel down to pick up everything that fell out, and try to peek under the curtain."

Norman glanced at elevated section of the dining room. Each booth had a curtain that could be drawn for privacy, but only one group of diners had taken advantage of that feature this evening. "I wonder who's dining in seclusion," he mused.

"I don't know, but it's some kind of special occasion."

"How do you know that?"

"I saw the waitress carry in a bottle of champagne in an ice bucket. I tried to get a look at the people inside, but she was really careful about closing the curtain behind her."

"Did the waitress bring champagne flutes?" Norman asked.

"Yes. I'm almost sure there were only two."

"It's a couple then. I wonder who they are."

"Do you want to walk past there on our way out?" Hannah asked him.

"Of course I do, but wouldn't it be obvious that we're snooping?"

"Not really. Janice Cox and her parents are up there in the end booth and they don't have their curtains drawn. We could stop and say hello to them and then walk past the private booth on our way out."

"You're devious, Hannah."

"I know. I learned from the best."

"Your mother?"

"That's right. So do you want to walk past?"

"I guess we could. It's a real invasion of privacy though."

"I know it is."

Hannah looked at Norman and Norman looked at Hannah. They locked eyes for several seconds and then both of them laughed.

"Let's do it," Hannah said.

"I'm with you," Norman agreed. "But it can't possibly be anyone from Lake Eden."

"Why do you say that?"

"Because people from Lake Eden know better. They realize that if they pull the privacy curtain, everybody out here is going to think something's going on. And then people are going to walk past and try to figure out who's behind the curtain."

"But what can they do if they really want privacy?"

"They can drive to a restaurant in The Cities where nobody knows them."

Hannah laughed. Norman was right. If someone from Lake Eden wanted privacy, they'd have to drive to Minneapolis.

As they climbed the steps to the elevated booths, Hannah kept her eyes on the one with the drawn curtain. It didn't extend quite to the floor and she could see two pairs of shoes. One pair belonged to a man wearing fawn-colored suede boots with beadwork on the sides. The boots were accompanied by two open-toed sandals crafted of shiny red leather straps and impressively high, implausibly thin heels.

"I wonder which man is responsible for her shoes," Hannah said in an undertone as they began to walk slowly toward Janice's booth.

"What shoes?"

"The red sandals behind the curtain. A woman doesn't wear impractical shoes like that unless she's trying to attract a man."

"Really?"

Hannah noticed that Norman was looking down at her feet and she could have kicked herself for her comment, especially since she was wearing her favorite but old moose-hide boots. "Of course that only applies if the man drops her off at the door. You'd never be able to walk to the parking lot in sandals."

"Right," Norman said and he looked much more cheerful.

"Hi, Janice," Hannah greeted Lake Eden's preschool teacher and then she turned to her parents. "Hi, Eleanor . . . Otis. How are those sled dogs coming along?"

"Just great, Hannah." Eleanor launched into her favorite subject. "We've got a new lead dog this year and she's breaking in just fine. Otis decided that he should retire Yukon. He's got a touch of arthritis and he's been limping a little."

"But doesn't Yukon miss it?" Hannah asked, wondering how the Siberian Husky with one brown eye and one blue eye was faring.

"He doesn't seem to mind at all. As a matter of fact, I think the cold was making his arthritis worse. He hardly limps at all now that he's a house dog."

"The least we could do," Otis said, and then he stopped speaking. He was a man of few words.

"So he sleeps on the bed with us now," Eleanor went on, "and he's a regular blanket hog. He watches the soaps with me, too."

"That sounds like a match made in heaven," Norman commented, which caused Otis to laugh.

Hannah loved to watch Otis laugh. He chortled a little, deep in his throat, and slapped his knee three times. That meant it was a good joke. If something really tickled his funny bone, he slapped his knees with both hands three times. That meant he thought it was hilarious. Norman's comment was a two-knee slapper.

Just then the waitress arrived with their entrees and Hannah and Norman said their goodbyes. Hannah noticed that Janice was having Sally's low-cal special, broiled red snapper with broccoli and three small red potatoes, and she figured that a diet must be in the works. She'd ask a couple of careful questions the next time she saw her and if Janice was trying to lose weight, she wouldn't tempt her by bringing her cookies at Kiddie Korner.

"Are you going to drop your purse when we get to the curtained booth?" Norman asked her as they moved away from Janice and her parents.

"No! That's what Mother always does."

"Does it work?"

"Well . . ." Hannah considered it for a moment. "Yes."

"Then why not do it?"

Hannah looked down at the purse her mother and her sisters had called a saddlebag. It was huge and it held all the essentials she needed in case of a national disaster and then some. "Mother has a much smaller purse," she told him. "It'll take us forever to pick up the contents from this one."

"And your point is?" Norman asked, grinning at her.

"Never mind." As they approached the curtained booth, Hannah slipped the strap from her shoulder. "Oops!" she said as her purse fell to the carpet and a myriad of things, some of them useful, some of them not, fell out.

"I'll help you pick it up," Norman said, bending down and craning his neck to the side so that he could see under the curtain.

"Thanks," Hannah answered, also dropping to her knees for a better view. As she shoveled paraphernalia back into her purse, she saw that the red sandals had moved. They were now very close to the suede boots with the beadwork on the sides, and they were not toe to toe any longer. That meant the woman had slid around the horseshoe-shaped booth and was now as close as close could be to her male companion.

"Hurry up!" Norman whispered, dumping handfuls of items into Hannah's purse.

"Why?" Hannah whispered back.

"Mother."

Hannah strained to hear. Norman's whisper was almost inaudible. "Did you say *mother?*" she asked, in a voice that matched his in volume.

"Yes. I'll tell you everything when we get outside."

Hannah's curiosity almost killed her as they exited the restaurant, walked through the bar, retrieved their coats from the cloakroom, traversed the lobby, and went out the front entrance. Once she'd finished shivering from the blast of crisp, cold air that assaulted them, Hannah repeated her question. "Did you say *mother?* As in my mother?"

"No. I said *mother* as in *my* mother. My mother was in that booth."

"But . . . how could you tell from just seeing her shoes?"

"I couldn't tell from her shoes. She never wears shoes like that. I could tell by the scar on her left ankle."

Hannah believed him. She was almost certain she could identify Delores by simply seeing her feet. But Norman could be wrong. "Are you sure it wasn't another woman with a scar on her left ankle."

"I'm sure. I heard her say *Oh, no!* in a very low voice when you dropped your purse. And after that, neither one of them made another sound. I think she must have gestured for him to be quiet. She probably thought it was Delores outside the booth since your mother pulls the same trick."

"Well . . . maybe." Hannah took a deep breath of the bracing air. "But if it was Carrie, who was the man with her? I didn't even know she was dating."

"Neither did I, but that explains why she canceled all those dinners with me."

"And why she told Mother she couldn't go to class with her. But who was the man? Do you have any idea?"

"Not a clue. I didn't recognize the boots. Did you?"

"No. But I think that the fact she was wearing those shoes shoots Mike's theory all to smithereens."

"What theory?"

Norman turned to look at her and almost tripped over a clump of snow. This was obviously unsettling to him and Hannah took his arm before answering. "Mike thought your mother was shoplifting."

"What?!"

"It wasn't an entirely crazy assumption. Mike's been helping with security at the Tri-County Mall and he's run into Carrie a couple of times. It's always when the mall is closing and she's loading packages into the trunk of her car. He told me she looks really guilty when she sees him, and that made him suspect that she could be shoplifting."

Norman gave a big sigh and his breath came out in a white cloud against the dark sky. "Let me get this straight. Mike *thinks* she looks guilty so he *assumes* she's shoplifting?"

"Yes. Of course Mike hasn't told anybody about it . . . except me. And I know he'll be really happy when we tell him he's wrong." Hannah stopped and cleared her throat. She had to be careful how she worded her next question. Norman might not be happy that his mother had a boyfriend. "I think your mother's doing all that shopping because she's trying to look good for someone new in her life. What do you think?"

"I think you're right. And that was well done, Hannah.

You were very careful not to use the word *boyfriend*, or *new man*."

"That's because I didn't know how you'd feel about it."

Norman slipped an arm around her shoulders and pulled her close to him. "I'm fine with it. Mother's been alone too long and if she's found some man to make her happy, more power to both of them. But I'm still mad about Mike. I can't believe he thought my mother was a shoplifter!"

"Well, he never thought she was doing it on purpose. He was concerned because kleptomania is a disease and he thought she might not be able to help herself. He wanted to help her, but he wasn't quite sure what to do."

"He should have come to me."

"I know, but he did the next best thing. He came to me instead."

Norman was quiet for a moment. "Okay. That's reasonable. Mike probably thought I'd fly off the handle. But we haven't addressed the real problem."

They arrived at the car and Norman opened the passenger door for Hannah. She climbed in, he shut it, and he walked around the car to get into the driver's seat. He started the engine immediately so that the car would warm up, and then he turned to her again.

"We have to find out who was in that booth with her. If he's a nice guy, I'm all for it. But I want to make sure he's not after her money."

Hannah understood completely. She and her sisters had been worried about the same thing when Delores had started getting serious about Winthrop. "I can ask Sally to ask her waitresses."

"I'd really appreciate it. Dad left her with quite a bundle and I don't want to see somebody try to take advantage of her."

"Of course you don't. But I didn't know your mother was that well-off."

"Neither did I until after the funeral. Dad never made a lot of money from the dental clinic, but he took out multiple life insurance policies right after I was born. Mother didn't know about them and neither did I until Doug Greerson called and said that Dad had a safe deposit box. When we opened it, we found a list of the policies. Dad made all the payments, even when he was sick. He was looking out for Mother right up until the end."

"Well, it's our turn now," Hannah told him, reaching out to take his hand. "We're going to find out who your mother's dating and make sure he's good enough for her."

TRIPLE THREAT CHOCOLATE CHEESECAKE PIE

Preheat oven to 350 degrees F., rack
in the middle position.

One 9-inch chocolate cookie crumb crust***

½ cup white (*granulated*) sugar
8-ounce package softened cream cheese
⅓ cup mayonnaise (*regular mayo, NOT Miracle
    Whip or sandwich spread*)
2 eggs
1 cup white chocolate chips (*I used Ghirardelli*)
½ teaspoon vanilla extract
1 cup semi-sweet (*regular*) chocolate chips

*** *You can make your own crust from chocolate cookie
crumbs, or buy one pre-made from your grocery store. It's
just like it says in "The Three Bears"—an 8-inch crust
will be a little bit too full (be careful carrying it to the
oven,) a 10-inch crust won't be quite full enough (you can
pile whipped cream on top after it's baked,) and a 9-inch
crust will be just right!*

Hannah's 1ˢᵗ Note: You can make this by hand, but it's a
lot easier with an electric mixer!

Beat the sugar with the softened cream cheese until it's
thoroughly blended. Add the mayonnaise and the eggs.
Beat well.

Melt the white chocolate chips in a microwave-safe bowl on HIGH for 40 seconds. Stir them to see if they're melted. (*Don't be fooled—chips may retain their shape even when they're melted.*) If they're not melted, microwave in 15-second intervals, stirring after each attempt, until you can stir them smooth. Set the melted chips on the counter to cool for a moment or two.

When you can comfortably cup your hands around the bowl holding the melted chips, mix them gradually into the batter. Then add the vanilla and mix well.

Remove the bowl from the mixer and stir in the semi-sweet chocolate chips by hand.

Spoon the pie batter into the cookie crust and smooth the top with a rubber spatula.

Bake the pie at 350 degrees F. for 30 to 35 minutes.

Cool the pie on a wire rack and then refrigerate. Take your pie out of the refrigerator 20 minutes before serving. Serve with sweetened whipped cream on top.

Hannah's 2nd Note: This pie is so deliciously rich, you have to serve it with strong coffee. I usually have a second pot all ready to go when the first one runs out.

Chapter
Fourteen

Their drive through the Lake Eden Inn parking lot to attempt to identify cars turned out to be an exercise in fu-
tility. There were simply too many cars they didn't recognize.
Carrie's car was not present. It was obvious that she'd ridden
out to the Lake Eden Inn with her dinner companion. Finally,
after the third round trip, Hannah decided to call off the
search.

"Forget it, Norman. This isn't doing any good. Unless you
want to sit here and burn gas until your mother comes out,
let's go pick up the check from Larry. Once we've got that,
we can take a detour past your mother's house to see if she's
home yet."

Norman looked surprised. "You want to go in and ask
who was in the booth with her?"

"Of course not. That would just put her on the defensive
and she probably wouldn't tell me anyway. I want to see if
there's a car parked in front of her house. If there is, all we
have to do is copy down the license number and ask Mike to
run it for us."

"Good thinking." Norman pulled out of the parking lot
and headed for the highway. They wound their way down
what looked like a huge, never-ending tunnel flanked by
snow banks. It was a little strange seeing snow banks as high
as the top of the car on both sides, and it was evident from

the height of the snow that Sally's husband, Dick, had used his mini-snowplow to clear the road multiple times this winter so that the guests could drive in.

Once they reached the highway, Norman increased his speed and Hannah leaned back to enjoy the ride. The radio was tuned to a classic jazz station, the interior of the car was warm, and the passenger seat was extremely comfortable. The phrase, *All's right with the world,* floated through Hannah's mind. Things were always right when she was with Norman. There were times, like right now, when she really couldn't understand her reluctance to marry him and be comfortable like this for the rest of her life. She loved him, she enjoyed being with him, and she'd love to live in the house they'd designed together. Norman would be a great husband, but just when she was about to say yes, thoughts of Mike got in the way. Perhaps she needed a shrink. But going to a psychotherapist would take time and time was one thing she didn't have. There were no spare fifty-minute hours during the Christmas season.

"Why so quiet?" Norman asked, taking her out of the dilemma she didn't seem to be able to solve anyway.

"I was thinking about time," Hannah said, telling him what she termed a *partial truth.*

"It must be pretty hectic for you this time of year with Christmas so close. Is there any way I can help you?"

"You're already helping me. You treated me to a wonderful dinner and now you're taking me to the Crazy Elf to pick up the check I failed to ask for this afternoon."

"I could do more. If you have any last-minute shopping to do, just let me know. I could run out to the mall for you. There's only ten shopping days left until Christmas."

"I know. Lisa reminded me today, but shopping for Christmas is the one thing I finished. I took Mother's advice and shopped early. Now all I have to do is remember where I put the presents I bought."

"And wrap them," Norman reminded her.

"Yes, there's that. And I hate wrapping presents. I'm really no good at it."

"I'm not a bad wrapper. I could help you wrap your presents. It would be more fun with the two of us."

"You're right. You could put your finger on the knot in my ribbon when I tie a bow."

Norman glanced over at her and smiled. "That's always been my goal in life," he said. "I love you, Hannah. I want to make your life easier."

"You do," Hannah said, and then she reached out to place her hand on his arm as he drove.

The Crazy Elf parking lot was chained shut and Norman parked on the street. As they got out of the car and headed for the entrance, the wind picked up and snow skittered across the sidewalk in little eddies and flurries. Hannah thought about dust devils and their bigger cousins, sand devils. If there were dust devils and sand devils, could there be snow devils? She'd have to look it up.

"What are you thinking about?" Norman asked.

"Dust devils and sand devils. And I was just wondering if there were snow devils."

"There are, but most people call them snowspouts. They happen when a mass of cold air hovers over a warmer body of water. That creates a kind of waterspout that freezes when it gets up in the cold air."

Hannah shivered slightly. It was a cold night and talking about freezing waterspouts was making her colder.

"Cold?" Norman asked, slipping his arm around her shoulder.

"Yes. I wish I could be magically transported to somewhere warmer . . . like the middle of a desert."

"Do you want to go to Palm Springs? It's only a few hours from here by plane."

"I'd love to, but I can't."

"Why not? We could fly in on a Friday night and spend the

weekend. And if you felt you had to get back to Lake Eden, we could fly back late Sunday night."

"Tempting," Hannah commented and it was. She'd love a weekend getaway. But she had a ton of work to do and she couldn't ask Lisa to do it all. "I'd love to, but we're right in the middle of our busy season. Could we table it until it slows down at the end of February?"

"We can do that. I'll ask you again on Valentine's Day. It should be cold enough to tempt you."

"I'm sure it will be!" Hannah wondered if she'd say yes. Valentine's Day was less than two months away and it would be equally tempting then. The snowbirds would be gone and everyone who was left would be sick of the ice and snow.

"Okay, it's a date."

"But I didn't say I'd go."

"I know that. I just meant it's a date to ask you."

"Okay." They arrived at the entrance to the Crazy Elf Christmas Tree Lot and Hannah opened the gate. "Follow me," she said. "I know where Larry's trailer is."

Everything looked different now that the main lights were off. They walked past the darkened and deserted log cabins that housed the shops and turned left on Rudolf Lane.

"This is strange without the lights and music," Norman said, and Hannah agreed. And although she'd never suspected she'd miss the loud, blaring Christmas carols, she did.

"Here's Elf Headquarters," she informed him as they turned down the path for the double-wide trailer where Larry lived. "The lights are on. He's waiting for us."

"Nice trailer," Norman said as they approached.

"I know. It's huge. Larry told me there are two bedrooms and he made one of them into an office. He's got a humungous flat screen television in the living room so he can watch sports."

"Larry's a sports fan?"

"I'll say! When Mike and I were here, he muted the sound but he left the game on."

"And most ordinary fans would have turned the game off until after you left?"

"Right." Hannah was always impressed at how fast Norman caught her train of thought.

They climbed up the low stairs to the trailer and Norman stepped aside so that Hannah could knock.

"Larry?" she called out, rapping sharply on the door.

There was a beat of silence and then another. They could hear the television playing inside and it sounded like it was a basketball game.

"Let me," Norman said, stepping forward to knock even harder. He waited a moment and then he tried again.

Nothing, absolutely nothing happened. There was no sound from inside except the voice of the announcer and roar of the crowd.

"Try it again," Hannah suggested.

Norman balled up his fist and pounded on the door while Hannah called out Larry's name. It had absolutely no effect and the door remained tightly closed.

Hannah turned to Norman. "What shall we do?" she asked.

"I don't know. Let's see if the door's open. He could have fallen asleep in front of the television."

Although Hannah couldn't see how Larry could sleep through such a racket, she stepped aside so that Norman could try the door. When the knob turned, she gave a little gasp. For some reason she didn't like this. She didn't like it at all. Maybe it was because the park looked so different with the main lights off and the crowd gone home. Or maybe there was something wrong and they ought to hightail it out of here.

"What?" Norman turned to her as her grip on his arm tightened.

"I don't know. It's just kind of strange, that's all."

"What's strange?"

"The door's unlocked. You'd think he'd lock it at night."

"He might not be worried about anyone walking in on him since the park's closed for the night," Norman suggested.

"Maybe you're right. But do you think we should go in?"

"He said he'd meet you here, didn't he?"

"Yes. But . . ." Hannah's voice trailed off and she swallowed hard. She couldn't seem to shake the feeling that something was horribly wrong.

"Come on. Let's go in and get out of the cold."

Norman opened the door and the light spilled out. He took her hand to pull her inside, but Hannah couldn't seem to make her feet move. She wasn't sure why, but she really didn't want to go inside Elf Headquarters. It was a lot like the reticence she'd experienced when Delores had asked her to go on a roller coaster with Andrea. That little excursion had ended in disaster and Hannah now knew that roller coasters and her stomach didn't coexist well. "Maybe we should come back tomorrow," she suggested, hoping he'd agree.

"Why? Larry should be back soon. He left the lights and the television on."

"I know, but isn't it rude to go in uninvited?" Hannah asked, trying to control her unreasonable urge to flee.

"The door was unlocked and it's pretty obvious he left it open for us. That counts as an invitation in my book. Come on, Hannah. It's silly to stand out here in the wind."

"Right," Hannah said, taking a deep breath for courage as she followed Norman inside.

There was a table just inside the doorway on her left. Hannah glanced at it and saw an envelope with her name written on the front. Larry had made out her check and receipt, just as he'd promised to do. She picked up the envelope, stuffed it in her purse, and followed Norman as he stepped deeper into the room.

Even though it was silly, she found herself holding her breath. There was something wrong. She was sure of it. And . . . there it was!

"What's wrong?" Norman asked, turning to her in alarm as she gasped out loud in shock.

"The TV," Hannah said, pointing at the huge flat screen

hanging on the wall. Something was drastically wrong with Larry's giant screen television set. Areas of the screen were glowing and other areas were dark. There were a couple of holes in the top part of the screen, but it continued to glow and fade almost like a light show and Hannah was mesmerized. And all the while the announcer continued to blather excitedly about the game they couldn't see.

The holes in the screen looked a lot like bullet holes to her! Hannah's mind went into overdrive. Had Larry gotten so angry with the outcome of the game that he'd shot his television set? Her gaze shifted to the coffee table in front of the couch. There were chips and a container of dip, along with a half-empty bottle of brandy and a snifter that had a bit of amber-colored liquid in the bottom. It was pretty evident that Larry had been drinking and that lent credence to her theory about the holes. "I don't like this," she said.

"I'm not exactly happy with it either," Norman replied. "But I don't think it's all that unusual. My dad threw a glass at the television once when they preempted his favorite show for a political debate."

As Norman spoke Hannah turned to survey the rest of the room. Nothing was moving, there was no sign of any other damage, and everything appeared to be perfectly . . .

"Hannah?" Norman turned to his suddenly silent companion. "What's the matter?"

"There," Hannah somehow managed to say and she pointed to the area on the other side of the door.

Norman turned to look. "Oh," he said. "There's Larry."

"Yes."

Norman moved a smidgen closer to the prone figure on the rug. "There's a brandy bottle on the coffee table. He could be dead drunk."

"Or he could simply be dead," Hannah said, swallowing again in an attempt to lubricate her suddenly parched throat.

"I'd better feel for a pulse."

Hannah stepped back. She wasn't about to fight about

which of them should feel for Larry's pulse. She didn't really want to touch Larry anyway. Instead, she averted her eyes as Norman knelt down next to Larry on the rug and that's when she noticed her platter on the floor, along with some scattered crumbs that could only have come from her Minnesota Plum Pudding. Larry must have been carrying the platter when he answered the door.

"No pulse," Norman said straightening up and turning to her. "He's dead."

"Dead," Hannah repeated, not liking that diagnosis one bit.

"I'd better call Mike," Norman told her, reaching in his pocket for his cell phone. "You can wait outside if you don't want to stay here."

"Alone?!" Hannah realized that her voice had turned into a frightened squeak and she regretted it. But she really didn't want to stand outside when she wasn't sure how Larry had died. "Was he . . . murdered?" she asked.

"I don't know. I won't know unless I turn him over and I'll leave that to the authorities."

"Right," Hannah said, leaning against the wall. She took a deep breath, shut her eyes so she wouldn't have to look at Larry, and listened to the sportscaster's voice as he gave a play-by-play account of the basketball game. She didn't know who was playing and she didn't care, but if she concentrated on what he was saying, she could avoid listening to Norman as he called Mike and told him why he should come out to the Crazy Elf Christmas Tree Lot right away.

Chapter Fifteen

"So he might have been expecting you when he opened the door?"

"It's certainly possible. He knew I was coming to get a check for the cookies, and I called him from the Inn to tell him we were on the way." Hannah refilled Mike's coffee cup from the carafe on her coffee table.

"What time did you call him?"

"It must have been close to nine. I could hear someone announcing that the park was about to close over the loudspeakers."

"And what time did you enter the park?"

Hannah shrugged. "It was probably after nine-thirty, but I didn't check the time."

"I did," Norman spoke up. "The clock on my dash read nine-fifty when we got out of the car. It's five minutes fast."

"So you're not late to work?" Mike asked.

"That's right. You do the same thing?"

"You bet."

Hannah wasn't interested in a discussion of tardiness in the workplace and she cut them off by asking Mike a question. "Was Larry shot?"

"We're waiting for a final determination from the coroner."

"Doc Knight couldn't tell if Larry was *shot*?" Hannah couldn't believe her ears.

"Of course he could tell." Mike turned to Norman who was sitting next to Hannah on the couch. "Describe everything you saw when you entered the park."

"Well . . . the music and the main lights were off. Only the dim lights they use at night were on. The gate was closed, but it was unlocked and that's how we got in."

"Did you see or hear anyone?"

Both Hannah and Norman shook their heads.

"No one," Hannah said.

"I guess someone could have been hiding in one of the shops or tents," Norman qualified it, "but we didn't actually see anyone."

"No noises that might have led you to believe that someone else was in the park with you?"

"No," Hannah answered that question. "Of course the wind was blowing and that might have masked any sounds."

"Did you notice any footprints outside the trailer?"

"No," Norman answered the question. "The wind had blown most of the snow away from the steps and the pathway."

"Hannah?"

Mike turned to her and Hannah shook her head. "If there were footprints, we didn't notice them."

"Okay." Mike jotted something in his notebook. "All right, Hannah. Describe everything you saw when you entered the trailer. I'm interested in your first impressions."

"Norman stepped in and I followed him. The second I stepped in the door, I thought something was wrong."

"Why?"

"There was no reason, not really. I hadn't noticed the television screen yet, and I didn't see Larry's body until later."

"But your *slay-dar* was working overtime?" Mike asked.

"I guess you could say that." Hannah smiled slightly, not really minding Mike's use of the word Norman had coined a few months ago to describe her affinity for finding murder victims. "When I first stepped inside, I looked to the left and

I saw an envelope on the table next to the doorway. It had my name written on the outside and . . . uh-oh!"

"What's wrong?" Norman asked when Hannah fell suddenly silent.

"It's just . . . When I saw my name, I assumed it was the check and receipt that Larry had promised to give me. I picked it up and put it in my purse, and that means I removed something from the crime scene!"

"You removed something from a place you didn't *know* was a crime scene," Norman corrected her.

"That's right," Mike said. "Do you still have the envelope?"

"Yes. Do you want it?" When Mike nodded, Hannah went to get the envelope out of her purse. "Here," she said, handing it to him.

Mike opened the envelope and took out the papers inside. "It's a check made out to The Cookie Jar, and a receipt for the cookies you delivered."

"That's what I thought it was. Do you need to keep it for evidence?" Hannah asked.

Mike thought about it for a moment and then he shook his head. "Not if it was just sitting on the table. I can't imagine any way this envelope could relate to the killer, but it wouldn't hurt to have a copy of it for the file."

"Would it work if I scanned the envelope and the contents?" Norman asked. "That way Hannah can deposit the check tomorrow."

"That'll do," Mike said, turning to Hannah as Norman went to use her computer. "What did you see next?"

"The holes in the television screen. And then the half-full bottle of brandy and the nearly-empty snifter on the coffee table. I remember thinking that Larry might have had one too many and shot his own television screen."

"But you still didn't know that Larry was dead?"

"No. Not then. I remember saying that I didn't like the way things looked, and Norman agreed with me. But then he said something about his father getting so mad when they preempted his favorite program that he threw a glass at his television set."

"And that reassured you?"

"Not really. I still had the feeling that something was wrong. That's when I turned around to look at the whole room and I saw Larry on the floor."

"And that's when Norman called me?"

"Not quite yet. First Norman went over to feel for a pulse and *then* he called you."

"Okay. Thanks, Hannah." Mike began to jot things down in his notebook again.

"Coffee?" Hannah asked him. "It should be ready by now."

"Sure."

Hannah went off to get the coffee, leaving Mike to his notes and Norman to print out the scans. By the time she came back into the living room, Norman was handing Mike the prints he'd made.

"You still haven't told us if Larry was shot," Norman reminded Mike.

"You wouldn't need to ask if you'd turned the body over. Thanks for not doing that. It makes our job easier if the victim's body hasn't been moved."

Hannah waited for the answer to Norman's query, but it wasn't forthcoming. It probably wouldn't be. She knew Mike well enough to predict that he'd give them as little information about the murder as possible. It was always a trade-off with Mike. If she tossed him a piece of information that he wanted, he'd feed her scraps about what he knew.

"I wonder if Larry's unorthodox business practices had anything to do with his murder," she mused. And then she waited.

Mike turned to her quickly. "What unorthodox business practices?"

"You'll have to ask Mayor Bascomb about that. He can explain it better than I can. How was Larry killed?"

"That's confidential."

"Not for long," Hannah went into her best argument. "Minnie Holtzmeier's son is Doc Knight's night ambulance driver. And he's fishing buddies with Jake and Kelly on the *News at O'Dark-Thirty* show. How long do you think it'll take them to broadcast it on KCOW radio?"

Mike thought about that for a minute and then he sighed. "He was shot through the heart, and I'm guessing it was a small caliber pistol. Maybe a twenty-two, but we won't know for sure until Doc fishes out the bullet and forensics gets through with it."

"So the killer shot Larry *and* the television screen?" Norman asked.

"In that order?" Hannah added her own question.

"That's probably right," Mike admitted. "The way I see it, Mr. Jaeger opened the door expecting you, and someone else was there. That someone pulled a gun and Mr. Jaeger was backing up in a futile attempt to get away from his killer when he was shot."

"How many times?" Hannah asked.

"Only once. Doc Knight found one entrance wound and no exit wound. After Mr. Jaeger fell, the shooter crossed over to the television set and put three bullets in the screen."

"I wonder why the killer shot the television," Hannah said.

"We won't know until we catch him," Mike said, and then he grinned. "Of course I've got my own personal theory."

"What's that?" Norman asked.

"He didn't like the way the game was going. Everybody's saying it's a miracle that the Knicks pulled it off." Mike reached for one of the cookies Hannah had brought to have with their coffee. He took a bite and looked slightly surprised. "Banana?"

"Yes. I'm trying out a new recipe for Banana Chocolate Chip Cookies. Lisa just got it from her cousin, Mary Therese. What do you think?"

"I like them," Norman replied, finishing the cookie he'd

taken when she'd set down the plate. "Banana and chocolate are really good together."

"You won't get any argument from me about that!" Mike smiled at Hannah and then he turned back to Norman. "There was a lot of blood. I was just wondering how long it took him to die."

"How much blood are we talking about?"

"I'd say maybe a quart. The stain on the rug was a little bigger than a basketball. If you spilled a quart of milk it would probably make a spot about that size."

"Okay . . . let me figure this out." Norman said, claiming the pad of paper and pen Hannah always kept on the table next to the phone. "If I remember the lecture on cardiac output correctly, the adult human heart pumps approximately seventy milliliters with each beat. That means it would take roughly fifteen seconds to bleed out a quart."

Hannah had heard quite enough. This latest topic bordered on the macabre. "Stop right there," she said, giving both men a stern look. "If you want to eat cookies and talk about dead bodies and quarts of blood, I'm going in my bedroom to watch television."

"Sorry," Norman said, looking apologetic.

"I didn't know you had a television set in your bedroom," Mike said, not looking in the least bit contrite.

"I don't. I just wanted you to stop talking about it, that's all."

"Okay, we're through here." Mike stood up, slipped his notebook in his pocket, and glanced over at her Christmas tree. "Are you going to decorate that? It looks kind of bare with just the lights, especially with those wires on the wall and . . . what are those wires doing there anyway?"

"Moishe," Hannah said by way of explanation.

"You're afraid he'll tip over the tree?"

"I *know* he'll tip over the tree. He's already done it once . . . before dawn this morning."

Mike turned to look at the guilty party who was sitting on the back of the couch washing his face. "It's time to talk turkey, Big Guy."

"Don't say turkey," Hannah said with a grin. "He knows that word. It's one of his favorite entrees."

"Okay, we'll talk tough. How's that?" Mike walked around the couch, sat below her errant feline, and lifted Moishe down to his lap. "That's Mama's Christmas tree over there in the corner," he told Moishe, who actually seemed to be listening. "You have to leave it alone. You've got your Kitty Kondo to climb. Uncle Norman bought it just for you. The Christmas tree is Mama's toy. You've got all your own toys to play with."

Moishe looked up at Mike and for several long seconds, they stared at each other. Then Moishe opened his mouth and gave a little yowl.

"Good," Mike said. "I'm glad you understand. And because you promised to be a good boy, I'm going to bring you a brand new toy the next time I come over."

Moishe yowled again, and Hannah was willing to testify that he'd understood every word Mike had spoken. Perhaps the cop-to-cat talk had been a success and her Christmas tree would be safe from feline attention.

"Gotta go," Mike said, giving Moishe a scratch under the chin. "Remember what I said, Big Guy."

Norman stood up and followed Mike to the door. "I'll see you out," he said. "There's something I need to tell you. It'll only take a minute or two."

The men went out and Norman closed the door behind them. That caused Hannah's curiosity to go on high alert. It wouldn't be right to listen to their private conversation. That would be snooping. But she thought she saw a smear of dirt on the rug very close to the door. One of them must have stepped in some slush and failed to wipe it off on the mat she kept outside her front door.

Armed with a napkin from the coffee table, Hannah hurried over to blot the rug. She wasn't quite sure where she'd seen the dirt, but if she blotted the whole area by the door, she couldn't miss it.

It was simply a coincidence that she could make out every word they spoke. At least that's what Hannah told herself. She certainly wasn't *trying* to overhear their conversation.

"I didn't exactly *accuse* your mother of shoplifting," Mike said.

"I know. Hannah told me." Norman said. "I just wanted to let you know that I'm almost positive Mother paid for all those things she bought at the mall. I'll check on it when the bills come in. I always go over there and help her with her online banking."

"That's good enough for me. I was just worried when I saw all those shoes. I mean . . . why would your mother buy six pairs of shoes?"

"Because she's dating someone and she's trying to impress him," Norman explained. "She probably bought a lot of new dresses, too."

"So who's the lucky guy?"

"We don't know. They were in a booth at Sally's with the curtains drawn and all we could see was their feet."

Mike laughed and Hannah noted he sounded amused. "What did you do? Crawl around on the floor?"

"No, Hannah dropped her purse. We had to kneel down to pick up the things that fell out."

"That's a good one. I'll have to remember she does that the next time I'm in one of those curtained booths."

Hannah began to frown. The *next* time? That meant Mike had been in one of Sally's curtained booths before!

"Anyway, now I know why Mother's been too busy to go out to dinner with me lately."

"Do you think it's serious?"

"I don't know. Hannah does."

"Why does Hannah think it's serious?"

"Because she saw the waitresses deliver a bottle of champagne to their booth. And Mother was wearing red sandals with really high heels."

"Hmmm." Mike was silent for a moment. "Hannah's probably right," he concluded. "How about you? Are you okay with that?"

"I'm fine just as long as he's not after her money. You always hear these stories about good looking guys cheating widows out of their retirement money. And look what happened to Hannah's mother. Delores almost got caught in a scheme like that."

"True. So what are you going to do about it?"

"I'm going to try to find out who the guy is. We were going to drive past Mother's house and take down his license number if we saw his car. But then we found Larry's body and you said you needed to take our statements, so we came straight here."

"I'll take a run past your mother's on my way back to the station," Mike offered.

"But it's out of your way."

"So what? You're a friend and I like your mother. I wouldn't want to see anyone take advantage of her."

Hannah backed away from the door and began to clear the table. Norman would probably be in any second and she didn't want to be caught eavesdropping. But all the while she was carrying in coffee cups and stashing them in the dishwasher, she was wondering when Mike had been in a curtained booth at the Lake Eden Inn, and who his dinner companion had been.

BANANA CHOCOLATE CHIP COOKIES

Preheat oven to 400 degrees F., rack
in the middle position.

2 sticks (*1 cup, ½ pound*) softened butter
1 and ½ cups powdered (*confectioners*) sugar
1/2 teaspoon lemon extract
1/2 cup mashed banana (*1 medium*)
1 teaspoon baking powder
¼ teaspoon salt
2 cups flour (*pack it down when you measure it*)
6-ounce package semi-sweet mini chocolate chips
   (*that's one cup*)

Hannah's Note: This is a lot easier to do with an electric mixer.

Beat the softened butter and the powdered sugar together until they look light and creamy. There's no need to sift the powdered sugar unless it's got big lumps. If you do end up sifting it, make sure you pack it down in the cup when you measure it.

Add a half-teaspoon of lemon extract and mix it in.

Peel the banana and break it into chunks. Mix them in until they're thoroughly mashed and the powdered sugar and butter mixture is smooth again.

Sprinkle in the baking powder and salt, and mix them in thoroughly.

Add the flour in half-cup increments, mixing after each addition. When the cookie dough is thoroughly mixed, take the bowl from the mixer and set it on the counter.

Mix in the chocolate chips by hand. You'll want them as evenly distributed as possible.

Line your cookie sheets with foil and spray the foil lightly with Pam or another nonstick cooking spray.

Use a teaspoon to drop cookie dough 2 inches apart on the cookie sheets, no more than 12 cookies to a sheet. *(I used a 2-teaspoon size cookie scoop to make small cookies. I've also used a 2-Tablespoon size cookie scoop to make larger cookies.)*

Use a metal spatula or the palm of your impeccably clean hand to flatten the cookies.

Bake the cookies at 400 degrees F. for 8 to 10 minutes, or until they're golden on top. Remove them from the oven and let them sit on the cookie sheet for 2 minutes. Then pull the foil off and transfer cookies, foil and all, to a wire rack to cool completely.

Yield: Makes approximately 3 dozen large or 5 dozen small cookies.

Mary Therese's Hint: (She wrote it out on the recipe card she sent to Lisa.) Be sure the butter is soft. I leave it out overnight. If you like bananas, you can use 2 medium bananas mashed, but you may have to add a little more flour.

Chapter Sixteen

When the alarm went off at four in the morning, Hannah sat up and rubbed her eyes. It had been an uneasy night filled with images of Larry prone on the rug at Elf Headquarters haunting her sleep. She hadn't really liked him all that much, but he hadn't deserved to be murdered.

It was time to get up, get dressed, drink all the coffee in the pot to wake up enough to drive, and go to The Cookie Jar to bake a zillion cookies. Once people heard that Larry Jaeger had been murdered and that she'd been there with Norman to discover his body, The Cookie Jar would be packed with curious customers.

Hannah thrust her feet into slippers and headed straight for the kitchen. A cup of coffee would perk her right up and get rid of that not-enough-sleep syndrome that usually plagued her in the morning. This morning it was even more severe than usual, perhaps because she'd stayed up until almost eleven with Norman, trimming her Christmas tree.

She was halfway down the hall when she heard a thumping from the living room. There was also a low rumbling noise that sounded a bit like a growl. At first she was hard-pressed to identify the origin, but as her steps brought her within a few feet of the living room, she heard a series of sounds she'd heard before. It was an ack-ack sound, a bit like the words GI's in World War II had used to describe anti-aircraft rounds going off in the distance. Except that this sound wasn't in the distance. It was in her living room. And the ack-ack in question wasn't coming from military weaponry. It originated deep within her feline's throat and it was a prelude to a leap, a pounce, and then, at least in Moishe's mind, the happy crunching of avian bones.

Hannah rounded the corner at the run, just in time to see orange and white fur in motion. Her cat appeared to be leap-ing straight up near the far corner of the room, and Hannah knew what that meant. It was a death rattle for Great-Grandma Elsa's birds, those lovely red cardinals and snow white doves that were fashioned from . . .

"Uh-oh!" Hannah groaned. And then, as she caught sight of the carnage that had been wreaked upon her living room rug, she uttered a phrase that would surely have been bleeped on network television. There were white and red feathers every-where, along with several bird feet that had been fashioned from wire and yarn. Five black beads that had served as bird eyes sat upon her coffee table, and Hannah almost chuckled despite the scene of utter devastation. There were bird's eyes on her bird's-eye maple coffee table. That coincidence seemed pretty funny until she remembered that Great-Grandma Elsa had dyed the feathers and handcrafted the cardinals and doves her-self. And now her great-great-grandcat, Moishe, had destroyed them.

Hannah turned to look at her feather-seeking missile, but he was no longer in the room. He'd vanished in a puff of cat dander, leaving one white feather floating slowly down to set-tle on top of the television set.

Cleanup and then coffee? Or coffee and then cleanup? It was no contest for Hannah. She averted her eyes from the avian massacre, turned on her heel, and stepped into the kitchen to get away from it all.

"I heard," Lisa said as Hannah walked into the kitchen at The Cookie Jar.

"Jake and Kelly?"

Lisa nodded and went to pour Hannah a cup of freshly brewed coffee. She carried it over to the stool Hannah had taken at the stainless steel workstation, and gave a little sigh. "I don't suppose you got a chance to . . ."

Before Lisa could finish her question, Hannah reached into her purse, pulled out the envelope, and held it up. "He must have been expecting us, because it was right there on the table next to the door."

"Thanks," Lisa said, taking the check and carrying it over to the file she kept for accounts receivable. The concept of accepting a check that had been so close to a murder victim might bother her a bit, but it was clear that it wouldn't deter her from depositing it.

"What do we have to bake today?" Hannah asked as she sipped her coffee.

"Everything. They're going to come through the door in droves. But you don't need to worry. I've got a good start on it. How about a little chocolate to get you going?"

"Sounds good to me. What do you have?"

"Chocolate Chip Crunch Cookies, German Chocolate Cake Cookies, Desperation Cookies, and a few Frosting Splatters.

"Frosting Splatters?" Hannah picked up on the cookie name she didn't recognize. "What are those?"

"They're something my mother used to make when she had leftover frosting. All you do is take out a splatter of soda crackers, tip it salt-side down, and . . ."

"Hold it." Hannah held up her hand. "What's a splatter?"

"That's what my Mom called four soda crackers in a sheet. They used to come in the box that way, remember?"

"I do, but I've never heard them called a *splatter*."

"I think it was Mom's word, a combination between *split* because that's what you do to them before you eat them and *platter* because they're flat."

"Makes sense to me."

'I don't think they come in splatters anymore. Or if they

do, Florence doesn't have them down at the Red Owl. The only crackers I could get were individual soda crackers in sleeves, but I'm still calling them splatters."

"I'd like to try a couple of Frosting Splatters."

Lisa hurried to the counter and came back with three Frosting Splatters. One was a soda cracker topped with German Chocolate Cake Cookie frosting, another was covered with the Mocha Frosting they used on their Cappuccino Cookies, and the third cracker had the frosting from Chocolate-Covered Cherry Cookies.

"See how the salt cuts the sweetness?" Lisa asked, as Hannah finished the first Frosting Splatter.

"I do. It works perfectly." Hannah made short work of finishing the other two.

"So you're all ready for baking?"

"I am."

"Good. I got talked into something last night and I'm hoping you'll approve. I said we'd make a dozen Christmas cookies for each family that benefits from Christmas For All."

"What's Christmas For All?" Hannah asked.

"It's a group that provides a family Christmas for kids whose parents can't afford a celebration. The men dress up like Santa and they deliver food and presents on Christmas Eve."

"I like that. We should definitely provide cookies."

"That's what I thought you'd say when your mother called me last night."

"My mother called *you*?"

"That's right. She said you weren't home from dinner with Norman yet, so she was calling me. That must have been when you were discovering . . . uh . . . Larry."

"You're probably right."

"Anyway, your mother and Carrie are involved."

Hannah frowned. "They don't have anything to do with the food, do they?"

"I don't think so."

"Thank goodness for that!"

"What do you mean?" Lisa asked.

"Mother cooks only when the restaurants are closed, and she alternates between two entrees, Hawaiian Pot Roast and EZ Lasagna."

"How about Carrie? Doesn't she cook either?"

"Carrie cooks. She cooked for Norman until he moved out."

"Was that one of the reasons Norman moved out?"

"I'm fairly certain it was. Carrie thinks it's her mission in life to influence people's diets. And she believes in a low-salt, low-fat, no-taste menu that's laden with powdered food supplements and rich in exotic vegetables that no one in Lake Eden grows in their gardens."

"Oh. Well then . . . maybe it's good that your mother and Carrie just provide the baskets to carry the food."

"It's very good." Hannah got up from her stool and carried her coffee cup over to the sink. "Let's get started."

"Okay. Everybody who comes in is going to ask what you saw when you found Larry's body."

"You'll tell them?" Hannah asked, hoping that Lisa would be the storyteller again this time and that she could hide out in the kitchen.

"I will, but you have to describe everything for me. We can do it while we're baking. If we don't get busy and bake at least a hundred dozen cookies this morning, we're going to run out."

FROSTING SPLATTERS

Leftover frosting of any type
Salted soda crackers in sheets of 4, *(if you can find them,)* or individual crackers packed in sleeves.

Lay out the crackers salt side down on a cookie sheet, counter, or platter. Spread the unsalted side with frosting.

Yield: Makes as many crackers as you have frosting to top.

Lisa's Note: Kids love these and so do adults. A few Frosting Splatters might just keep them from digging into the frosted cake until it's ready to be served.

There was a knock on the back door and Hannah sighed. "That's got to be Mother. She listens to KCOW radio when she drives to work in the morning and she's probably dropping by to accuse me of corrupting Norman."

"By taking him with you to find murder victims?" Lisa guessed.

"Exactly right. You know how she feels about my affliction."

"Is *that* what she calls it?" Lisa giggled and Hannah was reminded again how young her partner was.

"Among other things. It embarrasses her because none of her friends have daughters who stumble across murder victims."

"She's not entirely wrong, you know. You *do* seem to have a knack for it."

"A *knack*? Now there's a word she hasn't used to describe it." There was another knock at the door, a little louder this time, and Hannah got up from her stool. "I'd better open the door before she freezes out there."

"Good morning, dear," Delores said, as Hannah opened the door and ushered her into the kitchen. There was a smile on her face and Hannah knew instantly that she hadn't heard about Larry Jaeger. "I just dropped by on my way out to the college."

"It's good to see you, Mother. Would you like a cup of coffee?"

"I'd love to have a cup of coffee with you. I didn't have time for breakfast this morning. Do you have any cookies . . ." Delores stopped speaking as her gaze landed on the baker's rack that was filled with freshly-baked cookies. "That was a silly question for me to ask. Of *course* you have cookies!"

"We have Boggles, Raisin Drops, Spicy Dreams, or Orange Julius Cookies," Lisa told her, naming the cookies on the rack for Delores.

"Orange Julius Cookies? I don't think I've ever tasted those."

"I *know* you've never tasted them," Hannah said. "The recipe's from Andrea's friend, Kathy Bruns, and this is the first time we've baked them."

Lisa placed two of the cookies on a napkin in front of Delores. "I'm going to get things ready in the coffee shop," she said, heading for the swinging door that separated the two areas. "It was nice to see you, Mrs. Swensen."

"Lisa's always so formal and I've known her since she was a baby," Delores said, once Lisa was out of earshot. "What do I have to do to get her to call me Delores . . . or Mother?"

"You could adopt her."

"Perhaps that would do it," Delores said with a laugh. "Very good, dear."

As Hannah filled her mother's coffee mug, she thought about her choices. She could wait until Delores heard about Larry's murder on the radio, or she could take the bull by the horns and blurt it out now. Either way would result in upsetting her mother, but she might be a bit less upset if she heard it straight from the horse's mouth.

"I guess you haven't heard about Larry Jaeger," Hannah said, placing the coffee in front of her mother and jumping into what could be the frigid waters of motherly displeasure with both feet.

"What *about* Larry Jaeger?"

"Someone murdered him last night." Hannah waited for

her mother's predictable gasp. Once that occurred, she was about to go on when she had a brilliant idea. Although she'd been the one to spot Larry on the floor, Norman had actually discovered that he had no pulse and was dead. "Norman discovered him dead on the floor of his trailer."

"Norman?!" Delores stared at her daughter open-mouthed. "You said *Norman* found Larry's dead body?"

"That's right. We had dinner at the Inn last night and then we dropped by the Crazy Elf to pick up a check for the cookies I delivered yesterday afternoon. It was all arranged ahead of time and Larry left the gate open for us. When he didn't answer our knocks at Elf Headquarters, we thought he might be somewhere else in the park and we decided to wait for him inside. Norman opened the door to the trailer and he found Larry dead on the floor."

"Poor Norman!" Delores sighed and shook her head. "It must have been awful for him."

"He didn't seem to be terribly upset," Hannah said, pleased at the way this conversation was going. "I'd like to think that it was because I was with him."

"It's probably because he's a dentist," Delores contradicted her.

"What does being a *dentist* have to do with it?"

"Think about it, dear. Dentists are used to the sight of blood and other unpleasant things like that. This must have been just another unpleasant episode in a long line of unpleasant episodes for him." Delores took another sip of her coffee. "Well, I'm glad you told me about it before I heard it from someone else. Does Carrie know?"

"I'm not sure. It was late by the time Mike took our statements. Norman might not have called to tell her last night, but he probably talked to her this morning."

"No doubt you're right," Delores agreed, looking a bit disappointed that she couldn't break the news to her friend. She took another sip of her coffee and then something shocking must have occurred to her, because Hannah saw her carefully arched brows shoot up toward her perfect coiffure.

"What is it, Mother?"

"I just remembered. I'd better tell Nancy."

"Nancy?"

"Dr. Love. We've gotten to be great friends, dear. I know she's considerably younger than I am, but we're involved in a lot of the same things."

"Like what?" Hannah asked.

"Dorcas Circle, and the Lake Eden Historical Society. She just joined our Regency romance group, and then there's Christmas For All. That's where I first met her. It's an organization for . . ."

"Lisa told me all about it," Hannah cut her off before Delores asked her to join.

"Nancy says she considers me the mother she never had."

Too bad you're not the mother I *never had*, Hannah thought, but of course she didn't say so. She really didn't mean it. She loved Delores and she respected her as her mother. But it *was* a very funny comeback and it just about killed her not to say it.

"What's the matter, dear? You look strained."

"Nothing, Mother." Hannah put on a smile.

"Well, I really should see Nancy. She might not have heard about it. It won't take long, I promise."

Hannah frowned slightly. Why was her mother assuring her that her visit with Dr. Love wouldn't take long? Luanne opened Granny's Attic for business every day, and Delores and Carrie could come in as late as they pleased. Her mother's time was her own. She could stay out at the college for hours chatting as long as she liked.

"Nancy has office hours from eight to ten every morning, so we should be able to catch her."

"*We?*" Hannah asked, zeroing in on the plural.

"Yes, we." Delores stopped cold and looked very apologetic. "I'm sorry I didn't tell you, but I'm going to need you to follow me out to the college and then bring me back here. I have to leave my car in the parking lot."

"Why do you have to do that?"

"For Michelle. I'm just so scattered this morning, I forgot to tell you," she said, by way of apology. "And there's one other thing. Michelle can stay with you, can't she, dear? I'm having some painting done."

"Michelle's always welcome to stay with me, but I thought she wouldn't be home until Christmas Eve."

"That was the original plan, but it's changed. She's coming in late this afternoon and she needs to borrow my car. I'm going to park it in the college lot and she'll pick it up after rehearsal this evening."

"Why is Michelle coming to the community college?" Hannah asked, struggling to make sense of the disjointed facts she'd learned.

"Because she has a part in the Christmas Follies. Don't you remember that nice poetry professor telling us about it?"

"He's not nice," Hannah said, and then she wished she could take back the words. Her comment was sure to elicit a query from Delores. "Of course I remember," she said quickly, hoping to throw her mother off the track. "Do you know if Michelle's in a play? Or is it something else?"

"It's something else. She's going to sing."

"I didn't know Michelle could sing!" Hannah relaxed slightly. Her mother was off-topic and that was all to the good. She wasn't in the mood to discuss her former relationship with Bradford Ramsey, the Lothario of poetry professors.

"I'm just so proud of her!" Delores continued. "I'd assumed that she couldn't sing. You certainly can't, and Andrea's never been able to carry a tune. That's why I told you to whisper the words to the hymns in church. It was embarrassing when you girls tried to sing out loud. Everybody in the pew in front of us turned around to look."

Hannah remembered her mother's admonishment about

singing out loud in church. Delores had never told them why it was preferable for them to whisper, but now she knew why.

"Your father couldn't sing a note," Delores said, smiling fondly at some private memory. "He sounded like a dying bullfrog."

"Have you ever heard a dying bullfrog?" Hannah couldn't resist asking.

"Of course not. I was just hypothesizing, dear. In any event, I'm fairly certain that Michelle inherited her vocal talents from me."

I hope not! Hannah thought, remembering the night her mother and Carrie had entered a Karaoke contest. "Is Michelle part of a group?"

"No, she's doing a song and dance number from a musical that a Macalester graduate wrote. It's never been performed before."

"That's great," Hannah said, hoping that Michelle's number would be a huge success. "I can hardly wait to see it."

"So will you please follow me out to the college, dear? I know you're busy and I hate to ask, but I tried calling Carrie several times this morning and she's not answering her phone."

Maybe she's still with Mr. Suede Boots, Hannah thought, but she didn't say it. There would be plenty of time to tell her mother about Carrie's romance once they learned the identity of the man she was dating.

"And take some chocolate cookies, will you, dear? Nancy might need the endorphins."

It only took a moment to scoop up a half-dozen Chocolate Highlander Cookie Bars and stack them in one of The Cookie Jar's distinctive carryout bags. Then Hannah grabbed her parka, told Lisa she'd be back just as soon as she could, and headed out to her cookie truck to follow her mother.

It was snowing lightly as Hannah turned onto the highway behind her mother's car. Delores immediately increased her speed, widening the distance between them exponentially, and forcing Hannah to tromp on her accelerator just to keep up. What in the world had gotten into her mother? Delores was usually a careful driver who prided herself on the fact she'd never been in an accident, but that claim could change today. Hannah watched, open-mouthed, as her mother fairly flew down the roadway like a winged rodent emerging from eternal damnation.

There was nothing to do except follow and pick up the pieces if something happened. Hannah pushed her cookie truck to the max and hoped that she wouldn't get a speeding ticket in her effort to keep her mother in sight.

"Uh-oh!" she groaned, watching helplessly as Delores swerved on a patch of ice. Her father had done most of the driving in bad weather. Did Delores know how to steer out of a skid? Hannah had her answer several heart-pounding seconds later when the heavy sedan Hannah's father had bought only six months before he died stabilized and resumed a normal course. Hannah managed to avoid that very same patch of ice, and she hoped that her mother's reaction time was keen this morning. Delores was weaving in and out of traffic, kicking up the light coat of powdered snow that covered the asphalt and sending it airborne to shower against Hannah's windshield.

There was no way Hannah was going to risk life and limb to keep up with her mother. She slowed to a comfortable pace and made her way to the college, turning in at the parking lot just in time to see her mother exiting her car.

"Wait up!" she called out, pulling into the space next to her mother's car and jumping out. "Why the big hurry? You took some chances out there on the highway."

To Delores's credit, she looked quite contrite. "I know," she said. "I shouldn't have driven so fast. It's just that I was worried about how Nancy would take the news, and I wanted to be the one to tell her."

Hannah reached in to grab the cookies, locked her truck,

and scurried to catch up with her mother. "Why were you so worried about Nancy? Does she know Larry Jaeger?"

"Oh, my yes! You've heard her radio program, haven't you?"

"A few times, yes. I don't usually listen to talk radio, but she has some good advice to give."

Delores pulled open the door to Stewart Hall and they stepped inside. She took a moment to take off her gloves and slip them inside her pocket. "You must have heard her mention the Lunatic. She talks about him on almost every show."

"The Lunatic," Hannah said with a smile. "The worst husband a girl ever had. He taught Dr. Love everything she knows about what a husband should never do in a marriage."

"That's right."

"She's really funny when she talks about him." Hannah recalled several instances when she'd laughed out loud over the stories Dr. Love told on the air. "He's her ex-husband, isn't he?"

"He *was* her ex-husband."

It didn't take Hannah more than the time it took to take three steps to draw the obvious conclusion. She stopped cold and grabbed her mother's arm. "Don't tell me that the Lunatic is . . ."

"Lunatic Larry Jaeger," Delores confirmed it. "And that's why I want to be the first one to tell her."

ORANGE JULIUS COOKIES

Preheat oven to 350 degrees F., rack
in the middle position.

2 and ¼ cups flour *(don't sift—pack it down in the cup)*
¼ teaspoon salt
¾ teaspoon baking soda
2 sticks *(8 ounces, ½ pound)* softened butter
½ cup white *(granulated)* sugar
½ cup brown sugar
1 beaten egg
3 teaspoons grated orange zest *(that's the orange part of the peel)*
12-ounce bag white chocolate morsels *(2 cups) (I used Nestle's Premium White Morsels)*

Prepare your cookie sheets by spraying them with Pam *(or another nonstick cooking spray.)* You can also use a parchment-lined cookie sheet if you prefer.

In a large mixing bowl, combine the flour, salt and baking soda. Stir well and set aside.

In another bowl, beat the softened butter, white sugar, and brown sugar.

Add the beaten egg to the bowl with the butter and the sugars. Stir it all up. Then stir in the grated orange zest.

Stir in the flour, salt and baking soda mixture and mix well.

Stir in the white chocolate chips.

Drop by teaspoonfuls on a prepared cookie sheet, 12 cookies to a standard-size sheet. Flatten the cookies in a crisscross pattern with a fork, the way you'd do for peanut butter cookies.

Bake the cookies at 350 degrees F. for 10 to 12 minutes. *(Mine took 11 minutes.)*

Leave the cookies on the cookie sheet for a minute or two, and then remove them to a wire rack to cool completely.

Yield: 5 to 6 dozen cookies, depending on cookie size.

Hannah's Note: Delores thinks these cookies taste just like the drinks from the Orange Julius stand at the mall.

Chapter Eighteen

"Delores!" Dr. Love was clearly pleased when she saw who was knocking on her office door. "And Hannah, too! Come in. What brings you out here so early this morning?"

Dr. Love started to rise to greet them, but Delores waved her back down to her chair. "You'd better sit down, Nancy," she said. "I have some bad news for you."

Hannah saw Dr. Love's posture stiffen. It was clear she was bracing herself. "What is it?" she asked.

"Larry Jaeger is dead. Someone murdered him last night."

There was a moment of disbelief. Hannah could see it on Dr. Love's face. And then an expression replaced it, an expression that Hannah didn't understand, but could only be described as profound relief.

"Well, that saves me a whole lot of trouble!" Dr. Love said.

There was a moment of absolute silence. Both Hannah and Delores were at a loss for words.

"I . . . don't understand," Delores ventured at last.

"Of course you don't." Dr. Love gestured. "Sit. You probably think I'm in shock."

That's exactly what Hannah thought. She exchanged a glance with her mother, who made a gesture with her hands.

Hannah interpreted instantly and she set the bag of cookies on Dr. Love's desk.

"Chocolate?" Dr. Love asked with a small smile.

Hannah nodded. "Endorphins. Mother thought they might help if you were upset."

"How sweet!" Dr. Love smiled at Delores and then she turned back to Hannah. "Do you really believe that chocolate is a cure for anxiety, grief, and depression?"

"Maybe not, but it can't hurt," Hannah said, turning to her mother. It was time for Delores to take the lead in the conversation.

Delores caught on immediately. It was time to open the Larry Jaeger discussion. "I'm so sorry about your ex-husband," she said, reaching out to pat her friend's hand.

"He's not. He's *not* my ex-husband."

"You mean you weren't married to Larry Jaeger?" Hannah asked, slipping easily into question mode.

"Oh, I was!" Dr. Love reached for a cookie. "And I'm *still* married to him . . . or at least I was married to him right up until the moment he died. You see, we never divorced."

"Because you couldn't stop loving him?" Delores asked, sensing a romantic tragedy in the making.

"No, it's because I couldn't find him. I wanted to divorce him fifteen years ago, right after he left me high and dry, but I needed his address to serve him with papers."

"How awful for you!" Delores breathed.

"It wasn't one of the happier times of my life," Dr. Love agreed. "Since I was only months from graduating from college and I didn't have the money for a quickie divorce in another state, I simply let it go. I always thought Larry would turn up somewhere and I'd hear about it, and *then* I'd serve him with papers and divorce him."

"But what if you'd met someone else you wanted to marry?" Delores posed a dilemma.

Dr. Love gave a little shrug. "Then I would have been

forced to do something. But I *didn't* meet anyone I wanted to marry, so there wasn't any rush to divorce Larry."

"Did you hear from him during those fifteen years?" Hannah asked.

"Never."

"No calls? No letters? No e-mail?"

"Nothing. It was like he'd dropped off the face of the earth."

"And he didn't tell you where he was going?" Delores asked.

"I didn't even *know* he was going! It was a total shock to me. We were having trouble in our marriage, but I didn't expect him to vanish."

"What kind of trouble?" Delores asked her.

"What kind do you want?" Dr. Love gave a rueful chuckle. "He was dishonest, disloyal, and he couldn't hold down a job."

"That must have been frustrating for you," Hannah said.

"It was. I was working part time as a secretary at the college and taking a full load of classes. Whenever Larry got fired, I'd have to increase my hours so we could pay the rent. And then there was Brenda."

"Brenda?" both Hannah and Delores asked at once.

"Brenda lived in the apartment next door. She had an inheritance from her grandmother and she didn't have to work like the rest of us."

Hannah had a sinking feeling in the pit of her stomach. She thought she knew where this story was heading. "So Brenda was home all day?"

"That's right. I think it all started when Larry lost his job at the carpet store. He told me he went out looking for work every day, but several people I knew said he was spending his afternoons at the Indian Casino with Brenda."

"Gambling?" Hannah asked, remembering how Larry had kept track of the score of the basketball game while he'd discussed her cookie order and wondering whether he'd bet on the outcome.

"Larry loved to gamble and he was pretty good at it. That was the unfortunate thing. It was a game to him, like playing with Monopoly money, and he started believing that he couldn't lose."

"Did Brenda finance his gambling?" Delores asked.

"Yes, but I didn't know that at the time. All I knew was that when I got home from a three-day graduate seminar on *Marriage and the Family* at another university and opened our apartment door, every stick of furniture was gone. The only thing that was left was the pink plush teddy bear Larry won for me at a carnival when we were newlyweds. It was sitting on a huge pile of my books in the corner, and there was a note pinned to its chest."

"What did the note say?" Delores asked, clearly heartsick for her friend.

"It said, *I left your clothes in the closet.*" Dr. Love gave a little chuckle that sounded bitter to Hannah. "I still get mad when I think about it. And that's one story about the Lunatic that I'll *never* tell on the air."

"How about Brenda? Did you confront her?" Delores wanted to know.

"I couldn't. Brenda was gone, too. No one had actually seen her leave with Larry, but it was the logical conclusion."

"So what did you do?" Hannah asked the follow-up question.

"What *could* I do? I coped. My friends helped me out with the extra furniture they had, and my landlord was understanding about the rent. I worked overtime at the college and after a month or two, I managed to replace all the essential items Larry took with him, including the money in our joint checking account."

"He took the furniture *and* all the money?" It was clear from the tone of Delores's question that she was fuming over Larry's actions.

Hannah wasn't surprised when Dr. Love nodded. She'd

only met Larry briefly, but he'd struck her as the type of man who put himself first and rarely gave a passing thought to the feelings of others.

"When I found out he was in Lake Eden, I made an appointment with a lawyer. And that's why I'm relieved that Larry's dead," Dr. Love stated in no uncertain terms. "The killer saved me lawyer's fees, time in court, the airing of our dirty laundry in public, and the necessity of seeing Larry again. It's not nice to say, but I'm glad he's dead!" She stopped and gave each of them a searching look. "I hope you're not too shocked with me."

Delores reached out to pat her hand again. "Good heavens, no! I'm not one bit shocked after what you've told us."

"Hannah?"

Dr. Love turned to her and Hannah said the first thing that popped into her head. "I'd be shocked if you *didn't* feel that way. I don't blame you for being glad he's dead. You must have hated him for all the trouble he caused, and I can certainly understand why you wanted him out of your life for good."

There was a moment of silence when her words echoed back to her. *Glad he's dead. Hated him for all the trouble he caused. Wanted him out of your life for good.* And then Hannah stopped and stared at Dr. Love hard.

"What is it?" Delores asked, acknowledging the worried expression on her daughter's face.

"This isn't good," Hannah said, her eyes locked with Dr. Love's. "I wouldn't tell anyone else what you just told us, not unless you have an airtight alibi for the time of Larry's death."

"Hannah!" Delores looked shocked at the implication. "Surely you don't think that . . ."

Hannah interrupted her mother's question with a look. "Of course *we* don't, but someone else might."

"Someone like Mike?"

"Yes." Hannah turned back to Dr. Love. "*Do* you have an alibi?"

"I don't know. What time was Larry killed?"

"Sometime after I called him at a little before nine and when Norman and I got there at nine forty-five."

"Between nine and nine forty-five," Dr. Love repeated and as they watched, her face turned pale and she swallowed with difficulty. "This isn't good. This isn't good at all."

"You don't have an alibi?" Hannah asked, fearing the worst.

"I'm afraid not. I was home alone from eight o'clock on, grading term papers."

Of course she'd promised to help clear Dr. Love and Delores seemed relieved as they walked down the hall. Hannah was about to push open the heavy outer door when it opened from the other side and a woman dressed in a heavy parka and a ski cap pulled down low over her ears rushed in.

"Hello, you two," the woman said, pulling off her cap to reveal her features. "Were you looking for me so that you could turn in your homework?"

Hannah laughed. "Not exactly, Miss Whiting. I followed Mother here so she could drop off her car for my youngest sister. She goes to Macalister and she's in the Christmas Follies."

"How nice." Miss Whiting dismissed that bit of information quickly and turned to Delores. "Tell me, have you discovered the bad business practice on the handout I gave you?"

"We think we have. If we're right, it has to do with paying for supplies in cash and recording higher prices than were actually paid on supplier receipts."

"That is correct," Miss Whiting frowned slightly, "but you sound as if you had help. This was intended as an individual homework assignment."

Her mother looked a bit deflated and Hannah stepped in. "My mother and I discussed it, Miss Whiting. And several other people in the shop were interested, including my partner and Mayor Bascomb. I believe you met him?"

"Oh, yes. Mayor Bascomb. What a charming man." A smile flickered across Miss Whiting's face. "Don't tell me it took all four of you to unravel my little puzzle!"

"It took five," Hannah corrected her, "and we weren't completely sure we had the correct answer. You dish out some hard homework, Miss Whiting."

"It's my job to keep you on your toes and my duty to keep you from being cheated by people who employ nefarious business practices."

Delores cleared her throat. "Yes . . . well . . . thank you, Miss Whiting. And we'll see you in class on Monday evening."

"Yes, indeed you will. I haven't missed a class since I arrived here as a visiting professor three months ago."

Hannah waited until they had exited the building and then she turned to her mother. "Miss Whiting's an odd duck."

"Perhaps, but she's an excellent teacher." Delores headed toward the parking lot and then she turned back to Hannah with a frown. "I just saw something else odd . . . I think."

"What was it?" Hannah moved a little faster to keep pace with her mother.

"I thought I saw a student jump off the edge of the parking lot!"

"Where?"

"At the far end. Right over there by that big pine tree. It looked exactly as if he were on the end of a diving board and he dove off into space."

"Have you seen any programs about lemmings on the animal channel lately?"

Delores turned to give her a stern look, but the corners of her lips twitched up. "Very funny, dear."

"Don't worry, Mother. Midterms are over and the students have no reason to commit suicide in hordes. Your eyes must be playing tricks on you. I notice that you're not wearing your glasses."

"They're for reading, not distance. And this was in the distance, dear. It was right over . . ." Delores pointed and then she gasped. "There goes another one over the edge! You're wrong, Hannah! They're jumping off like lemmings!"

Hannah looked where her mother was pointing. Delores was right. Another student was hurtling off the edge of the parking lot and disappearing into thin air. "Wait here. I'll see if I can find out what's going on."

It didn't take Hannah long to discover exactly what phenomenon was occurring. It wasn't an illusion at all. The students really were jumping off the edge of the parking lot, or very close to it. Three or four feet beyond the asphalt was the crest of a steep hill. A rack of stiff plastic sheets sat next to the precipice with a sign that read, *Take a Slider Made by the Lake Eden Community College Shop Class. Ride and Return Please.*

Hannah watched as a girl in a parka grabbed a green plastic Slider from the rack. It had a handle at the top that was fashioned of plastic rope and the rest was simply a sheet of industrial plastic. The girl grabbed the handholds on either side, held the sheet against her chest, and raced to the crest of the hill to throw herself over on her stomach.

"Want to try one?" the girl's companion, a student Hannah didn't think could be any older than twelve, asked her with a grin.

"No, thanks. I think I'm a little old for that type of sledding."

"You'll never know unless you try it," the boy encouraged her, holding out the top slider on the rack, a bright red one.

Hannah wavered. Red was her favorite color, but her mother was waiting. "Maybe later," she said, giving him a smile and heading back to tell Delores that she wasn't imagining things after all.

"Colored plastic sheets?" Delores looked amazed as Hannah finished telling her about the Sliders the shop class had made.

"It makes sense. That's a great sliding hill and the plastic is probably impervious to the elements. I had a plastic disk when I was a kid, didn't I?"

"Yes, but I took it away."

Hannah started her cookie truck and turned to look at her mother. "Why did you do that?"

"Because it made you sick. You never were any good with things that whirled around."

Hannah had a flashback to the Tilt-A-Whirl at the last county fair and shivered slightly. "You're right," she said. "The Sliders don't whirl, though. I watched and they go straight down the hill."

"You weren't any good with sleds that went straight, either. You never could control them. You always ran into trees unless Uncle Ed was with you. Then he took the big blue sled and he did the steering."

"I'd forgotten all about that!" Hannah said, smiling at the memory. Her Uncle Ed had taken the front seat and she'd ridden behind him with her arms clasped around his waist.

"You loved it and so did your sisters. It's really too bad Ed never married. He was so good with children, and he should have had some of his own."

"You're right," Hannah said, wondering if someday people might say the same about her.

Delores leaned back in the passenger seat and closed her eyes as Hannah pulled out of the parking lot and headed down the access road to the highway. "I've got to rest my eyes, dear. I didn't get much sleep last night."

"Why is that, Mother?"

"I kept thinking about Carrie and imagining all sorts of horrid things that could be wrong."

Hannah frowned. There was no way she could keep her mother in the dark any longer. She had to tell her what they suspected even though they didn't know the full story. "I think I found out what's wrong, Mother."

"You did?" Delores's eyes flew open. "Tell me!"

"Norman and I think she's dating."

"Dating? Carrie?"

"That's right. We're almost positive that Carrie and a date were at the Lake Eden Inn last night for dinner."

As her mother listened, Hannah explained everything that had transpired. And then she ended her account with their dilemma. "But we don't know who she's dating yet."

"Dating." Delores sounded bemused. "Well, that's certainly less disastrous than I imagined. We have to identify the man, though. He may not be right for our Carrie."

"Don't worry. We will. We've even got Mike working on it."

Delores smiled and reached out to pat Hannah's arm. "Thank you, dear. You've relieved my mind and I feel so much better. I just hope Carrie's found someone wonderful."

"So do we, Mother. Why don't you catch a short nap now? I'll wake you when we get back to town."

By the time she reached the highway, her mother was sleeping. Hannah glanced over to make sure she had her seatbelt fastened, and mentally patted herself on the back. Her mother felt much better now that she knew about Carrie's dinner companion. It was never good to keep secrets from family . . . unless, of course, they involved Christmas presents.

Chapter Nineteen

"Take a break, Hannah. You look beat," Lisa said, as she took the last sheet of her friend Nancy's Chocolate Oatmeal Cookies out of the oven. "We've still got at least a half hour before the noon rush starts, and I can answer any questions they ask about last night."

"Okay."

"And eat one of Nancy's cookies. The oatmeal's nutritious and the chocolate will give you a lift. Besides that, they're really good."

"Thanks, I will," Hannah answered, reaching for one of the cookies she'd wanted to try anyway. She could certainly use a break. The morning had been hectic to say the least. Everyone and their cousin had come in to hear the story of how Norman and Hannah had found Larry's body. "Call me if you need me. I'll stay right here in the kitchen."

Once Lisa had gone back to the coffee shop, Hannah sat down at the stainless steel workstation and pulled out the steno pad she'd come to think of as her personal murder book. So far the pages were blank, but she'd learned quite a bit about Larry Jaeger over the past few days. Some of what she'd learned could mesh with facts she had yet to discover, other tidbits could guide her to questions she needed to ask, and still other facts could give her clues to the identity of the killer.

She started as she always did, with a page listing the suspects. Dr. Love's name headed the list. After her unhappy marriage to Larry, she might have hated him enough to kill him.

Courtney was next. If Larry's fiancée suspected that Larry was cheating her out of her investment, she could have killed him in spite. There was also the possibility that she'd found out about his marriage to Dr. Love and the fact they'd never divorced. If Courtney believed that Larry was stringing her along for her money and he never intended to marry her, she could have been so angry, she'd done him in.

There was also Mayor Bascomb. Hannah felt a bit strange writing down his name, but he'd said that he was going to ask Larry about those blank receipts Lisa had signed. While Hannah didn't think that the mayor would actually pull out a gun and shoot Larry over a bad business deal, it was within the realm of possibility. And if Mayor Bascomb was a suspect because of his business relationship with Larry, then so were the other investors in the Crazy Elf Christmas Tree Lot.

Who were the other investors? Hannah would have to ask the mayor if he'd name names. But what if Mayor Bascomb didn't know all of Larry's investors?

Hannah flipped the page and wrote *INTERVIEWS* at the top in block letters. She'd start with Mayor Bascomb and ask for the names of every investor he knew. Then she'd talk to Luanne and ask her if there had been a list of names on any of the papers that Courtney had given her. It was also possible that the names of the investors could be a matter of public record and she could get them by going to the courthouse. She'd have to find out about that.

Then there was the man with the briefcase she'd seen going into Larry's trailer the night she'd ridden Santa's Magic Sleigh with Mike. He could be an investor. He'd reminded her of Earl Flensburg so that's where she'd start. She'd ask Earl if he had any cousins or relatives that might have had a business meeting with Larry.

Hannah flipped the page again and wrote MOTIVES on

the top in block letters. Almost every killing had a motive and she needed to list them. Robbery came first. Larry could have entered his trailer and interrupted a robbery. By now Mike should know if anything had been stolen. The trailer hadn't looked as if it had been ransacked, but the killer had shot Larry's giant flat screen television set. Perhaps Larry's killer had broken in to steal it, but had found it too bulky to take and had been so frustrated, he'd used it for target practice.

Money could be a motive for murder. What if one of Larry's investors had killed him because the Crazy Elf Christmas Tree Lot wasn't making the money that Larry had promised? She'd have to find out if the business was showing a profit or not. Local gossip said it wasn't, but local gossip had been known to be wrong.

Then there was the gambling angle. Players with a gambling addiction didn't stop gambling when they had no money. They borrowed or stole money to try their luck one more time. She had to find out if Larry had any gambling debts he couldn't pay. If so, the person he owed could have killed him.

Love was always a motive. Again, the killer could be Larry's faux fiancée, Courtney, or his legal wife, Dr. Love. It could even be some other woman who'd been spending time with Larry.

Hannah realized she'd come to the bottom of the page and she flipped it over. Suddenly the blank lines of the steno pad seemed endless and she put her head down on the counter of the workstation to rest her eyes. She was so tired, she couldn't think straight. She'd take a little break and concentrate on something to relax her, something pleasant, and something that had nothing to do with Larry or his murder. And then she'd get back to work.

"Hannah?"

She sat up with a jolt as Lisa called her name.

"Wake up, Hannah. Andrea and Tracey are here."

"Here," Hannah repeated, lifting her head and blinking

several times. "Sorry, Lisa. I didn't get much sleep last night and I must have drifted off for a minute or two."

"Try thirty, but that's not a problem. I'll get them settled back here with coffee, milk, and cookies, while you duck into the bathroom and splash some water on your face."

That was exactly what Hannah did. The cold water was refreshing and she felt much more alert as she opened the bathroom door and stepped into the kitchen to greet her sister and her oldest niece.

Both Andrea and Tracey were dressed beautifully, but Hannah had expected no less. Her sister had always been fashion model material and today was no exception. Andrea's shining blond hair was perfectly styled in an elaborate twist that must have taken her hours to perfect, her makeup was flawless, and her dark blue wool suit was exquisitely cut to highlight her perfect figure.

Tracey was a chip off the old block, or in this case, a child model in the making. She wore a quilted lavender and white sweat suit with a lavender ski cap on her head that sported a fluffy white pom-pom on top.

"Hi, Aunt Hannah!" Tracey said, taking off her ski cap and smiling widely to display the gap where one of her front teeth had been. "I lost a baby tooth last night!"

"Did the Tooth Fairy visit?"

"There aren't any fairies, Aunt Hannah. At least not any real ones. They're fictional."

"Do you mean the Tooth Fairy didn't come into your room while you were sleeping and leave a quarter for your tooth?"

Tracey laughed. "Daddy did that. He thought I was sleeping, but I saw him. He tiptoed in all sneaky-like and left a dollar under my pillow."

"A whole *dollar*? Maybe I should write to Tooth Fairy Headquarters and complain. All I ever got was a quarter."

"That's inflation, Aunt Hannah. Things cost more now, even baby teeth. I watched a program on television about it." Tracey turned to her mother. "Is it okay if I go back to the coffee shop and help Aunt Lisa until Grandma McCann comes to get me?"

"Aunt Lisa might not want any help just now, honey."

"Yes, she does. She said I could come back and wait on customers at the counter if it was okay with you. Besides, I know you and Aunt Hannah want to talk about the Crazy Elf murder."

"Well . . ." Andrea paused and glanced at Hannah who gave a slight nod. "Okay then, honey. Just don't try to pour hot coffee, okay?"

Tracey gave a little sigh. "That's exactly what Lisa said when I asked her if I could help. I can pour water, can't I?"

"Yes, if Aunt Lisa wants you to."

Hannah watched as Tracey picked up her cookie and milk, and headed for the door. Once she'd gone through to the coffee shop, Hannah turned to Andrea. "Tracey knew we wanted to talk about Larry. That's definitely precocious."

"And how! And I didn't say a word to her about it." Andrea took a sip of her coffee and then she asked, "You're going after Larry's killer, aren't you?"

"Of course. I have to clear Dr. Love."

Andrea looked bewildered. "What does Dr. Love have to do with Larry's murder?"

"She was married to Larry, and they never got a divorce."

"But that's impossible! Larry was engaged to Courtney!"

Hannah shrugged. "I guess he figured a little thing like being married already shouldn't stop him."

"No wonder someone shot him!" Andrea nibbled at her cookie. "I like these, Hannah. What are they called?"

"Chocolate Oatmeal Cookies."

"Oatmeal?" Andrea gave a delicate little shudder, and Hannah knew she'd made a mistake by telling her. Ever since childhood, Andrea had hated oatmeal.

"It's really rolled oats," she explained, hoping that her sister wouldn't know that was a term for uncooked oatmeal.

"Rolled oats, but not oatmeal?"

"That's right."

"And they're different things?"

"Yes, they are."

"That must be why I like them. I hate oatmeal, but rolled oats taste just fine."

It was time to change the subject before more questions about oats were forthcoming. The list of Crazy Elf investors should do it. "I need your help, Andrea," she said.

"What do you want me to do?"

Promise me you'll never compare the definitions of oatmeal and rolled oats, Hannah thought, but instead of replying with something that would surely cause a sisterly fissure, she said, "I need to find out who invested money in Larry's Christmas tree lot. Do you have any idea how I can do that?"

"I'm going to the bank at noon to talk to Doug about setting up a college fund for the girls. I'll ask him if investors have to file any sort of paperwork."

"Private investors," Hannah reminded her. "I don't think Larry ever went public."

"You're probably right. He was too small time for that. And if Doug doesn't know anything, I'll talk to Al when he comes back from lunch." Andrea reached for another cookie and took a bite. "What do you need from Bill?" she asked.

"Crime scene photos aren't essential. Norman and I were there. I could use the autopsy report and maybe the crime lab sheet. Anything you can get would be good."

"Then I'll get it all. How about Larry's bank records? If he had a lot of money, he could have been killed for that."

"That's true." Hannah thought about possible gambling debts and her theory about failure to pay. "And if he *didn't* have much money, he could have been killed for that, too."

"Huh?" Andrea looked completely bewildered.

"Never mind. It might not even be important. Can you really get Larry's bank records?"

"I think so. All I have to do is get Bill to ask for them. I think they'll have to give them to him if he gets a subpoena."

Hannah thought about that for a minute and then she got up and began to pack candy in a box.

"What are you doing?"

"Packing some of the Chocolate Raspberry Truffles that Lisa made this morning."

"For me?" Andrea asked, looking hopeful.

"No, for Lydia Gradin. She still works at the bank, doesn't she?"

"Yes. She got a promotion and now she handles all the special customers. But it won't do any good to ask her about Larry. Lydia's a stickler for the rules, and Larry's bank records are confidential. Lydia won't give them to you."

"I don't need Larry's bank records. I just need some information about his accounts."

"She won't give you that, either."

"Maybe she will. I think I just figured out a way to get what I need."

"By bribing her with truffles?"

"That might help, but I've got something else to give Lydia that's even more important."

Andrea looked dumbfounded. "What could be more important than Chocolate Raspberry Truffles? Lydia's crazy about truffles."

"A deposit," Hannah said, tying a bow on the top of the box and then leading the way to the door.

CHOCOLATE OATMEAL COOKIES

Preheat oven to 325 degrees F., rack
in the middle position.

½ cup softened butter *(1 stick, 4 ounces, ¼ pound)*
1 cup white *(granulated)* sugar
2 one-ounce squares unsweetened chocolate *(I used
   Baker's)*
1 beaten egg *(just whip it up in a glass with a fork)*
1 teaspoon baking powder
½ teaspoon salt
¾ cup flour *(pack it down in the cup when you
   measure it)*
1 and ½ cups dry oatmeal *(either quick cooking or
   old fashioned will do)*

In a large bowl, mix the softened butter and the sugar
until it's fluffy.

Unwrap the squares of unsweetened chocolate and melt
them in the microwave according to package directions.
Add them to the butter and sugar mixture and mix well.

Feel the bowl. If the mixture is cool enough, add the
beaten egg, mixing until it's thoroughly incorporated.

Mix in the baking powder and the salt.

Add the flour, mixing it in thoroughly.

Mix in the oatmeal and stir until the mixture is completely blended.

Drop by teaspoonfuls onto greased *(or sprayed with Pam or other nonstick cooking spray)* cookie sheets, 12 cookies to a standard-size sheet. *(I used a 2-teaspoon scoop.)*

Bake at 325 degrees F. for 13 to 15 minutes or until slightly brown.

Let the cookies cool on the cookie sheet for 2 minutes and then remove them to a wire rack to cool completely.

Nancy says that these cookies are better if they are soft so don't over-bake them. If you store them in a cookie jar and they get too hard, use Grandma Ingrid's trick of adding an orange peel or slice of apple to the cookie jar to soften them up.

Yield: Makes about 3 dozen chewy, chocolaty cookies.

Nancy's Note: If you don't have the squares of unsweetened chocolate in your pantry, you can substitute 3 Tablespoons of cocoa and 1 Tablespoon vegetable shortening for each square of chocolate needed. Just blend in the shortening with the butter and add the cocoa with the flour.

Chapter
Twenty

Hannah spotted Lydia Gradin the moment she walked through the door at Lake Eden First Mercantile Bank. Lydia was hard to miss. Her hair was streaked with bright purple and she was wearing shiny purple leather pants and a matching midriff-hugging top that might have looked stunning on one of Jordan's High's cheerleaders, but did nothing to enhance the appearance of a much older, much less shapely woman.

As she gave a wave and settled down in a chair in the lobby to wait until Lydia was free, Hannah wondered, not for the first time, why Lydia felt the need to dress like a teenager. There was no doubt she did so intentionally. Delores had mentioned she'd seen Lydia coming out of *Umpteen*, a clothing shop in the mall that specialized exclusively in teenage fashions. Hannah's mother and Lydia had been classmates multiple decades ago, and that meant Lydia had to be *Umpteen*'s oldest customer. Was this a case of arrested development? An effort to stop the clock at a happier time in her life? Or just wishful thinking?

Lydia finished with her customer and she motioned to Hannah. As Hannah approached the private cubicles the tellers manned for their customers, she noticed that the purple streaks in Lydia's dark hair actually looked good. Hannah usually avoided making any comment at all about Lydia's appearance, heeding the words of Thumper in *Bambi* when the young rabbit repeated his father's advice, *If you can't say something nice, don't say nothing at all.* This time, though, Hannah had something nice to say. "Your hair looks good, Lydia," she said, sitting down in one of the two cushioned chairs in front of Lydia's desk.

"Thanks, Hannah!" Lydia looked quite surprised. "You don't mind the purple?"

"I think it goes really well with your natural hair color," Hannah said, hoping that the rest of Lydia's hair *was* her natural color.

"I'll tell my niece. She spends hours picking out my clothes and trying out new hairstyles on me. She wants to be a beautician when she graduates from high school."

Hannah gave a fleeting thought to Tracey and Bethie, and decided that an aunt's love should stop short of outlandish. There was no way she'd let either Tracey or Bethie near her with fashion advice or a bottle of purple hair dye.

"What can I do for you, Hannah?" Lydia asked.

"It's what I can do for you," Hannah countered, placing the box on the desktop. "They're Chocolate Raspberry Truffles."

Lydia gave what could only be described as a little whimper. "Chocolate Raspberry Truffles. What could be more wonderful? This is really sweet of you, Hannah. How did you know that my birthday's tomorrow?"

Hannah managed to keep the surprise off her face. "There are no secrets in Lake Eden," she said, smiling sweetly. "Happy early birthday, Lydia. Why don't you have a truffle now? They're something new and I'd love to know what you think of them."

Lydia opened the box and reached in daintily for a truffle. She took a bite, gave another little groan of pleasure and smiled. Then she popped the other half of the truffle into her mouth and closed her eyes in bliss. "Perfect," she said.

"Oh, good. Do you think we should sell them at The Cookie Jar over Christmas?"

"Definitely. I'll be first in line. Thank you for the best birthday present ever, Hannah."

"You're welcome."

Lydia wiped her fingers on a tissue from the dispenser on her desk and went into customer service mode. "May I help you with any banking needs today?"

"Actually, yes." Hannah drew out the check she'd taken back from Lisa's deposit folder. "Lisa was a little worried about this check, so I said I'd bring it down with me. She thought the account might be closed, or something."

Lydia glanced at the check, typed in some numbers on her keyboard, and nodded as information came up on her screen. "Lisa is correct to be concerned. This account's not closed, but I'm glad you brought the check in today because the balance is quite low. Did you want cash, or would you like to deposit it to your business account?"

"We'll deposit it to The Cookie Jar account." Hannah waited while Lydia filled out the paperwork and signed where she indicated. "One more thing," she said.

"Certainly, I'm here to help." Lydia was all business.

"I believe we have more checks from this same person." Hannah leaned closer. "They're in payment for the cookies we provided."

"I understand. Is there a problem with those checks?"

"I don't know. I'm hoping you can tell me that. I just glanced at the deposit Lisa planned to make later today, and it seemed to me that the checks from this particular person looked different than the one I just gave you."

"How were they different?"

"I've been trying to remember, but I'm just not sure. They might have been a different color, or a different number, or something like that. All I know is that they didn't look like the check I just deposited. Could they be drawn on another account?"

Lydia tapped on her keyboard for a few seconds and then she glanced at the screen. "Yes, they could be drawn on another account."

"Then the person has two accounts here?"

"That is correct." Lydia reached out for another truffle and this time she popped the whole thing in her mouth. "Wonderful!" she said after she'd savored and swallowed.

"That certainly explains why the checks looked different." Hannah brought Lydia's attention back to Larry's accounts. "Is there any way you can tell me if they'll bounce if we don't deposit them today? We're awfully busy with the Christmas rush and all, but I don't want anyone to close that second account or put a hold on it, or anything like that."

"They'd have to go through legal channels to do that and it would take a few days. You're safe, Hannah. It's a private account and there's only one name on the signature card."

"But what if other people have checks drawn on the same account and they cash them? Could they clean it out before we get a chance to deposit ours?"

Lydia took another truffle and popped it into her mouth as she tapped away on the keyboard. She studied the screen and then she smiled at Hannah. "That's extremely unlikely, Hannah. The account was opened on November first of this year. Since then there's a record of frequent deposits, but there have been no withdrawals."

"So we may have the only checks drawn on that account?"

"That could easily be the case. Would you say the total of the checks you hold is over two hundred and fifty thousand dollars?"

"No, of course not." Hannah's mind reeled at the prospect. There was no way she could even imagine selling enough cookies to earn a two hundred and fifty thousand dollar check.

"Then take your time about depositing those checks. I'd say you have absolutely nothing to worry about."

Hannah was back in the kitchen adding what she'd learned to her murder book when Lisa came in. "Your mother's here," she announced.

"Great. Would you ask her to come back and have coffee with me? I've got something I'd like to discuss with her."

By the time she'd poured two cups of coffee and set out a few Chocolate Raspberry Truffles for her mother to sample, Delores came in through the swinging door from the coffee shop. "Hello, dear," she said in a cheery voice.

"Hello, Mother. You look as if you got a little rest."

"I did. Luanne saw how tired I was and she sent me home to take a nap."

"And you managed to get some sleep," Hannah said, noticing that the dark smudges under her mother's eyes were no longer visible.

"I slept for over two hours, dear. Now that I know why Carrie's so secretive, I don't have to worry. I know you and Norman will make sure he's the right sort of man for her. I *do* wonder who it is, though."

"So do I," Hannah confessed.

"Before I forget, here's something Luanne sent over for you," Delores set a large envelope on the stainless steel surface of the workstation. "She said to tell you that she made copies of all the papers Courtney gave her because that's what Miss Whiting taught them to do in accounting class. Luanne thought the papers might be useful in light of Larry's death."

"Great. It's possible they will be. The more information I have about Larry and his business, the better. Thank Luanne for me, will you please?"

"Certainly."

Hannah pushed the small dish of truffles closer so her mother could take one. "Try one of these truffles, Mother."

Delores complied and took a dainty bite. One bite was all it took for her to finish the first and reach for a second. "The combination of raspberry and chocolate is divine, dear."

"I'll tell Lisa you like them. She goes to a candy exchange every year and Amy Kocias brought these. Lisa liked them so much, she asked for the recipe."

"I'd like to take two or three with me if that's all right, dear. Carrie and Luanne are handling Granny's Attic for the afternoon and I need to go out to the Tri-County Mall for a bit of last-minute Christmas shopping."

"You do?" Hannah was surprised at that news. Her mother always shopped the January sales for her Christmas presents. Because of her urging, Hannah had tried it once, but she'd placed the presents she'd purchased eleven months early in a nice, safe place and she still hadn't found them!

"I'm getting an extra present for Michelle. She mentioned that she had to have her boots re-soled and I thought I'd buy her another pair . . . perhaps something a bit more feminine than the pair she's wearing now."

Hannah wisely held her tongue. If she argued with her mother about Michelle's right to wear the boots she liked, Delores might focus on Hannah's old moose-hide boots and decide her elder daughter also needed a new, more feminine pair.

"That shouldn't take me more than an hour," Delores continued. "And then I'm free for the rest of the afternoon. Is there any way I can help you in your investigation?"

"I'm sure there's something," Hannah told her, paging through her steno pad. "How about talking to Dr. Love about a possible alibi again?"

"I'd be glad to do that, but Nancy already told us she was home alone grading term papers."

"She could still have an alibi. How about phone calls? Did she make or receive any? Did she see anyone walking by on the sidewalk between nine and nine forty-five? Does she remember a noisy truck driving past during that time period? How about a siren she heard on her street? Any of those things could prove she was home and not at the Crazy Elf Christmas Tree Lot."

"Very good, dear! I'll ask all those questions and see if we can place her firmly at home and not at the murder scene."

"That's exactly right, Mother. Good for you! You caught on to the concept right away."

Delores looked pleased at Hannah's praise. "Is there anything else I can do for you?"

Hannah glanced down at her book again. "There *is* one more thing."

"Anything, dear. I wouldn't mind doing some undercover work again. I had so much fun the last time!"

"I think you could call this undercover," Hannah said, attempting to think of a way to put a covert spin on what she was about to ask her mother to do. "I need you to question Earl Flensburg."

"Earl? You don't think he's a suspect, do you?"

"He's here on my suspect list." Hannah tapped her notebook.

"But why?"

"When Mike and I were riding on Santa's Magic Sleigh the night before Larry was killed, I saw someone who looked just like Earl going into Larry's trailer with a briefcase. And when Larry talked to us earlier, he said he had a business meeting in a few minutes."

"Earl? Going to a business meeting with a briefcase?" Delores looked as if she couldn't believe what Hannah had just told her. "I can't picture Earl at a business meeting, not unless one of the executives needed a car towed. And the only thing I've ever seen Earl carry with him is his lunch. It must have been someone else, dear . . . someone that merely looked like Earl."

"Maybe. It's something we have to check out. I thought because you went to school with Earl, you might be able to coax more information out of him than I could. I want you to be an investigator going undercover as an old friend."

"Oh! Well . . . that's intriguing, dear. I'm sure I could do it. Exactly what do you want to know?"

Hannah ticked off her concerns on her fingers. "I need to

know if the man I saw that night was Earl. And if it was, I need to find out if Earl was one of Larry's investors. If Earl says he wasn't anywhere near the Crazy Elf Christmas Tree Lot, ask him about any lookalike cousins that live around here."

"Lookalike cousins," Delores sounded excited at the prospect of identifying Flensburg progeny that resembled Earl. "That's an excellent suggestion, dear. Earl's father was a twin, and if I'm not mistaken, he married Earl's mother's sister. If they had children and they're still in the area, they could resemble Earl."

"So you'll ask him?"

"Yes, indeed." Delores thought for a moment. "I think I'll ask Earl where he was at the time of the murder."

"You think Earl killed Larry?" Hannah was shocked. Earl Flensburg was one of her mother's oldest friends.

"Of course not, but we should alibi him anyway."

"That's true."

"It should be easy for me to find out. Earl never could lie to me. When I asked him if he drew that awful picture of our sixth grade teacher on the blackboard, he admitted that he was the guilty party."

"Did you tell on him?" Hannah asked, not even noticing that she'd slipped back to grade school vernacular.

"Of course not! I didn't tell a soul."

"Because Earl's friendship was important to you?"

"Yes, but not entirely. To tell the truth, I couldn't stand our sixth grade teacher either."

CHOCOLATE RASPBERRY TRUFFLES

Hannah's Note: Amy told Lisa that this recipe's so easy, she almost hates to call it a recipe. But everyone just adores these truffles. Lisa told me she's going to try it with white chocolate and raspberry, or maybe white chocolate and peach, or white chocolate and some other jam or jelly. Since it's white chocolate, she'll roll her truffles in powdered sugar rather than cocoa.

6 ounces *(1 cup)* semi-sweet chocolate chips
2 Tablespoons *(⅛ cup)* seedless raspberry jam
Cocoa powder to coat truffles

In the top part of a double boiler over simmering water, melt the cup of chocolate chips with the raspberry jam. Stir occasionally. Heat until the mixture is of a fudge-like consistency, similar to the inside of a chocolate truffle.

Let the mixture cool on a cold burner and then shape it into truffle-sized balls with your fingers. It's best to roll them fairly small because they are VERY rich.

Roll the balls in cocoa powder and store them in a covered container in the refrigerator.

These Chocolate Raspberry Truffles are best served at room temperature. Take them out of the refrigerator thirty minutes before you plan to serve them.

Yield: 18 sinfully delicious truffles, depending on the size you roll them.

Hannah's Note: Lisa and I tried refrigerating the truffles without rolling them in cocoa. We melted some chocolate, pierced the cold truffles with a food pick, dipped them quickly in melted chocolate and then placed them on waxed paper to harden. They were fantastic! Lisa also suggested a couple of alternatives including rolling the truffles in shredded coconut, or in finely chopped nuts.

Chapter Twenty-One

"Busy?" Hannah asked, as Lisa came through the swinging door with a display cookie jar in her hand and headed for the baker's rack to fill it.

"And how! Andrea's out there covering for me while I get more cookies. I'll send her back here in a couple of minutes."

"Great." Hannah sliced the apples she'd peeled and spread them out in the bottom of a cake pan she'd sprayed with nonstick cooking spray.

"What are you making?" Lisa asked her, filling another cookie jar from the extras lined up on the counter next to the baker's rack.

"Dixie Lee's German Apple Cake."

"I love that cake! It smells so good while it's baking."

"I know. After that, I'm going to mix up more cookies. What questions are people asking about the murder?"

"Mostly they want to know about the holes in the flat screen," Lisa said, giving a little shrug. "I guess there's something universal about wanting to shoot a television set. And they love your description of how it looked when Norman opened the door to the trailer."

"How did it look?" Hannah asked. She'd given Lisa a brief description and counted on her partner's imagination to do the rest.

"It was like the Northern Lights inside the room, that faint kind of glow you see when it's overcast and there's something bright glowing and flashing, hidden under the clouds. It was eerie. You weren't sure if you should enter the trailer or not. And then there was the announcer's disembodied voice, calling out a play-by-play description of a basketball game with no image there."

"So what did I do?" Hannah was fascinated. Lisa really had a way with words.

"You took a step inside and just stared at the ragged holes in the mammoth, expensive flat screen. You couldn't stop staring as the sportscaster went on and on about the Knicks' chances now that they were finally on a roll. Your eyes dropped to the coffee table and you noticed the nearly-empty brandy bottle. For a brief moment you wondered whether Larry had thrown his glass at the screen, but you decided that a glass hurled as hard as a man could throw couldn't leave a jagged hole like that. And there were three holes, glowing, flashing, occasionally sparking like fireflies. Should you and Norman look for the remote to shut it off? Or should you take the chance that the whole trailer might go up in flames from twisted wires, smoking circuitry, and sparking resistors?"

"What did I decide?" Hannah asked.

"You didn't get the opportunity to decide. As you turned to pose the question to Norman, you saw a huddled figure on the floor, a man curled into semi-fetal position. His hands were splayed out as if he were trying to ward off the devil himself, and a glossy puddle of his lifeblood had gathered around him."

"Yuck!"

"Oh, I know. But they love it, Hannah."

"I'm sure they do. Go on, Lisa."

"At first all you could do was hold out one quaking hand. Tremors shook your whole body as you gestured toward the unmoving form you hoped and prayed was merely an apparition. Then, after you'd swallowed several times to ease your parched throat, you managed to croak out one word."

"Which was?"

"*Look!* you uttered, your voice trembling like a stalk of grain in a tornado. And then you took a deep bracing breath and uttered two more words. *There! Look!*"

"Bravo!" Hannah clapped her hands together. "You're really good at this, Lisa. I think the Lake Eden Players have dropped the ball by not snagging you as their leading lady."

"Thanks," Lisa said, blushing. "I'd better get back and let Andrea come in. She says she has news for you."

Hannah had no sooner covered the apple slices with the batter she'd mixed up earlier and slipped the pan into the oven than Andrea fairly flew through the door.

"Oh, boy!" she said pouring herself a cup of coffee before Hannah could do it. "It's a zoo out there!"

"Lots of questions about the crime scene?"

"Yes, but they don't dare talk to me about it, being that I'm the sheriff's wife and all. The only question anyone asked me was when Lisa was coming back."

"Lisa's got quite a story to tell," Hannah said, pouring her own coffee and taking a seat at the workstation across from her sister.

"That's what everyone said. Bertie pulled me aside and told me it was simply hair-raising."

"Hair-raising is something she's qualified to talk about," Hannah said with a laugh, referring to the fact that Bertie Straub owned the local beauty parlor, the Cut 'n Curl.

"What do you have to eat?" Andrea asked. "I didn't have time for lunch."

"I could make you a sandwich. There's tuna in the pantry."

"No, thanks. I'm really in the mood for something sweet."

"Then help yourself to anything on the baker's rack. I'd offer you some apple cake, but it won't come out of the oven for almost an hour, and it has to cool before I frost it."

"Cookies will be fine." Andrea walked over to take a look and gave a little sigh of contentment. "Lisa's Pieces," she said taking one of the macadamia nut, white chocolate chip cookies. "They're just about my favorite. And here's my Pecan Divines. I just love those. And Blueberry Crunch. Those are so good! And just look at these beautiful Cherry Winks with red and green cherries. They're so nice and Christmassy. I think I'll have a red one and if I'm still hungry, I'll come back for a green one."

Hannah just shook her head as Andrea loaded four cookies on a napkin and carried it to the workstation. Her sister had a perfect figure, but if she kept this up, she'd be eating nothing but salads with low-cal dressing before long. "Did you find out anything for me?" she asked once Andrea had finished her first cookie.

"Yes." Andrea took a sip of coffee and drew a piece of paper from her pocket. "I wrote it down so I could give you the exact words. I asked Doug about investing and whether there were any records of the people who'd invested in Larry's business. He said, *Larry probably kept records. There should be contracts between the investors and Larry, but I don't believe it's necessary to file any legal papers.*"

"Okay," Hannah said. "How about Al? Did you get a chance to talk to him?"

Andrea nodded. "Al said, *If they didn't have a signed contract with Larry, they're dumber than dumb.* And when I asked him if he'd invested with Larry he said, *Are you kidding?* And then he laughed like crazy."

"Anything else?" Hannah gave a little sigh.

"Yes. I called Howie Levine and asked him if you had to fill out any paperwork to invest in a private corporation. He said no, but you'd be an idiot if you didn't get a signed contract clearly stating all the terms."

"Did he mention whether anyone in town had hired him to draw up such a contract?"

"I asked him that and he told me that information like that was confidential."

Hannah rolled her eyes at the ceiling. "That sounds like Howie."

"I know. So I asked him a couple of other legal questions to throw him off the track and then I went in the backdoor."

"How did you do that?"

"That's not important. What's important is that Howie drew up contracts for two businessmen in Lake Eden. One was Mayor Bascomb, but we already knew about him. And the other was Jon Walker."

Hannah flipped open her notebook and reached for her pen. She was about to add the owner of Lake Eden Neighborhood Pharmacy to her suspect list when she remembered who'd been in the last private booth at the Inn last night when she'd passed by with Norman.

"Aren't you going to write him down?" Andrea asked her.

"No. Jon and his wife were at the Lake Eden Inn for dinner last night and they were just being served their entrees when Norman and I left."

"Oh, drat!" Andrea looked very disappointed. "I thought we had another live one."

"Another live one?"

"Yes! I forgot to tell you. Right before I left the office, Mayor Bascomb came in to see Al. I already knew he'd signed a private contract with Larry when he invested in the Crazy Elf, so I asked him whether he'd visited Stephanie last night and how she was doing in the hospital."

"Smart," Hannah said.

"He said Stephanie's still there and he stayed with her until visiting hours were over. And I promised to go see her tonight and take her something." Andrea turned and stared at the baker's rack.

It didn't take a particle physicist to understand Andrea's gesture. "I'll pack up some cookies for you," Hannah said.

"Anyway, I called the hospital to check on visiting hours and I found out that everyone has to leave at nine. It's only about ten minutes from the hospital to the park, and that means Mayor Bascomb might not have an alibi for the time of Larry's murder."

"Bingo," Hannah said, flipping to the suspect page again and putting a star by Mayor Bascomb's name. "I'll send Mother to see him. She's fearless."

"Good! If anybody can intimidate Mayor Bascomb, it's Mother." Andrea picked up her last cookie and by the expression on her sister's face, Hannah knew that if there were a little gauge from Andrea's mouth down to her stomach, it would be full to the brim. "Can I take this one with me?" she asked.

"Of course. Let me go pack up those cookies for Stephanie."

Andrea nibbled at her one remaining cookie as Hannah packed a dozen of Lake Eden's first lady's favorite Carrot Cake Cookies. By the time she turned back to her sister, the Cherry Wink had disappeared and Andrea was blotting her lips with the napkin.

"I couldn't help it. They're so good," Andrea said by way of explanation. "I'm showing a house at four, but I'm free until then. Is there anything else I can do for you?"

Hannah was about to shake her head when she thought of a bit of legwork that Andrea could do quite easily. She pulled out one of the papers that Luanne sent with Delores and referred to it again. "How about dropping by to see Jessica Murphy?"

"She's not a suspect, is she?"

"No. I just need to know what Larry paid her for those crocheted animals she makes. And I also need to know if he asked Jessica to sign any blank receipts."

"I can do that. I need to talk to Jessica anyway about finding a bigger place now that they have two children. That house is going to be too small for them really soon now. Anything else I can do?"

Hannah glanced down at the sheet again. "Larry got his Christmas trees from Winnie Henderson's farm. I need to ask her what he paid and whether she signed any blank receipts."

"You got it," Andrea got up from her stool, took the box of cookies Hannah handed her, and headed for the door.

"Don't worry. I won't eat these cookies. I know they're really good, but I've finally had enough."

It was almost five in the afternoon when Hannah finished frosting the last apple cake. She was about to carry it to the walk-in cooler to join the others she'd made when Norman came into the kitchen.

"Hi, Hannah," he greeted her with a smile and came up to give her a hug. But when he was close a worried expression replaced his smile. "You look tired. How about going out for a steak at The Corner Tavern with me?"

Hannah didn't hesitate. "I'd love to!" she said quickly. "A steak is exactly what I need. Thanks for asking me, Norman."

"And after the steak, I can help you wrap those presents," Norman offered. "If you're not too tired, that is."

"That would be perfect. We can even have dessert at my place. I want to try out a new bar cookie recipe."

"Hi, guys!" Andrea breezed into the kitchen wearing a huge smile. "I just sold another house!"

"Congratulations!" Hannah said.

"From me, too," Norman added. "How about a celebratory steak at The Corner Tavern? Hannah and I are going and we'd love to have you join us."

Andrea's smile grew wider, something Hannah hadn't thought was possible. "That's just perfect," she said. "Tracey's going out to Karen Dunwright's house for a sleepover, Bethie has a little case of the sniffles so Grandma McCann is putting her to bed early, Bill has to work late, Mother's having dinner with Dr. Love, and I have absolutely no plans for dinner."

"You do now," Norman told her. "Just let me call for a reservation. What time can you leave, Hannah?"

"Now," Hannah said, glancing at the clock and making an executive decision. "I'll tell Lisa to lock up right now and leave a little early. Her throat's probably sore from all those stories she's been telling about us finding Larry."

Thirty minutes later, they were sitting in a circular booth

at The Corner Tavern, enjoying the chef's famous Caesar salad. Hannah and Norman had anchovies while Andrea had opted for none. They were just picking up their forks when the owner, Nick Prentiss, came over with a bottle of champagne in a silver bucket.

"I understand congratulations are in order," he said, popping the cork. And then he turned to Hannah. "Is tonight a special occasion for you and Norman?"

There was dead silence for a moment and then Andrea jumped into the breach. "It certainly is!" she said with a smile. "Hannah and Norman just ordered the porterhouse for two and that's worthy of a celebration in its own right. But we're here because I just sold another house this afternoon."

"Congratulations!" Nick reached out to shake Andrea's hand and then he leaned closer. "Did you order the garlic bread?"

"Of course. It's the best in Minnesota."

"Thank you. And are you having your usual order to go for Sheriff Todd?"

"Yes, I am."

"Then please let me include a nice half bottle of Chianti with my compliments. It goes so well with the garlic bread. Mayor Bascomb was quite impressed with it last night."

"Mayor Bascomb was here for dinner?" Hannah asked, suddenly attentive to what Nick was telling them.

"Oh, yes. He drove here right after he visited his wife in the hospital. Such a lovely lady. I hope she recovers soon."

"So do we," Norman said, picking up on the questioning as Nick poured their champagne. "None for me please. I'm driving. Do you know what time the mayor arrived here last night?"

"A few minutes after nine. He drove here directly from the hospital." Nick leaned in a little so people in the neighboring booths couldn't hear him. "He said he needed a good meal after he saw what they served to his wife in the hospital. Why can't they cook something good in that place? Sick people need good food."

"Oh well," Andrea sighed after Nick had poured champagne and left. "I didn't really think Mayor Bascomb did it anyway." She took a sip of her champagne and reached over to give Norman a hug. "Thank you for the celebration."

"My pleasure. I'm just sorry Bill isn't here to enjoy it with us."

"Me, too." Andrea turned to Hannah. "Do you want to know what I found out from Jessica and Winnie?"

"Yes." Hannah pulled her steno pad from her purse and flipped it to the proper page. "How about Jessica?"

"Larry paid her ten dollars for each stuffed animal she made and he never had the receipts ready. She signed blank copies and he paid her in cash."

"So it was a hundred percent profit on Jessica's toys, and not the twenty percent Courtney thought it was!"

"That's right. Winnie signed blank copies too, and Larry paid her in cash. She gave me her price list and I remember what I paid for my tree. It was a twenty dollar markup over Larry's cost."

Norman whistled. "If that's true across the board, Larry wasn't losing money after all."

"He was losing money on paper," Hannah said, spearing an anchovy with her fork. "Luanne went over the books for Courtney and they showed that Larry was in the red. And there was barely enough to cover the check he gave us for his cookie order in his business account."

"Hold on," Norman said. "If Larry was making a profit on everything he sold, where was the money going?"

"To his private account at Lake Eden First Mercantile Bank and probably to accounts at other banks, too."

"You're right," Andrea agreed. "It's pretty clear that Larry was cooking the books."

"We suspected that all along, but now we've got proof. The next thing we have to do is find out who else proved it."

"And killed him because of it," Norman said.

DIXIE LEE'S GERMAN APPLE CAKE

Preheat oven to 350 degrees F., rack
in the middle position.

4 cups peeled and sliced apples *(4 or 5 medium size apples)*
3 eggs
1 cup vegetable oil
2 cups white *(granulated)* sugar
1 teaspoon vanilla
1 teaspoon baking soda
2 teaspoons cinnamon
½ teaspoon salt
2 cups all-purpose flour *(pack it down in the cup when you measure it)*

Grease *(or spray with Pam or another nonstick baking spray)* the inside of a 9-inch by 13-inch cake pan. *(I used Pam baking spray, the kind with flour in it.)*

Peel, core, and slice the apples as you would for a pie. Place the sliced apples on the bottom of the prepared cake pan.

Hannah's Note: You can mix the cake batter by hand or with an electric mixer. We use our electric mixer down at The Cookie Jar because we quadruple the recipe and make 4 apple cakes at once.

In a medium sized bowl, whisk the eggs with the oil until they're thick. Then add the sugar and beat it in.

Mix in the vanilla, baking soda, cinnamon, and salt. Mix thoroughly.

Add the flour in one-cup increments, mixing after each cup.

Scrape down the bowl, give a final stir with a spoon, and then drop the batter over the apples in spoonfuls. *(Don't worry if it doesn't completely cover the apples – the batter will spread out during baking.)*

Bake at 350 degrees F. for 60 minutes. *(Mine took only 50 minutes.)* Cool the cake in the pan on a cold burner or a wire rack.

Dixie Lee's German Apple Cake Frosting:

- 8-ounce package softened cream cheese *(the brick kind not the whipped)*
- 2 teaspoons vanilla extract
- 1 Tablespoon lemon juice *(freshly squeezed is best of course)*
- 4 Tablespoons *(½ stick, 2 ounces)* melted butter
- 2 cups confectioner's *(powdered)* sugar *(no need to sift unless it's got big lumps)*

If you forgot to take the cream cheese out of the refrigerator to soften naturally, unwrap it, place it in a microwave-safe bowl and heat it for 20 seconds on HIGH. Check it to

see if it's soft. If it's not, give it another 15 seconds or so, until it is.

Stir the vanilla extract into your cream cheese. Then add the lemon juice and the melted butter. Mix until it's smooth.

Beat in the confectioner's sugar in half-cup increments, checking the consistency after each addition. When the mixture is the consistency of frosting, stop adding sugar. (*I ended up using all of the powdered sugar.*)

Dixie Lee has given us a win-win frosting for her apple cake. If it's too runny, add more powdered sugar. If it's too stiff, add a little more lemon juice or vanilla.

Frost your cooled German Apple Cake, cut a slice to have with a nice cup of coffee, and enjoy.

Lisa's Note: I'm going to try this with peaches instead of apples when they're in season.

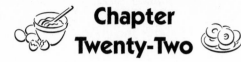

Chapter
Twenty-Two

Hannah put her key in the lock, pulled open the door, and braced herself for the furry onslaught that greeted her every homecoming. But this time it didn't happen. No orange and white feline launched himself into her arms. "Uh-oh," she said.

"Let me." Norman stepped into Hannah's condo and when he gave a little gasp, Hannah expected the worst. Moishe was hiding because of a misdeed. Moishe was ill, stretched out on the floor. Moishe was . . . she didn't even want to think it!

"What . . . ?" Hannah queried, stepping in and surveying the room. There was no sign of mayhem or destruction, no orange and white cat on the couch breathing lethargically with a fever, nothing wrong that she could . . .

"Do you have a stepstool, Hannah?" Norman asked, interrupting her assessment of the situation.

"Yes, but why . . ." Hannah looked to see why he was staring at the ceiling and gave an identical gasp to the one he'd given earlier. Moishe was clinging precariously to one of the top branches of the Christmas tree, the last bird Great-Grandma Elsa had made in his mouth. He'd obviously missed one this morning and consequently his avian appetite had struck again. He'd climbed up the tethered Christmas tree to grab his prize, but now he couldn't get down by himself.

The last of Great-Grandma Elsa's birds. Hannah felt like

sitting right down on the rug and crying. But then her errant cat gave a pathetic, feather-muffled mew and she rushed for the kitchen stepstool. Moishe's safety was more important than antique Christmas ornaments. And now that she thought about it, she was almost positive they'd left one of each kind in the ornament box.

Norman took the stepstool from her and climbed up to retrieve Moishe. Instead of scratching, as most cats would do, Moishe went limp in Norman's arms and started to purr. Hannah truly believed it was a purr of contrition. At least that's what she *wanted* to believe as she took the bird's mangled body from her unresisting cat.

"Coffee?" she asked Norman, figuring that both of them needed a cup after their scare with Moishe.

"That would be great. Tell me where you keep your wrapping paper and ribbons, and I'll get them organized."

For once Hannah was glad she'd taken her mother's advice. All her Christmas wrap, ribbon, and tape were in one of the red and green boxes her mother had ordered from a catalogue for each of her daughters.

"Everything's in a red and green box under the bed in the guest room," she told him. "I'll put on the coffee and slip a couple of pans of Nancy Dunns in the oven for dessert."

"What are Nancy Dunns?"

"They're bar cookies with oatmeal and dates. I got all the ingredients ready to go last night, but I was too busy cleaning up feathers after you-know-who to bake them this morning. I'll bake one pan for us and another to try at The Cookie Jar tomorrow. They're supposed to be unbelievably rich and luscious."

"You've never made them before?"

"No, I just got the recipe in the mail last week. If everybody likes them I'll add them to the menu for catering."

Hannah hurried to the kitchen to preheat the oven, put on the coffee, and assemble the bar cookies for baking. Since the dry ingredients were already out on the counter, all she had to do was gather the rest of her baking supplies from the refrigerator and prepare the pans. She'd cooked the dates with the orange juice the previous evening and they were all ready to go. The recipe was simple and in less than ten minutes, the bars were baking.

"That was fast," Norman said, coming over to take his mug of coffee from her hand. "I think we have everything we need . . . except for the presents, of course."

"Right." Hannah set her coffee on the end table by the couch and went off to get the presents she'd bought. She was about to carry them out when she realized that Norman's present was among them. She quickly stuck it back in the bottom of her closet, made a mental note to wrap it later, and carried out the various bags and boxes that made up what Michelle still called *Christmas loot.*

"Get out of the box, Moishe!" Hannah called out as her cat's whole head disappeared inside.

"I'll get him," Norman said, picking Moishe up and setting him on the back of the couch. "He's just curious."

Past scenes of Moishe's curiosity flashed before Hannah's eyes. Her designer couch pillows completely de-stuffed with pieces of foam and other unidentifiable fibers scattered over her living room rug like snow. The wires from her cable box, video recorder, and television set pulled out and tangled like a bird's nest on the floor. The pile of dry cat food in the bottom of her closet after Moishe attempted to move his food supply. And in the last two days, the fallen Christmas tree, the destruction of her great-grandmother's handmade ornaments, and the feline who'd been stuck like a tree topper on the highest branch. Curious? She supposed so, but she could think of several other words that would also describe Moishe's behavior, the nicest of which was *naughty.*

"He'll probably leave us alone to wrap if we give him something to play with," Norman said, cutting off a length of ribbon and carrying it over to Moishe. "Here you go, Big Guy."

Moishe glanced at her and then he turned to look at Norman. Hannah could swear he was grinning as he batted at the ribbon and purred. Norman balled it up and tossed it to him, and then he walked back over to the box. "Coffee table, or floor?" he asked her.

"Floor. I've got a couple of big things that won't fit on the coffee table." Hannah gestured toward the whiteboard and erasable markers she'd purchased for the back of Tracey's bedroom door.

"Fine with me." Norman opened the first bag and assessed the contents. "We'll need to wrap this one in the gold foil with the little green Christmas trees. It's the only thing you have that's wide enough."

"Right." Hannah sat down on the other side of the red and green box and handed him the roll of paper.

"I'll unroll it on the rug. You set the whiteboard in the center about six inches from the end. Then we'll know where to cut."

"Got it." Hannah waited until Norman had unrolled the paper, but just as she was about to set the whiteboard down on the paper, a furry shape hurtled from the top of the couch, ducked under Tracey's present to skid on the paper with claws out and all four feet extended like miniature rakes.

"Uh-oh," Norman said, reacting to the loud, ripping sound.

"Uh-oh is right, but I think we know where to cut. It's right before the paper you *didn't* unroll."

"Very funny. Will you throw one of his mice for him so we can get this done?"

"Sure, but we'll have to hurry. That'll only distract him for a minute."

"A minute's better than nothing." Norman waited until Hannah picked up one of Moishe's play mice. "Wiggle it a little with your right hand so he knows you're going to throw it. Then put your left hand down on the edge of the paper. I won't unroll it until the mouse leaves your hand."

"Okay. Ready?"

Hannah clamped down the edge of the paper with one

hand and wiggled the mouse with the other. When Norman said he was ready, she pegged the mouse down the hallway, picked up the whiteboard and plunked it down in the proper position and intercepted Moishe as he came flying back. "It worked," she said.

"Don't speak too soon." Norman cut off the paper and reached for the tape. "I still have to wrap it and tie a ribbon around it. Maybe you'd better throw the mouse again."

Hannah lugged her pet over to the Kitty Kondo and snatched another mouse from the stash on the second level. The first mouse she'd thrown was still in the hallway. Moishe had left it there and raced back as he saw Norman begin to roll out the paper. "I'm sure not this is going to work twice," she said, "especially when you unwind the ribbon."

"Let's try. I'm going to need you to put your finger on the ribbon so that I can tie a knot."

Hannah kept a tight hold on her pet as she wiggled the mouse in what she hoped was an enticing manner. He seemed interested, but his attention was definitely divided between the mouse and reel of ribbon that Norman was holding.

"Now!" Norman said, and Hannah sent the play mouse flying to the very end of the hallway. Then she whirled and placed her finger on the knot Norman had just made with the ribbon. There was time for him to make one loop of a bow before disaster struck in the form of a furry paw with unwavering aim that knocked the spool of ribbon out of his hand and sent it flying.

Norman groaned. Hannah did the same. And then they turned to stare at the cat that was gleefully chasing red velvet ribbon all over the living room rug. Hannah was the first to speak.

"The way I see it," she said, "there are only two possible solutions to our problem, other than taping all four of Moishe's paws together."

"And you wouldn't do that . . ." Norman paused and cocked his head. ". . . would you?"

"Of course not. That would be cruel. I have another solution, though."

"You're not going to lock him up, are you?"

Hannah shook her head. "I've got something even better in mind."

"What's that?"

"I'm going to open a can of salmon and dole it out piece by piece. And you're going to wrap presents alone as fast as you can."

Things had turned out rather well Hannah thought. An eight-ounce can of salmon had been just the right size to distract an overly curious feline during the wrapping of sixteen presents. Perhaps the bows were not as elaborately tied as they might have been without a cat in the room, but Hannah knew it was a much better job than the one she would have done by herself.

The Nancy Dunn Cookie Bars were out of the oven and cooling on wire racks, Moishe was stretched out blissfully on the top of the couch snoring lightly with salmon-scented breath, and Hannah and Norman sat on the couch discussing Larry Jaeger's murder case.

"I wonder what Larry did before he came to Lake Eden," Hannah mused. "I know he left Dr. Love fifteen years ago, and she doesn't know where he was for all those years."

"We might be able to find out where he was if he used the same business name," Norman suggested.

"I know what name he used," Hannah said, remembering the conversation she'd had with Mike and Larry at Elf Headquarters. "Larry was talking about the sign that he made when he was in high school and how it's hung at the front of every business L. J. Enterprises has ever owned."

"Then we'll start with L. J. Enterprises," Norman said, getting up and going to Hannah's computer. "You don't mind if I use your computer?"

"Not at all. Do you want more coffee and a couple of Nancy Dunns? I think they're cool enough to cut."

"Sure. This shouldn't take long, especially if some of his businesses had Web sites."

By the time Hannah came back with more coffee and a plate of Nancy Dunns, Norman had the printer running. "You found something?" she asked.

"I found the business he opened before he came to Lake Eden," Norman told her. "It was called Hollywood Home Theater and it was in Madison, Wisconsin."

"He sold movies?" Hannah guessed.

"He sold big screen television sets," Norman corrected her. "Technicians called the Cast and Crew installed them in people's living rooms, complete with theater seats and sound. Unfortunately the business didn't make it for long."

"How long?"

"It went bankrupt after only five months. There's a link to a newspaper story. Hold on while it downloads."

Norman clicked on the link and read the text. "It's a story that was carried by the *Wisconsin State Journal*. It's about Salvatore Bianco, one of Larry's investors in Hollywood Home Theater. When the business went bankrupt, he lost his entire retirement and he committed suicide."

"That's awful!" Hannah said.

"Yes, especially if Larry pulled the same kind of scam and cheated his investors."

"He probably did. You'd think big screen televisions would go over big in a city as large as Madison. Practically everyone there follows the Packers and . . ."

"What?" Norman asked as Hannah suddenly stopped talking.

"Big screen television sets. I just remembered. That's what Miss Whiting's homework was about."

"And you think it might not be a coincidence?"

"That's *exactly* what I'm thinking. But how did Miss Whiting find out about Larry's last business?"

Norman smiled. "There's only one way to find out."

"Right. I'll drive out to the college and ask her first thing tomorrow."

"Correction. *We'll* drive out to the college and ask her first thing tomorrow."

"Good. Your car's more comfortable and your heater's . . ."

Hannah stopped in mid-sentence again, but this time Norman didn't ask why. "Larry's flat screen?" he asked her.

"That's right. Do you think there's a connection?"

"There could be. Somebody killed Larry *and* his TV. And Larry owned a business that sold them and went bankrupt, cheating at least one investor we know out of his retirement and his life. That's a lot of coincidence to swallow."

"It's too much of a coincidence." Hannah reached for her steno pad and proceeded to write down what they'd learned, what they suspected, and the interview she needed to have with Miss Whiting. She was just closing the cover when there was the sound of a key in the lock.

"Hi, Hannah," Michelle breezed in with a smile on her face. "Hi, Norman. What smells so good?"

"Nancy Dunn Bar Cookies." And then, before her sister could ask, Hannah explained. "They're date and oatmeal cookie bars, and they're so good they melt in your mouth."

Michelle looked disappointed. "If I'd known you were baking I wouldn't have stopped for a chocolate sundae on the way here."

"Too bad," Norman said. "I just had one and they're fantastic."

"Well . . . I probably have room for a small one." Michelle made a beeline for the plate and picked one up. "Your tree's beautiful. I'm so glad you got one this year."

"Me, too," Hannah said. Michelle was right. The tree *was* beautiful.

"Where's Moishe?"

"Right there on the top of the couch," Hannah told her, pointing at her sacked out cat.

"But he always comes over to greet me." Michelle looked worried. "Is he sick?"

Hannah shook her head. "It's just a food coma. I had to feed him a whole can of salmon to keep him distracted while Norman wrapped the Christmas presents."

"Well, you'd better not put them under the tree!" Michelle gave a little laugh. "I talked to Andrea and she said you've already had a couple *cat*-astrophies this year."

"That's true. We're just hoping the tree's secure enough to last until Christmas Eve."

"Oh, that reminds me," Michelle said, taking another Nancy Dunn. "Are you doing Christmas Eve dinner this year?"

"Of course. I *always* do Christmas Eve dinner."

"And you're doing it here?"

"I *always* do it here."

"Oh, good. Do you think I can invite someone from the college for dessert? They're doing a dinner out there, but you always have something really fantastic for dessert."

"Of course. Invite anyone you like. Just make sure to tell me how many friends you're bringing. We'll start at six with appetizers and I'll serve the Minnesota Plum Pudding at eight."

"Thanks, Hannah. That'll be perfect. Mother already told me about your plum pudding and she said it was incredible." Michelle glanced at her watch and sighed. "It's only nine-thirty, but I'm beat and I'd better get to bed. We went through the whole show three times today and tomorrow morning's dress rehearsal."

"Good night, Michelle," Norman called out as she turned to go.

" 'Night, Norman. 'Night, Hannah." Michelle hesitated and then she walked back to the coffee table and took another cookie bar. "I have to keep up my strength," she said, heading off to the guest room with a grin on her face.

NANCY DUNN BAR COOKIES

Preheat oven to 350 degrees F., rack
in the middle position.

8-ounce package pitted dates, coarsely chopped
1 and ½ cups orange juice *(I used Minute Maid)*
2 and ½ cups all-purpose flour *(pack it down when
   you measure it)*
1 and ½ cups firmly packed brown sugar
½ teaspoon salt
1 and ½ cups softened butter *(3 sticks, 12 ounces, ¾
   pound)*
2 cups Quaker Oats *(quick or old fashioned,
   uncooked)*
1 cup shredded coconut *(for the batter)*
1 cup chopped nuts *(walnuts or pecans)*
½ cup shredded coconut *(for a topping)*

In a medium size saucepan combine the dates and the
orange juice. Do not cover. Bring the mixture to a boil.

Reduce the heat to simmer and cook for 15 to 20 minutes, or until thickened, stirring occasionally.

Move the saucepan to a cold burner and let it cool.

In a large bowl, combine the flour, sugar, and salt. Mix
it thoroughly.

Cut in the softened butter with a pastry blender, or two
knives until the resulting mixture is crumbly. *(You can also
do this with a food processor and cold butter cut into*

pieces. Use the steel blade in an on and off motion until the mixture is crumbly.)

Stir in the oats, coconut, and nuts. Mix thoroughly.

Spray a 9-inch by 13-inch cake pan with Pam or another nonstick cooking spray.

Measure out 4 cups of the oat mixture and set it on the counter to use for a topping. Press the remainder of the oat mixture in the bottom of your baking pan.

Spread the date mixture evenly over the crust to within a quarter-inch of the edges.

Sprinkle the date mixture with the remaining oat mixture.

Sprinkle the remaining half-cup coconut on the top and pat it down gently.

Bake at 350 degrees F. for 35 to 40 minutes, or until light golden brown on top. Cool completely in the pan on a wire rack.

When completely cool, cut into bars. Store them in a tightly covered container.

Yield: Makes 36 rich, delicious bars.

Chapter Twenty-Three

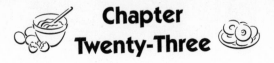

"I'd better be going, Hannah." Norman stood up and carried his coffee mug into the kitchen. "It's almost ten and you need your sleep."

"That's true. What time shall we go out to the college? I know Miss Whiting has an eight o'clock class."

"I'll pick you up at The Cookie Jar at eight-thirty and we'll catch her after her class. I've got the morning clear tomorrow."

"Thanks, Norman." Hannah was about to get up to walk him to the door when someone knocked.

"I'll get it," Norman told her, heading to the door. "Who is it?"

"It's Hannah's mother," Delores called out so loudly that Hannah could hear her right through the closed door. "Let me in, Norman. It's cold out here."

Norman wasted no time ushering Delores into Hannah's living room and Hannah got up to take her mother's coat. "How about a cup of coffee?" she asked.

"Only if it's made, dear. I don't want to put you to any trouble."

"It's made. And I wouldn't mind making it if it weren't." Hannah hurried to the kitchen to pour coffee and came back out with several more bars to slip onto the plate Michelle and Norman had come close to devouring. "Have a date bar with your coffee, Mother."

"Well . . . perhaps one. Nancy made dinner for us and it was lovely. She said she didn't feel like going out."

"How about the alibi?" Hannah asked, hoping her mother had been successful in finding a way to prove that Dr. Love was nowhere near the Crazy Elf Christmas Tree lot when Larry was murdered.

"I struck out, dear. No phone calls made or received, no one walking by on the sidewalk, no noises that she could remember, nothing to place her at home when Larry Jaeger was killed."

"Okay. It was a long shot and I know you gave it your best try. We'll just have to prove that someone else shot Larry," Hannah said, trying to look confident for her mother's sake. "How about Earl? Did you have more luck with him?"

"Actually . . ." Delores frowned deeply and shook her head. "No. I didn't have any luck at all. He said his uncle and aunt didn't have children and he had no cousins in the area. I asked him about investing with Larry and whether you might have seen him out at the Crazy Elf Christmas Tree Lot and he never gave me a straight answer. And then, when I asked him where he was between nine and nine forty-five on the night Larry was killed, he said, *Somewhere. I dunno.* I thought I was asking the right questions, but Earl was terribly evasive." Delores stopped speaking and gave a deep sigh. "Maybe I'm not very good at this after all."

Norman reached out to squeeze Delores's hand. "You're *very* good at this. Don't think you aren't, not for a second. You're forgetting that you discovered a very important clue when you went undercover in that Karaoke bar."

"Well . . . yes. But that was then and this is now. This time I didn't get anything at all."

"Nonsense," Norman said, and Hannah could have kissed him for being so nice to her mother. Actually, she could have kissed him just for being Norman.

"It's possible you were given an important clue, and you just haven't realized it yet," Norman went on reassuring Delores. "Tell us all about your afternoon."

"Well . . . I hope you're right," Delores said, brightening considerably. "The first thing I did was go to the mall to get . . ."

When her mother stopped speaking, Hannah knew what caution had just crossed her mind. "Go ahead, Mother. She's in the guest room sleeping."

"I went out to the mall to get a new pair of boots for Michelle," Delores said in a much lower voice. "I found just the thing at The Glass Slipper and I brought them up here to show you."

Delores opened the bag she'd brought in with her. She pulled out a boot-size box and lifted the lid. "Aren't they just perfect for Michelle?" she asked.

"Perfect," Hannah agreed, exchanging glances with Norman. The boots were fawn-colored suede with lovely beadwork butterflies on the sides.

"They were terribly expensive, but I just knew Michelle would wear them and love them." Delores turned to Hannah. "I'm right, aren't I, dear?"

"Absolutely. Michelle's going to adore them."

"Are they suede?" Norman asked, pulling Hannah back to the more important issue.

"That's right."

"They have beautiful beadwork," Hannah commented. "Did they happen to have any men's boots?"

"No. The owner told me there was a pair and someone came in and bought them. They were only for display, but the owner sold them because it was too late to special order any more before Christmas. It was the same with Michelle's boots. I'm just lucky they were her size."

"That's interesting." Hannah exchanged another glance with Norman. "Did you happen to ask who bought the man's pair?"

"Yes, but the owner didn't know his name. All he could remember was that he was from Lake Eden. I was curious because the boots were so expensive. I couldn't help but wonder which local man paid that much for dress boots."

"Yes, we're wondering that, too," Norman said.

Delores turned to give him a sharp look. "Is there a special reason you're wondering?"

There was another meaningful look between Hannah and Norman. Norman gave her a nod, giving his consent to tell Delores about Carrie and the man with the suede boots.

"It's the man I told you about this morning, Mother." Hannah turned to her mother.

"The one in the private booth with Carrie?"

"Yes. He had suede boots similar to the ones you bought for Michelle. And from what you just told us, he must have bought them at The Glass Slipper."

"Do you think I should go back to The Glass Slipper and have a little talk with the salespeople to see if I can find out more about the man who bought them? I wouldn't mind a pair of new boots for myself."

"That's a great idea," Hannah said, handing her mother the package of cookie bars she'd wrapped for her to take home.

"Thanks for the information, Delores." Norman stood up and grabbed Delores's coat. "It's a big relief to know that the man Mother is dating is local."

Delores shrugged into the coat that Norman was holding for her. "Goodbye, dear," she said to Hannah. "Goodbye, Norman."

"I'll see you to your car," Norman told her, grabbing his jacket and putting it on. "I'm leaving now anyway. Hannah needs her sleep."

Hannah waved and as the door closed behind them, she gave a relieved sigh. She was tired and she wanted to go to bed. Her alarm clock was set for four in the morning and it was already past ten-thirty. If she wanted to get more than five hours of sleep, she had to turn in right now.

It only took a moment to put the coffee mugs and dessert plate in the dishwasher and make sure the cake pans with bars inside were tightly covered with cat-proof lids. Hannah switched off the bright kitchen light and was about to pick up her lethargic feline to carry him into the bedroom when there was a knock at her door.

Hannah knew there were only two possibilities for callers who'd knock on her door this late. It was either Mike or a home invasion robbery. Hannah was betting on the former when she crossed to the door and opened it.

Mike looked surprised. "Don't you ever ask who's there?"

"Why should I do that? I knew it was you."

"How did you know that? You didn't even stop to look through the peephole."

"The peephole doesn't work. The security light's too bright and all I can see is a dark shape in front of it."

Mike gave an exasperated sigh. "Are you going to invite me in? Or are we going to stand here and argue all night?"

Hannah had the urge to shut the door. She was tired and she wanted to go to bed. But then Mike smiled and her irritation vanished in a wave of longing for a bit of private time with Winnetka County Sheriff's Department chief detective. There was also the fact that Mike was investigating the same crime that she was, and she might be able to pry some official information from him.

"Come in, Mike. It's good to see you," Hannah put on the cheeriest voice she could muster. "I'll put on the coffee if you'd like some."

"That would be good. I've been out in the field all day."

Food. He wanted food. Hannah felt like groaning, but she managed to keep the pleasant expression on her face. "You didn't eat dinner?"

"Yeah, I ate. I stopped for a patty melt and fries at the café before they closed. I didn't have dessert, though. All Rose had left was a piece of raisin pie."

There was a pregnant silence. Hannah let it go on for several seconds. "I'll see what I can do," she said, waving him over to the couch. A half-dozen Nancy Dunn Cookie Bars ought to elicit some information from the man who didn't like raisin pie.

It didn't take long to brew the coffee. Hannah sneaked out a cup before the whole pot had brewed, and emerged from the kitchen with a steaming mug and a plate of cookie bars. "Here you go," she said, setting them down on the coffee table in front of her erstwhile boyfriend.

"These look good," Mike said, and took one. He took a bite, smiled, and said, "They *are* good. What are they?"

"Date and oatmeal bar cookies." Hannah figured it was time to ask him some questions before she fell asleep. "Do you have any suspects yet?"

"Only one."

"And that would be . . . ?" Hannah waited, but no answer was forthcoming.

"When you and Norman entered the trailer, how far did you go?"

"Not far. I told you before, I just had a funny feeling something wasn't right."

"A premonition?"

"Were there any subliminal clues that warned you that something was wrong inside?"

Hannah just stared at him for a minute and then she laughed. "If they were subliminal, I wouldn't have consciously registered them."

"Sorry. You're right. Let me rephrase that. Were there any clues that warned you that something was wrong inside the trailer?"

"I don't think so, at least none that I remember. It was probably just that Larry said he'd be there, but he didn't answer the door."

"Okay," Mike took a sip of his coffee. "Back to the important stuff. Did you, at any time, approach the flat screen television set?"

"No. I saw the bullet holes though. At first I thought maybe Larry got mad and threw something at the screen. And then I realized that they were probably bullet holes." Hannah stopped speaking and stared at him. "Why do you want to know if I was close to Larry's television set?"

"Because there was a bloody footprint and the crime lab just got back to us this afternoon. The blood was Larry's and they're ninety-nine percent positive the footprint was made by a woman. I just stopped by to eliminate your prints. What boots were you wearing that night?"

"The only ones I have, my moose-hide boots."

"Could I see them please?"

Hannah got up to get them, but then she turned back to Mike. "You're not going to take them, are you? I'm going to need them in the morning."

"All I need is the left one. And I may not have to take it."

"Thanks," Hannah said a trifle sarcastically, already envisioning a one-footed hop down the stairs in the early morning to her cookie truck.

Her boots were on the rug by the side of the door. Hannah picked up the left one and carried it over to Mike. "Here," she said.

Mike turned the boot over, took one look, and handed it back. "Okay," he said. "The print's not yours."

"You can tell if there's blood on the sole of my boot by just looking?" Hannah was amazed at his investigative skills.

"No. Your boot is a lot bigger than the boot that made the print. What size is it anyway?"

"Six," Hannah said, cheating by several integers. She was lying to the authorities, but she felt justified since her boot had already been eliminated. "How about Courtney? What size boot does she wear?"

"Five, but it has a different type of heel. Mr. Jaeger's fiancée left the park early and drove out to the Inn. A couple of the employees told me that she had an altercation with Mr. Jaeger before she left, but Sally said she was sitting in the kitchen talking to her from nine-twenty until almost ten."

"Are there any other women suspects?" Hannah asked, knowing that there was at least one more. If Dr. Love was lucky, Mike hadn't found out about her marriage to Larry yet and Hannah could clear her before he did.

"There were several women involved in Mr. Jaeger's case. We found three local females who were having . . . uh . . ." Mike stopped and looked slightly embarrassed.

"Play dates?" Hannah suggested.

"That's good. I like that! These three local women were having play dates with Mr. Jaeger, but they all have alibis for the time of the murder."

"So that's it for the women suspects?" Hannah asked, wondering if she dared cross her fingers.

"No, there's one more. Thanks to your tip about Mr. Jaeger's business practices, we did an extensive search of his financial records. That's when we discovered that one woman suspect had a very compelling motive. Now all we have to do is gather more evidence and then we can make an arrest."

Hannah felt her spirits take a nosedive. She thought she knew, but she had to ask. "Who's your suspect?"

"Mr. Jaeger's wife. She stands to gain the most from his death. I just came from interviewing her and I like her."

Hannah knew that Mike's *like* was not the same as her *like*. When Mike said *like*, it referred to the person he'd like to arrest for Larry Jaeger's murder. But what if Larry's current wife wasn't Dr. Love? What if he'd filed for a quickie divorce in another state and married someone else?

"She has no alibi for the time of the murder, and over two million in various banks in the tri-state area is one heck of a motive. When her boots come back from the crime lab we'll know for sure."

Hannah swallowed hard and asked the question. "Who is it?"

"You probably know her as Dr. Love. She's a psychology professor at the community college and she has this cock-and-bull story about how she hasn't talked to her husband in fifteen years."

Chapter
Twenty-Four

The alarm clock was set for four in the morning, but Hannah awoke before it went off. She sat up in bed and glanced at the clock. It was three forty-seven. What had happened to wake her up eight minutes before the alarm went off?

All was silent in her darkened condo. Hannah had just laid her head back on the pillow and closed her eyes when there was a bloodcurdling yowl. It was the kind of sound that would have made her hair stand on end if it hadn't already been impossibly mussed by an uneasy night's sleep.

Another yowl, equally loud, followed the first, and Hannah sprang into action. She jumped out of bed, no time for her slippers, and raced down the hallway. No time to flick on the light. Moishe was in trouble and she had to help him.

Enough light spilled in from the outside for Hannah to see what was wrong. Her cat was hanging perilously from the top branch of her Christmas tree in a repeat performance of last night's gravity-defying stunt.

It was a good thing she'd forgotten to put away the stepstool. Hannah positioned it quickly and climbed up to rescue her pet. Something had to be done about her Christmas tree and fast.

She'd just poured her first cup of coffee when Michelle appeared in the kitchen doorway. "What happened?" she asked. "I heard Moishe yowling."

"He climbed the Christmas tree again and he couldn't get down."

"That's bad. I know they say cats climb down from trees eventually, but I'm not sure I believe it."

"Me, either." Hannah filled a second cup with coffee and handed it to her sister. Then she led the way to the almost-antique kitchen table and they both sat down.

"So what are you going to do about it?" Michelle asked. "Enclose the whole tree in a cat-proof cage?"

Hannah gave a little shrug. "It's either that or enclose the whole cat in a tree-proof cage."

Of course Lisa had urged her to go and not give a second thought to their business at The Cookie Jar. And when Hannah worried aloud about how Lisa could handle everyone alone, Lisa said she'd already called Herb's Aunt Patsy who was coming down to wait tables for her. Hannah was free to go search for Larry's killer. Lisa and Patsy would take care of everything else.

Hannah watched the weather go by outside the passenger window of Norman's car. The weatherman on KCOW radio was predicting snow later tonight with an increase in wind velocity.

"Did you hear that?" Norman asked her, taking the access road to the college and driving up the big hill where Hannah had seen the students sledding.

"I heard. I hope it's not the beginning of a big storm. Michelle said they're giving several more performances before they close with a matinee on Christmas Day."

"I checked with the national weather service on the computer this morning and the maps didn't show anything big in the works for the rest of this week. Next week is anyone's guess."

"I'll guess snow," Hannah said with a grin. "There's always snow this time of year."

Once Norman had parked and they'd crossed the road to

the campus, Hannah led the way to Stewart Hall. "Miss Whiting's classroom is on the second floor, third from the end on the left," she told him, and opened the door to the stairway.

Since they hadn't rushed from the car to Stewart Hall, Hannah wasn't out of breath when they reached the top of the stairs. As they stepped out of the stairwell, they heard a bell ring and the deserted hallway that stretched before them was suddenly filled with students. Norman took Hannah's arm and steered her toward the end of the hall.

Miss Whiting looked up when she saw them in the doorway. "Hello, there," she said. "Did you come to turn in your homework?"

"Not yet," Hannah said. "I'd like you to meet Norman Rhodes. He's a dentist in Lake Eden."

"You might be interested in my class," Miss Whiting told him, "especially if you own your own practice. Do you?"

"Yes, I do."

Miss Whiting opened her center desk drawer and pulled out a folded packet of papers. "This is our syllabus. I teach four business courses and the curriculum for each is enclosed. It's very important for a professional to have a business plan. Do you have one?"

"Yes."

Hannah decided it was time to rescue Norman from Miss Whiting's questions. "Do you mind if I ask you something, Miss Whiting?"

"Not at all as long as it pertains to your homework. Does it?"

"As a matter of fact, it does. Was the handout you gave us from a Madison, Wisconsin business called Hollywood Home Theater?"

Miss Whiting looked shocked. "Don't tell me I failed to screen out the business name!"

"No. You covered it completely. But are they records from Hollywood Home Theater?"

"Well . . . yes. Yes, they are."

"It's an amazing coincidence," Norman said, stepping in to continue the questioning. "That business was owned by Larry Jaeger and he was murdered two nights ago in Lake Eden."

"Really? What was the owner of Hollywood Home Theater doing in Lake Eden?"

"Running another business, the Crazy Elf Christmas Tree Lot," Hannah said, catching the conversational ball. "And unless we're mistaken, it looks as if he was involved in the same sort of bad business practices."

"And you think that's why he was murdered?"

"That's right. What we'd like to know is why you chose Hollywood Home Theater for a homework assignment."

"Well, that's simple. My graduate thesis involved bad business practices leading to bankruptcy. I researched all the bankruptcies in a five-state area to pick the most egregious cases, and Hollywood Home Theater was one of my examples."

"How about future homework assignments?" Norman asked her. "Do they involve other businesses that went bankrupt?"

"Yes. That's my area of concentration. Next week we'll examine a used car dealership in Fargo. That will be followed by assignments concerning a video game franchise in Pierre, a fast food business in Des Moines, and an exotic juice bar in Rochester."

"Thank you, Miss Whiting," Hannah said, as the next class of students began to file into the classroom.

"You're quite welcome." Miss Whiting turned to Norman. "Do think about taking one of my classes, Dr. Rhodes. I think you'd enjoy it . . . and I'm sure I could teach you a thing or two."

Norman didn't speak until they'd left the classroom, walked out of the building, and were several feet from the door. "Am I crazy, or do you think she was flirting with me?" he asked Hannah.

"She was flirting with you."

"You're sure?"

"I'm sure."

Norman looked pleased at her answer. "Not that I'm interested or anything like that, but I'm glad she didn't just want her teeth whitened for free."

"I hope he's got the coffeepot on," Norman said as he pulled up to the county tow truck and snowplow driver's house.

"No, you don't. I once heard Cyril Murphy refer to Earl's coffee as one step worse than motor oil. And Cyril's coffee comes in second on the worst coffee scale."

"Who's number one?"

"Jon Walker. He hasn't washed his pot in years. The baked on old coffee residue is probably the only thing that's keeping it from falling apart."

Norman digested those comments for a moment and then he laughed. "Thanks, Hannah. I was craving a cup of coffee a minute or two ago."

"And now you're not?"

"That's right. Tell me why we're here, especially after Mike told you the killer was a woman."

"Mother said Earl was evasive about where he was when Larry was killed. And he refused to tell her if he was one of Larry's investors. It may not have anything to do with Larry's murder, but I want to find out why Earl's not talking to Mother. They've been friends for years and he hurt her feelings. I could tell."

"Good answer. What do you want me to do?"

"When we start talking about where he was at the time of the murder, I'm going to go into the kitchen for a glass of water. That way, if he was somewhere doing something he's embarrassed to admit in front of Mother or me, he'll tell you and then you'll tell me later."

"Okay. Let's do it. I've got that urge for coffee again and I don't know how long I can fight it."

Earl looked surprised to see them when he opened the door. "Hannah," he said, stepping back. "And Norman. Is somebody stuck in the ditch?"

Hannah shook her head. "No, Earl. We just wanted to talk to you for a minute. Can we come in?"

"Well . . . yeah . . . sure. Sure you can come in." Earl stepped aside and let them enter his living room. "What do you want to talk to me about?"

"Tuesday night," Hannah said jumping in quickly. "Where were you on Tuesday night, Earl?"

Earl swallowed hard. Hannah could see his Adam's apple bob up and down as he glanced at Norman and then back at her. "Why do you want to know?"

"Because it's important. Why don't you want to tell us?"

"I . . . I can't." Earl looked so uncomfortable Hannah took pity on him. She gave a little cough, cleared her throat, and said, "I need a glass of water. I'll be back in a minute."

As she went into the kitchen, Hannah heard Norman say something about certain subjects he wouldn't want to discuss in front of women. Hannah smiled and hoped the man-to-man camaraderie would work. It was clear the two men liked each other. There was a good chance that Earl would tell Norman what he wouldn't tell Delores or her.

It was a pleasant kitchen, nicely decorated and well maintained. It certainly wasn't what she'd expected. Most bachelors she knew went for function, not appearance. Earl seemed to like both, or perhaps the house had come complete with charm and good taste.

Hannah considered what she knew about Earl, which wasn't a lot. He'd gone to school with Delores, he was a nice pleasant man, and he worked for the county. That wasn't much. She wasn't sure if Earl had inherited the house from his parents or if he'd purchased it himself. Of course Andrea would know. Her sister knew the provenance of every house within a ten-mile radius of Lake Eden.

She opened the cupboard and took out a glass, noticing

how neatly everything was stacked and how clean the dishes appeared. For a bachelor, Earl was a good housekeeper. She ran some water in the glass, set it down on the counter, and took a little trip around the kitchen to see what was there. A sheaf of bound papers on the table caught her eye and she walked over to see what Earl was reading. It was a government report on the state of the economy.

An old roll top desk sat under the window in an alcove and Hannah went to look at that. There was a laptop computer on the desk and Hannah was surprised to see that it was hooked up to the only satellite internet provider in their area. And right there, by the side of the desk, was a pair of fawn-colored suede boots with fancy beadwork on the sides.

Hannah's breath slid out of her open mouth in a low, almost inaudible whistle. Earl was Mr. Suede Boots, the man that Carrie was cuddling up to in the private booth at the Lake Eden Inn, and the reason she'd canceled so many plans with Delores and Norman.

"So you see, Norman, I can't really tell you who it was," Earl was saying when Hannah walked in carrying the boots.

"New boots?" she asked him, grinning at Norman.

"Yeah. I got them earlier this week."

"Looks like you haven't worn them much," Norman said, locking eyes with Earl.

"Not much. I wore them out to dinner, but that's it."

"A champagne dinner with my mother," Norman said, "in a private booth at the Lake Eden Inn."

There was a moment of complete silence and then Earl sighed. "That's right and I'm glad it's out in the open. Carrie made me promise not to tell anyone until she had a chance to talk to you. If it's okay with you, I'd like to marry your mother." Earl stopped and frowned slightly. "Actually . . . I'd like to marry your mother even if it's *not* okay with you."

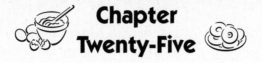

Chapter
Twenty-Five

"I still can't believe *that's* why Earl was so evasive with me."

Delores gave a little laugh and Hannah glanced over at her mother as she pulled into the parking lot at the college. Delores looked happier than Hannah had seen her in weeks and the worry lines on her forehead had completely vanished. "You're not angry that Carrie kept the news from you?"

"No. Carrie explained everything to me this afternoon. Her romance with Earl was so wonderfully sudden and unexpected, she was afraid to talk about it. She said it was like a beautiful dream that would vanish if she woke up and opened her eyes."

The parking lot hadn't filled up yet, and Hannah found a space right next to her mother's sedan. She noticed that Michelle had unwound the extension cord that had been coiled around the bumper and plugged it into the power pole between the two spaces. Hannah copied her sister actions and plugged in her cookie truck. And then she opened the passenger door for her mother.

"When was Carrie planning to tell you about Earl?" she asked, waiting for her mother to emerge.

"On Christmas Eve. She planned to bring Earl to our dinner and tell us all then."

"How about Norman? She was planning to tell him before

then, wasn't she?" Hannah took her mother's arm since Delores was wearing fashionable boots with high heels.

"Yes, tonight. Carrie said she was going to have a talk with him when he picked her up for the Christmas Follies. And then, if Norman took it well, they were going to meet Earl in the auditorium so they could all sit together."

"Was she afraid that Norman wouldn't approve?" Hannah asked as they crossed the road to the well-shoveled sidewalk that led to the college auditorium.

"Yes. She thought he might have issues with her marrying again, especially to someone he didn't know that well."

The auditorium was just ahead. Hannah and Delores stepped into the foyer and joined the line that was waiting to be seated.

"I'm a little nervous about Michelle's number," Delores confessed in a whisper.

"So am I, but I talked to her this morning and she wasn't worried at all. She said they're going to tape it and show it to angels."

Delores reared back and stared at Hannah in shock. "*What* did you say?"

"Michelle said they're going to tape it and show it to angels. That's what they call the money men who finance new theatrical productions."

"Oh. *Those* kinds of angels!" Delores looked relieved. "For a moment there, I thought that you were so nervous, you weren't making sense."

The college orchestra was playing as they were led inside by one of the ushers. Michelle had arranged for two seats in the center section quite near the front, and Hannah waved as they passed Andrea, Bill, and Tracey who were sitting in the front row on the side. Delores nudged Hannah and they both gave a wave as they spotted Norman, Carrie, and Earl. Mike wasn't there, and Hannah knew he probably wouldn't be. He was too busy working on Larry Jaeger's murder case.

Once they'd reached the center of their row, Hannah and Delores sat down and slipped off their coats. The auditorium was dark and warm, and the seats were comfortable. That was three strikes out for someone like Hannah who'd had only four hours of sleep. To keep herself from emitting embarrassing snorts or snores on the eve of her sister's big musical comedy debut, Hannah busied herself by reading the program the usher had handed to her.

"Look, Mother," she pointed to a section listing the songs the college choir would perform. "They're singing *O Christmas Tree* in German."

"*O Tannenbaum*," Delores said with a smile. "I still remember my grandmother singing that."

"And here's *Feliz Navidad* in Spanish and English."

"Wonderful. That's such a happy song. What else are they singing, dear?"

"It says they're singing *White Christmas* in Italian."

"*Bianco Natale*," Delores said, smiling at Hannah.

"I didn't know you spoke Italian!"

"I don't. Your father hired an Italian immigrant to help out in the hardware store when we were first married. I invited him to Christmas dinner since his family was still in Italy and he sang *Bianco Natale* for us."

"That's nice, Mother," Hannah said. And then, as she glanced down at the program again, her eyes widened. Bianco was the last name of the man who invested in Larry's Hollywood Home Theater company and committed suicide when he lost his retirement. Miss Whiting was the teacher who gave them the handout of financial date from Larry's Hollywood Home Theater company. Larry's company sold giant screen television sets. A woman had shot Larry's television set after she'd killed Larry. And *bianco* meant *white* in Italian. What if Miss Whiting's name had been Bianco and she'd Americanized it?

"What's the matter, dear?"

Hannah didn't realize she'd gasped out loud until her mother asked the question. "Just something I remembered," she said, and settled back in her seat to think it through once again. She was almost certain that a woman who had a connection to the

Hollywood Home Theater bankruptcy had killed Larry Jaeger. There were just too many coincidences. But how could she prove that Miss Whiting was connected to Salvatore Bianco?

The moment a probable answer occurred to her, Hannah turned to her Mother. "Miss Whiting said she was a visiting professor. Do you happen to know where she's from?"

"I think she mentioned it at the beginning of the course, but I'm not sure, dear. I believe it was a college town in a neighboring state, perhaps Iowa? Or Wisconsin?"

Another coincidence? Hannah was collecting far too many to believe, but she still had no proof of anything. If she could tie Miss Whiting to Wisconsin, that would help. Hannah reviewed her brief conversations with their business teacher in her mind. Miss Whiting had been here for three months. She'd mentioned that. Perhaps she'd been so busy she hadn't gotten around to applying for a Minnesota driver's license or re-registering her car.

"What kind of car does Miss Whiting drive?" Hannah asked.

"A little silver compact. I can never tell the difference between them. They all look alike to me."

That was enough for Hannah, especially when she remembered that a little silver Honda had been parked in front of The Cookie Jar when she'd come in to find Miss Whiting sitting at the table with Delores.

"I have to do something, Mother," Hannah said. "I'll be back in a couple of minutes."

"All right, but hurry. Your sister's act is third on the program."

"I'll be back in plenty of time," Hannah promised, and then she began to squeeze past people's knees to make her way to the end of the row. She had to go out to the parking lot to find Miss Whiting's silver Honda to see if it had Wisconsin plates.

For once KCOW radio's weatherman had been right. The wind was picking up and snow had started to fall. It felt at least ten degrees colder than it had when they'd walked to the auditorium less than fifteen minutes ago, but Hannah didn't think the actual temperature had fallen. It was wind chill that was robbing heat from her body much faster than still air could do.

Her hands were cold. Hannah thrust them into the pockets of the black dress coat her mother had given her as a present, and pulled out the dress gloves that had come with it. She'd worn the coat and the gloves to please her mother, but she'd drawn the line at dress boots. Delores had offered, on more than one occasion, to buy her a pair, but Hannah had steadfastly refused. She loved her moose-hide boots. They were an acquisition from the Helping Hands Thrift Shop and she'd decided to let the original owner, whoever she might be, feel the guilt about supporting an industry that made footwear out of animal skins. The boots were already made, the moose was long deceased, and Hannah was certain that no rational person could blame her for purchasing second-hand moose-hide boots from a store that supported a soup kitchen for the needy.

The wind whistled harder and picked up loose snow to pelt against her face. She hadn't worn a hat because her knitted ski cap had looked ridiculous with her dress coat. Now she wished she'd had the foresight to stuff it into her pocket. There was no one to see her. Everyone who was coming was already inside the college auditorium where the Christmas Follies were about to begin.

Hannah rushed across the road with the wind and dashed down the first aisle in the parking lot, only to find that there were two silver Hondas. Did one of them belong to Miss Whiting? How could she identify the teacher's car?

One glance at her mother's car answered Hannah's question. There was a blue parking sticker with *STUDENT* written across it on the lower right-hand corner of Delores's windshield. Were faculty parking stickers a different color?

Hannah walked down the first aisle of cars again, checking the stickers. The two silver Hondas had blue student stickers, but the car at the end of the row had a red parking sticker with *FACULTY* written across it.

Now that she'd identified her quarry, Hannah moved faster, stopping only at silver Hondas to identify their parking sticker color.

It was cold work and Hannah felt like a walking block of ice by the time she'd finished. She'd found six silver Hondas, but not one of them had displayed a red faculty parking sticker. Either Miss Whiting wasn't here tonight, or she'd ridden to the college in someone else's car.

Hannah was about to leave when a car turned into the lot. She watched as it drove past one of the argon lights that illuminated the area, and her heart began to beat faster. It was a silver compact and the driver found a spot at the very end of the center row. Hannah couldn't tell if it was a Honda from this distance, and she hurried over for a closer look.

It was a Honda and a woman was opening the driver's door. It was Miss Whiting and she waved as she saw Hannah.

"Hello, Hannah. What are you doing out here all alone?"

Hannah thought fast. She needed a plausible excuse. "I left my purse in the truck, and I had to come back out here to get it," she said.

"We'd better hurry if we want to get inside before the program begins," Miss Whiting said.

"Yes." Hannah tried to get a look at the license plate, but Miss Whiting was blocking it with her body. The teacher just stood there, waiting for Hannah to turn around and head back to the auditorium, but Hannah couldn't do that. She had to get a look at Miss Whiting's license plate.

"Are you coming?" Miss Whiting asked, and that was when Hannah remembered the tactic she'd used at the Lake Eden Inn. There was no reason why it wouldn't work now.

"Oops!" Hannah exclaimed, and dropped her purse. Then

she bent down to pick up the items that had spilled out, moving from spot to spot to retrieve them, and attempting to read Miss Whiting's license plate at the same time.

She managed to catch a glimpse of the top right hand corner of the license plate. It was a graphic of a barn with a silo. Any state in the heartland could have a barn with a silo on its license plate.

"I think my pen dropped over here somewhere." Hannah leaned to the left and searched in the freshly fallen snow. She extended as far as she could and spied the letter "W" on the upper left hand corner of the plate.

She still didn't have enough. The "W" could stand for Wyoming, or West Virginia, or Washington. She needed one more letter to be sure.

That was when Miss Whiting moved three steps to the side, exposing the entire license plate to Hannah's view. "Is that a little easier for you?" she asked.

She knows what you're doing! Hannah's suspicious mind shouted. But as she got to her feet, Hannah told herself that perhaps Miss Whiting had moved over so that more light would fall on the dropped items.

"Thanks," Hannah said, holding the purse in both hands. "I think I've got everything I need."

"I'm sure you do, especially now that you've seen my Wisconsin plates."

"What do you mean?" Hannah did her best to look innocent, but her heart sank to her toes. She was out here alone with Miss Whiting. And Miss Whiting had killed Larry Jaeger.

Miss Whiting took a step closer.

Hannah jumped back.

"What's wrong?" Miss Whiting smiled a chilling smile. "Are you frightened of me?"

There was nothing to be gained by avoiding an answer. "Yes," Hannah said.

"Why?"

"Because I think your name is Bianco. And you shot Larry Jaeger because of your connection with Salvatore Bianco."

"Well, well. You're smarter than I thought you were." Miss Whiting smiled that chilling smile again. "Salvatore Bianco was my father and Larry killed him. Oh, he wasn't there physically, but his finger was on the trigger. And it was all because I convinced my father to invest every cent of his retirement money in Larry's business."

"That's . . . awful!" Hannah's mind was buzzing at warp speed, trying to figure out how she could get away from Miss Whiting. She'd killed once. She had nothing to lose if she killed again.

"Yes, it's awful. I loved him, you know."

"Your father," Hannah commiserated.

"And Larry. I loved Larry, too . . . or at least I thought I did." Miss Whiting reached into her purse and pulled out a gun. "That's enough talking. Walk."

Hannah walked. What else could she do? But she kept talking as they stepped closer and closer to the edge of the hill. "Why did you shoot Larry's television screen?" she asked, even though she already knew the answer.

"That was a mistake, but I got so angry when I saw it."

"Because of Hollywood Home Theater?"

"Yes. I let my anger get in the way of my good sense, and I left an arrow pointing in my direction. If I'd just killed Larry and walked away, you never would have connected me with his murder. No one but you put that last piece together. You're a good student, Hannah. I could make you into an excellent C.P.A. You have a logical mind and it's a pity I have to kill you."

Her goose was cooked if she didn't do something. They were at the edge of the parking lot and Hannah's eyes darted left and then right, searching for some avenue of escape. That was when she saw it, the stack of Sliders the shop class had made. If she could just throw Miss Whiting off balance, she could grab one and . . .

"That's far enough," Miss Whiting ordered, and the steely tone in her voice told Hannah that this was the time to act. She whirled around, threw her purse directly in Miss Whiting's face, raced to the rack, and grabbed the top Slider. Even though she wanted to turn and see if Miss Whiting had recovered from the blow she'd received, Hannah just held the Slider to her chest, took three steps to the precipice, and hurtled over the edge into space.

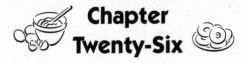

She landed so hard it knocked the breath out of her body, but somehow Hannah managed to hold onto the Slider. She slid several feet before she got the hang of it, just in time to keep from hitting a huge pine tree. She had to pull up on one of the handholds cut into the side, and push down on the other to change her course so that she could avoid obstac . . .

There was a loud pop and almost immediately something whizzed past her ear. Miss Whiting was shooting at her! She must have recovered from the blow to the head quickly because . . .

There was another loud pop, but this time Hannah didn't hear the whiz. She didn't feel anything either and that meant she hadn't been hit.

Hannah pulled up on the right handle just in time to avoid a hillock that certainly would have overturned her like a turtle and left her soft underbelly exposed to Miss Whiting's bullets. And speaking of bullets, how many did she have left?

Hannah tried to remember the gun she'd seen in Miss Whiting's hand, but it was no use. All she could visualize was the round, dark hole in the end of the barrel, the hole that would release the bullet that would end her life. As she zoomed down the hill, she thought of the ballistic tally that Mike had given her. One shot in Larry, three in the flat screen TV. That meant four shots were gone, and most revolvers had six shots . . .

didn't they? Miss Whiting had just shot once past Hannah's ear, and once more only the winter birds in the trees knew where. That was a total of six shots. Miss Whiting could be out of ammunition, unless she'd reloaded after she'd killed Larry.

Another shot hit the snow about three feet in front of Hannah's Slider, kicking up a puff of snow that almost blinded her for a moment. Another shot thunked into a pine tree ahead of her and to the left. Forget the revolver and counting shots. It seemed Miss Whiting had plenty of ammunition. All Hannah could do was hope that the business teacher knew more about balance sheets than bull's-eyes.

Hannah gasped when she saw a thicket of prickly thorn bushes dead ahead. She twisted and turned the handholds on the Slider, desperately seeking to change her course and avoid what promised to be a painful encounter. Delores was right. She'd never been able to steer a sled by herself, but at least, this time, it wasn't a tree!

There were several moments that occurred in slow motion, reminding Hannah of several movies she'd seen. There was her hand on the Slider twisting, twisting to no avail. There was a single gust of snow, peppering the smooth skin of her cheek. There was her mouth, open in a silent scream as the Slider moved inexorably forward. And finally there was one barbed thorn as big as the sun, quivering in anticipation of her arrival.

And then real time took over and she hit the prickly thorn bushes. Hard. Still tumbling forward, she smashed into the spiked branches that attempted to make ribbons of her skin.

Perhaps the freezing air acted as an anesthetic. Or perhaps she was simply too frightened to feel much of anything. Hannah wasn't sure which theory was accurate, but something kept her from feeling the sting of barbs and the sharp pricks of thorns. She jumped to her feet, grabbed her Slider, and ducked behind the biggest tree she could find.

Her rational mind, the one her would-be killer had praised

just moments ago, was thankful that her Slider was forest green. It would blend in with the winter foliage and perhaps escape Miss Whiting's notice.

Hannah huddled against the pine tree and wondered how long it would take Miss Whiting to find her. There was probably a path left by her Slider from the top to midway down the hill. Miss Whiting would see it and know that Hannah was here. She had to move.

Risking a glance at the top of the hill proved almost fatal. A bullet thudded into the pine tree where Hannah was attempting to hide. She'd been spotted. The Slider had left a telltale trail.

Hannah's mind flew through the possibilities. Would Miss Whiting climb down here to kill her? And where was Mike? Mike always rescued her when she was in trouble. Didn't he have some sort of sixth sense that told him when someone was about to kill her? Mike always came to the rescue.

Another shot brought Hannah back to the present with a snap. She had to move again. Right now! The only question was whether she should crawl, or hold up the Slider as a shield and run to another big pine tree.

It was dark and overcast, with snow still falling in flurries. The wind whipped up, providing a perfect opportunity, and Hannah crawled through the snow straight back from her pine to the pine behind it.

When she got there she waited expectantly, but there were no more shots. She'd made it! She wanted to stop and rest, but it couldn't hurt to put one more tree between her trail and Miss Whiting.

Hannah dropped to her stomach and prepared to crawl once more. She felt like a crab as she inched her way back, pushing with her feet and pulling with her hands against the snow-packed earth. She was halfway there when she heard a sound that couldn't have been made by the wind, or the snow, or any forest creature. It was click of metal against metal, and she looked up to see Miss Whiting standing over her.

"Good try," Miss Whiting said, leveling the gun directly at Hannah's head. "One shot through the brain should do it. It's a pity to waste a good mind, but it can't be helped."

It was over. She'd run out of options. Hannah shut her eyes and wondered whether her life would flash before her eyes. It didn't. All she could think about was Moishe and how she hoped Norman would take him and give him a good home with Cuddles. She's miss him dreadfully, and even though he was a bad boy at times, he was *her* bad boy.

And then she heard the shot. It was loud and it hurt her ears. Miss Whiting had shot her through the head. Her life was over. She was dead.

Dimly, she heard a crashing as someone ran down the hill. How could that be? Dead people weren't supposed to hear anything except celestial music. Perhaps she wasn't dead yet. Perhaps she was still dying.

And then she was gathered up into two strong arms, and someone was smoothing back her hair. Not dead, then. And the arms and the hand felt good.

"Are you okay?" Mike asked, lifting her up into his arms.

"I . . . think . . . so." The words were an effort and it seemed to take forever to speak them.

"Don't worry. She's dead," Mike said, carrying her up the hill. "Just relax, Hannah. Lonnie's coming to cover the crime scene and I'm taking you straight to the hospital."

"Miss Whiting shot me?" Hannah asked, fearing the worst.

"No, but you need to take care of those scratches on your face. And you might have a concussion from running into those thorn bushes so hard. I need to make sure you're okay."

Hannah smiled, even though it hurt to do so. Mike cared. But she couldn't resist asking, "Why?"

"Because I'm worried about you."

It was a good answer. Hannah's relief at being rescued and happiness at being alive grew even stronger as Mike bent down to place a light kiss on her lips.

"You have to get well in a hurry so you can cook that bang-up Christmas Eve dinner you promised to make for me."

Chapter
Twenty-Seven

The mood was festive and the guests around Hannah's dinner table were enjoying the excesses of the season. It was Christmas Eve and candles glowed softly down the length of the folding library table Hannah had borrowed from Marge Beeseman. Andrea's shiny gold tablecloth graced its surface and Michelle had helped Hannah make the edible place cards. They'd wrapped tiny truffle boxes that contained one chocolate raspberry and one white chocolate apricot truffle in Christmas paper with the guests' names written on the top. Delores had arrived early to set the table and she had rearranged the place cards so that Hannah was seated between Mike and Norman. Again.

Christmas carols were playing softly in the background. Hannah's sound system and Moishe's Kitty Kondo were still in place, but every other stick of living room furniture had been moved to other rooms to make space for the long table.

"Your tree looks so good," Michelle said, taking another cracker with Shrimp Louie Spread.

"It certainly does . . . except for the mice," Delores said with a delicate little shudder. "They're just too realistic for me!"

"They're not too realistic for Moishe," Mike said, watching Hannah's pet go after one of the mice on the tree.

They'd solved the problem of the Christmas tree without caging either the tree or the cat. Mike and Norman had been frequent visitors the weekend Hannah had spent recovering from her near brush with death and her thorn bush injuries, and they'd caught Moishe in action. Both men agreed that something had to be done, but they didn't want to admit defeat and take down her Christmas tree. There had been measurements, discussions of pulleys and levers with Rick and Lonnie Murphy, and a trip to buy the necessary hardware. Hannah had gone back to work on Monday, and by the time she'd come home that night, her tree had been reliably cat-proofed.

"It turned out okay," Norman said, gazing at the tree. "It's not exactly your normal tree, but it's better than no tree at all."

Hannah agreed wholeheartedly. She'd grown to like her upside-down tree, hung by its trunk from a pulley attached to the highest point of the exposed beam on her cathedral ceiling. It was fully decorated with lights, glass balls, and Great-Grandma Elsa's remaining two birds, the way any regular Christmas tree would be. And just in case Moishe felt frustrated because he could no longer climb it, Mike and Norman had hung six new toy mice on almost invisible fishing line from the tip of the tree. Since the tip was almost four feet from the rug below it, Moishe could bat at the mice to his heart's content without any danger of coming into contact with the tree itself.

The Christmas Cheese Round was almost gone and the Shrimp Louie Spread was going fast. It was time to start serving the first course. Hannah rose to her feet, and headed for the kitchen, followed by Michelle, Andrea, and Tracey.

"What can I carry, Aunt Hannah?" Tracey asked. "I promise I won't drop anything."

Hannah reached out to give her niece a little hug. "I know you won't, honey," she said. This was the first Christmas Eve that Tracey had been allowed to help instead of staying at the table with Grandma McCann and Bethany, and she was taking her duties seriously.

The first course was Holiday Squash Soup. It was accompanied by condiments of sour cream and parsley. The soup was hot and would be dished up in the kitchen and carried to the table in individual bowls.

"How would you like to carry the sour cream?" Hannah asked her, knowing that her sisters could easily handle the trays with the bowls of soup. "I can follow you with the parsley. You'll have to hold the bowl while people take some."

"I can do that," Tracey said. "Do you think a lot of people will want sour cream?"

"Grandma Delores will. She loves sour cream. And I think Mike and Norman will, too. And then there's your dad, and maybe Grandma McCann, and . . ."

"So it's almost everybody!" Tracey looked delighted with her assignment.

Once the soup was served and everyone had embellished their bowls with sour cream and parsley, Hannah went back into the kitchen to stage the rest of the meal. She took the Jeweled Pork Roast out of the oven and set it on a rack to cool slightly before carving, and then she found the perfect platter for Andrea's Jell-O. Unmolding it was almost always an easy task because the Jell-O had ridden in the back of Andrea's Volvo on the trip to Hannah's condo, and the vibration from the road had already done the lion's share of the work.

The serving platter went over the top of the ring mold Andrea had used for her Jell-O. A quick flip of Hannah's wrists turned the mold upside down, and once she'd given it a little shake, she heard the Pineapple Cranberry Jell-O Salad break loose and settle down on the platter. Hannah lifted the ring mold and smiled. Andrea really was the Queen of Jell-O. This one was as pretty as a picture.

The Christmas Bell Salad was next. Hannah had prepared

it an hour before the guests were due to arrive and it was waiting in a bowl in the refrigerator. She took it out, pulled off the plastic wrap she'd used to keep it fresh, and set it next to the Jell-O on the counter.

The salted water was gently simmering for the Petite Green Pea Boats and Hannah turned up the heat. Then she went to the refrigerator to get the "boats" she'd made by removing the fruit from orange halves, and arranged them on a pretty platter. When the water was boiling, she put in the petite frozen peas, and gave Michelle and Andrea the high sign. It was time to stage the rest of the meal while Tracey carried in the empty soup bowls.

Andrea and Michelle knew exactly what to do. They'd worked it all out in advance. Andrea stuck the toothpicks with the little sails on the orange "boats" that would receive their cargo of buttered petite peas, and Michelle started the Lingonberry Gravy, which was actually flavored with apricot jam since Hannah hadn't been able to find lingonberry jam.

The peas were ready. Hannah poured them out into a strainer and then quickly doused them in the ice water she had waiting to preserve the bright green color. It took only a moment to toss them with butter, salt, and pepper and spoon them into the boats Andrea had decorated.

The Scandinavian Spuds were waiting in the oven in their ovenproof serving dish. Hannah took them out with her best pair of oven mitts and set them at the end of the lineup on the counter.

"Pork roast, gravy, and we're done," she said, grabbing a cutting board and her electric knife.

The Jeweled Pork Roast sliced like a dream. Hannah cut it into one-inch-thick slices and transferred them to her meat platter. By the time she was finished slicing, Michelle had poured the gravy into the pitcher Hannah preferred to use in place of a gravy boat, and they were ready to serve.

"What do you want me to carry, Aunt Hannah?" Tracey asked.

"How about all the serving utensils?" Hannah scooped up the meat forks, serving spoons, and the cake server she'd been planning to use for Andrea's Jell-O salad, and plunked them into a basket. "All you have to do is follow us to the table and we'll get the serving utensils from you."

Hannah turned to look at the counter again, and frowned. "I'm missing something," she said. "I wonder what it is."

"Bread?" Tracey guessed. "You always have rolls or something, don't you?"

"Good call!" Hannah praised her, reaching up to grab the towel-lined basket of Cranberry Scones she'd removed from the oven shortly after her guests had arrived. "Is everyone ready?"

There was a chorus of assent from Michelle, Andrea, and Tracey. Hannah stepped to the front of the line with her Jeweled Pork Roast and within moments they'd lined the long table with the dishes that made up their festive meal.

Hannah took her place at the table. There was nothing more for her to do until it was time for dessert and coffee, and she was looking forward to enjoying the fruits of her labors.

Other than the occasional "Mmmm!" from one diner or another, they all ate in contented silence for several minutes. And then, when ravaging appetites had been partially appeased, the conversation began to flow again.

"Did you hear what Nancy is going to do with Larry's money?" Delores asked them.

"Who's Nancy?" Michelle asked.

"Dr. Love," Delores answered. "She's Larry Jaeger's legal widow."

Mike looked interested. "I haven't heard."

"Neither have I," Carrie said, and Hannah noticed that she was holding her fork in left hand so that she could hold hands with Earl.

"She's going to refund the money to all of Larry's investors."

"There's *that* much money?" Michelle was shocked.

"There's more than enough," Delores told them. "Nancy and Courtney went through all of Larry's papers. They found the ledger he used to list the investors in every business he ever owned and they're writing checks to all of them."

"So is your name on the list, Earl?" Delores asked him.

"Not mine. I went out there to talk to Larry the night Hannah saw me. He wanted investors for the spa he was planning to open in Duluth. I asked him a couple of questions about financing and I didn't like his answers so I turned him down flat."

"Smart man," Carrie said, smiling at Earl.

"I'm really glad you think so," Earl said, and smiled back.

"I have some news about the show." Michelle said, putting down her fork. "Did anybody see the DVD we made of my number in the Christmas Follies?"

"I did," Hannah said, grateful that her sister had shown it to her. While Michelle had performed her song and dance number, Miss Whiting had been shooting at her in the woods.

"There's an important money man in New York who likes it. He says he might finance the show if he sees a couple of the other numbers performed live."

"You're going to New York?" Delores asked, barely able to contain her excitement.

"That's right, Mother. We're leaving on Monday and we're going to his theater to perform it for him."

Andrea began to frown. "But what if he decides he wants you for the part and he offers you a contract? Will you take it and live in New York?"

"Oh, you don't have to worry about that," Michelle said with a laugh. "He wouldn't want an unknown college student like me!"

The conversation turned to other things then, but no one mentioned Miss Whiting. Mike was handling the fact that he'd killed her to defend Hannah quite well, but no one wanted to broach the subject.

When everyone at the table had put down their silverware

and leaned back slightly in their chairs, Hannah gestured to her sisters and they began to clear the table for the dessert.

The coffee was ready. Hannah had dashed to the kitchen to flick the switch midway through the dinner. Now she transferred the coffee to a serving pot and took down the tray she'd prepared earlier with cups, spoons, and sugar. Once the cream had been added to the tray, she sent Andrea out to serve the coffee while she put on a second pot. Then she scraped and rinsed dishes, and Michelle slipped them into the dishwasher.

When Andrea came back, she put away the leftovers, stashing them in the refrigerator. "All done," she said, wiping down the counter where they'd staged the dinner.

"Time for dessert," Hannah announced, handing them bowls of Hard Sauce and Soft Sauce, and giving them both a little shove toward the living room. "You go sit down. It'll only take a couple of minutes."

"Tracey's all ready with the lights," Andrea informed her. "She knows her cue word. She wrote it on her arm with a felt-tip pen."

"Uh-oh. I hope it's not a permanent marker," Michelle said.

"It may be, but it'll wear off eventually."

When her kitchen was sole occupancy again, Hannah got out the bottle of brandy she'd purchased specially for this occasion, and poured some in a small saucepan. She turned on the heat, warming it slowly as she lifted the domed cover on her cake carrier. Her Minnesota Plum Pudding sat inside, and it was going to be a spectacular dessert.

The brandy was almost warm enough. Hannah could see the vapors rising toward the overhead lights. She heard the doorbell ring and Michelle call out that she'd get it. Her friend from college had arrived right on time!

Hannah pulled the saucepan from the heat and drizzled the brandy over the top of her plum pudding. Then she picked up the long lighter she used to light the pilot light on her gas fireplace whenever it blew out, and held it close to the top of her dessert.

When the brandy ignited, Hannah made a circle over the top with the lighter. It was flaming beautifully and it was time to give Tracey her cue.

"Don't you just love Christmas Eve?" she called out, watching the light level in the living room. Tracey must have been standing right by the switch, because the room went dark almost immediately.

From the glow cast by her upside-down Christmas tree, Hannah carried in her spectacular dessert. She set it down in the center of the table and looked up with a smile as everyone applauded.

"Bravo! Well done!"

A deep voice praised her, and Hannah recognized it in an instant. It was the same voice that had murmured sweet nothings in her ear, told her she was the only woman for him, and promised her he'd love her forever. Her startled eyes darted to the chair they'd saved for Michelle's college friend and met the gaze of Bradford Ramsey.

SHRIMP LOUIE SPREAD

Hannah's Note: This is best served well chilled with a basket of crackers on the side.

8 ounces softened cream cheese
½ cup mayonnaise
¼ cup chili sauce (*I used Heinz*)
1 Tablespoon horseradish (*I used Silver Springs*)
⅛ teaspoon pepper
6 green onions
2 cups finely chopped cooked salad shrimp***
   (*measure AFTER chopping*)
Salt to taste

*** - *It's best to use frozen cooked salad shrimp that you've thawed according to package directions and dried on paper towels. You can also use canned salad shrimp, but they will be more salty, which is why you should salt to taste after everything is mixed up together.*

Mix the cream cheese with the mayonnaise. Add the chili sauce, horseradish, and pepper. Mix it up into a smooth sauce.

Clean the green onions and cut off the bottoms. Use all of the white part and up to an inch of the green part. Throw the tops away.

Mince the onions as finely as you can and add them to the sauce. Stir them in well.

Chop the salad shrimp into fine bits. You can do this with a sharp knife, or in the food processor using the steel blade and an on-and-off motion.

Mix in the shrimp and check to see how salty the spread is. Add salt if needed.

Chill the spread in a covered bowl in the refrigerator for at least 4 hours. You can make it in the morning if you plan to serve it that night.

Yield: Makes approximately 3 cups.

HOLIDAY SQUASH SOUP

2 ten-ounce packages winter squash (*the kind that's in a solid block and already pureed*)
½ cup chopped onion
2 teaspoons chicken bouillon beads (*or whatever measure it gives to make 2 cups of chicken broth*)***
2 cups heavy cream
¼ teaspoon pepper
8-oz package cream cheese, unwrapped and softened in the microwave for 1 minute

sour cream and/or parsley for toppings

*** - You can use a can of condensed cream of chicken soup instead of the bouillon beads, but then you'll have to reduce the cream to one and a half cups. You can also use the bouillon cubes, but you'll have to mix them with a VERY small amount of hot water and mash them before you put them into the blender.

Hannah's Note: If you don't have a large enough blender to do this all at once, blend half of it at a time and stir it all together when you get it in the crockpot.

Cook the squash according to package directions, drain it and put it in a blender.

Add the chopped onion and the chicken bouillon beads.

Add the heavy cream.

Zoop it up in the blender and make sure all the onion pieces are pureed and the mixture is smooth.

Add the pepper and the softened cream cheese.

Zoop it up again until it's all smooth and then dump it in the crockpot you've sprayed with Pam.

Once your soup is in the crockpot, give it a final stir and taste a little bit for seasoning. If it needs more salt, DON'T ADD IT. Add another teaspoon of bouillon beads instead to make it really chickeny. If you want to make your soup sinfully rich, this is the time to cut a half-stick of butter *(4 ounces, ¼ pound)* into little pieces and throw them in the crockpot.

Turn the crockpot on LOW and cook for 4 hours. *(This can go an hour or two longer if your company doesn't arrive on time.)*

Check for seasonings again right before serving. When you dish it into the bowls, you can top it with a dollop of sour cream and a sprinkle of fresh parsley if you like.

Yield: approximately 4 cups.

Hannah's Note: If your soup gets too thick in the crockpot, thin it with a little chicken broth.

PINEAPPLE CRANBERRY JELL-O SALAD

6-ounce package raspberry Jell-O
1 and ¾ cup boiling water
16-ounce can jellied cranberry sauce
8-ounce can crushed pineapple *(do not drain)*
¾ cup orange juice
1 teaspoon lemon juice *(freshly squeezed is best)*
½ cup chopped walnuts

Dissolve the Jell-O in the boiling water. Stir for at least 30 seconds to make sure it's dissolved.

Add the cranberry sauce and stir until well blended.

Add the pineapple *(with the juice)*, orange juice, lemon juice, and walnuts.

Mix everything together and pour in a ring mold.

Refrigerate until firm. This should take about 4 hours, but you can make it the night before your dinner and keep it in the refrigerator until you're ready to unmold it and serve it.

Hannah's Note: Andrea got this recipe from Sally Hayes.

CHRISTMAS BELL SALAD

1 large red bell pepper *(cleaned, seeded, and cut into thin strips)*

1 large yellow bell pepper *(cleaned, seeded, and cut into thin strips)*

1 large green bell pepper *(cleaned, seeded, and cut into thin strips)*

6 green onions *(cleaned and minced—use up to one inch of the stem)*

¼ cup chopped fresh parsley

4 cups fresh spinach *(or a bag of spinach salad from the store)*

½ cup golden raisins

½ cup roughly chopped nuts *(I used walnuts)*

⅛ cup *(2 Tablespoons)* raspberry vinegar *(or red wine vinegar)*

¼ cup extra virgin olive oil

¼ cup white sugar

Freshly ground black pepper

¼ teaspoon salt

Hannah's Note: If fresh bell peppers are not available in your area, use a bag of frozen, multi-colored bell pepper strips. Let them thaw naturally in your refrigerator overnight and dry the strips with paper towels before using.

Assemble the pepper strips, onions, parsley, and spinach in a large salad bowl. Mix in the golden raisins and nuts and toss.

Put the vinegar, olive oil, sugar, pepper, and salt in a small bowl. Whisk them until they are well blended.

You can dress the salad now and refrigerate it for up to an hour, or dress and toss it at tableside.

Yield: Serves 4 to 6 people.

JEWELED PORK ROAST

5-pound boneless loin of pork, center cut
2 bags mixed dried fruit***
3 Tablespoons butter
3 Tablespoons virgin olive oil
Salt
Freshly ground black pepper
1 cup white wine
1 cup heavy cream
Extra milk

*** - *My bags contained prunes, peaches, pears, apricots, and apple slices. I used some of every kind. Even though I'm not fond of prunes, they were excellent inside the pork roast!*

Cut your pork loin into 2 pieces. Each piece should be no longer than 8 inches.

Stand one piece of pork loin on the cut end and run a barbeque skewer all the way down the middle lengthwise, just like you're skewering a giant hotdog from one end to the other.

Move the skewer around and turn it to enlarge the hole you've made through the middle of the pork loin. If you have a second skewer, push it in right next to the first skewer to assist in enlarging the opening.

When you've enlarged the hole as much as you can with the skewers, withdraw them and insert the handle of a wooden spoon. Again, twist it around to stretch the meat

and enlarge the hole. Work at this until the hole through the middle of the pork loin is large enough for you to insert your finger.

Lay the fruit out on a sheet of wax paper so that you can pick and choose. This is going to be an awe-inspiring entrée if you alternate fruit color as you're stuffing. Start by examining the prunes to make sure they're pitted. You don't want one of your guests to crack a tooth!

Insert a prune into the hole. Push it down to the halfway point with your finger or the end of the wooden spoon. Follow that with an apricot, then a pear, a peach, and two apple slices. Insert as much fruit as you can stuff into the hole.

Now go at it from the other end, stuffing the fruit in random order, alternating types and colors. When your piece of pork loin is chock-full of fruit and it's practically popping out the ends, either skewer the ends closed or sew them closed with kitchen string and a large needle. *(I lived dangerously – I just left mine open and was very, very careful when I browned the pork.)*

Repeat with the second half of the pork loin and then heat the butter and olive oil in a skillet large enough to hold both pieces of pork.

Brown the outside of your pork roasts, turning them with tongs so that they're brown all over. Salt and pepper your pork as you go so it's seasoned all over.

Take out a roasting pan large enough to hold both roasts and deep enough to also hold the cream, wine, and milk. Spray the inside of the roasting pan with Pam or another nonstick cooking spray and pour in the white wine and cream.

Place the roasts in the roasting pan. If you haven't sewn or skewered the ends closed, try to jam them up against each other and the sides of the pan so the fruit won't fall out during baking.

Pour enough milk into the pan so that the liquid comes halfway up the sides of your roasts.

Cover your roaster with the lid or with a piece of heavy foil tucked down around the sides, slip it into the oven, and turn the oven on to 350 degrees F.

Bake the roasts for 2 hours or until the meat no longer resists when poked with the tip of a sharp knife.

Remove the pan from the oven. Remove the foil or cover carefully—steam will escape. Then remove the roasts from the pan and place them on a cutting board, cover them loosely with foil and let them rest for at least 10 minutes. *(15 minutes is okay, too.)*

Throw away the liquid in the pan. It won't make good gravy.

When your Jeweled Pork Roasts have rested, use a very sharp knife to slice off the very ends. Then slice the roasts into 1-inch thick pieces and arrange them on a platter.

Pat yourself on the back when you carry the platter to the table and everyone oohs and ahhs. You deserve it.

Yield: Serves 6 to 8 guests.

LINGONBERRY GRAVY
(OR APRICOT IF YOU CAN'T FIND
LINGONBERRY)

Hannah's Note: This is not homemade pork gravy. Since you cook the pork in milk, you don't have all that wonderful brown stuff in the bottom of your pan that makes gravy taste so yummy.

If you want to make this the way my grandma did and you can find lingonberry jam, by all means use it. If you can't find lingonberry jam, you can substitute apricot jam, seedless raspberry or blackberry jam, or even apple jelly.

3 packets of Pork Gravy Mix *(I used Schilling's—the kind that makes 1 cup of gravy for each packet)*
Extra packet of Pork Gravy Mix
½ cup lingonberry jam *(or your choice of a substitute jam or jelly)*

Make the 3 packets of Pork Gravy Mix following the directions on the package. When it's ready, add the half-cup of lingonberry jam *(or substitute.)*

If the jam thins the gravy too much, use as much of the other gravy package as you need to thicken it.

SCANDINAVIAN SPUDS

12 baking potatoes, about 4 inches long and
    2 inches wide
2 Tablespoons softened butter *(¼ stick, 1 ounce)*
8 Tablespoons melted salted butter *(1 stick, 4
    ounces, ¼ pound)*
1 teaspoon salt
2 Tablespoons dried crumbled sweet basil *(I used
    Spice Island sweet basil)*
1 teaspoon paprika
4 Tablespoons bread crumbs *(I used the flavored
    kind)*
8 Tablespoons cold salted butter *(1 stick, 4 ounces,
    ¼ pound)*

Choose a bowl large enough to hold all of the potatoes
and fill it with cold water. Add a teaspoon of salt and a squirt
of lemon juice to the water. Set it on your counter and . . .

Peel a potato, rinse it off, and find a wooden spoon or
serving spoon that will cradle the peeled potato almost
halfway up its sides. Put the spoon on a bunched up towel
on the counter so it won't roll from side to side, and nestle
the potato inside. Turn the spoon sideways so that the long
side of the potato faces you. Start about a half-inch from the
end and slice straight down in quarter-inch intervals, stopping a half-inch from the other end of the potato. The bowl
of the spoon will stop your knife from cutting through the
potato all the way so that it's only partially sliced. Drop
the partially sliced potato in the cold water so that it won't
discolor and start in on the next one.

Hannah's Note: The peeling and slicing of the potatoes can be done several hours in advance as long as you store them in cold, salted water in the refrigerator.

If you do slice all the way through a potato, don't worry. Just bump the two pieces tightly together in your baking pan when the time comes and no one will be the wiser.

One hour and ten minutes before you want to serve your potatoes, preheat your oven to 425 degrees F., rack in the middle position.

Once your oven comes up to temperature, the potatoes will take about one hour from start to finish.

Choose a baking pan that will hold all of your potatoes in a single layer. If you don't have one that large, use two smaller ones.

Use the 2 Tablespoons of softened butter to coat the inside of your baking pan. *(If you have a pretty one that can be carried to the table, by all means use it!)*

Take the potatoes out of the water and pat them dry with paper towels. Place them in the buttered pan, cut side up in a single layer.

Drizzle the melted butter over the tops of the potatoes and sprinkle on the salt.

Sprinkle the Scandinavian Spuds with sweet basil and paprika.

DO NOT sprinkle on the bread crumbs yet.

Place your pan in a 425 degree F. oven, UNCOVERED, and set your timer for 30 minutes.

When the time is up, take your pan out of the oven and sprinkle the bread crumbs over the top of your potatoes *(the slices will have spread out a bit so some will go between the slices)*.

Melt the cold stick of butter. Drizzle it over the top of the breadcrumbs.

Slip your pan back into the oven, uncovered, for an additional 25 minutes.

Test your potatoes to make sure they're done by spearing one gently with a fork. If it shows no resistance, take the pan out of the oven and let the potatoes cool for at least 5 minutes before serving.

Yield: 12 potatoes.

You can cut this recipe in half, of course. Or you can double it if you've invited Mike to your Christmas Eve dinner. He's been known to eat three on occasion.

CRANBERRY SCONES

Preheat oven to 425 degrees F., rack
in the middle position.

3 cups all-purpose flour (*pack it down in the cup
when you measure it*)

2 Tablespoons white (*granulated*) sugar

2 teaspoons cream of tartar (*important*)

1 teaspoon baking powder

1 teaspoon baking soda

½ teaspoon salt

½ cup softened salted butter (*1 stick, 4 ounces, ¼
pound*)

2 large eggs, beaten (*just whip them up in a glass
with a fork*)

1 cup unflavored yogurt (*8 ounces*)

1 cup sweetened dried cranberries (*Craisins, or their
equivalent*)

½ cup whole milk

Use a medium-size mixing bowl to combine the flour,
sugar, cream of tartar, baking powder, baking soda, and salt.
Stir them all up together. Cut in the salted butter just as
you would for piecrust dough.

**Hannah's Note: If you have a food processor, you can
use it for the first step. Cut ½ cup COLD salted butter into
8 chunks. Layer them with the dry ingredients in the bowl
of the food processor. Process with the steel blade until the
mixture has the texture of cornmeal. Transfer the mixture**

to a medium-sized mixing bowl and proceed to the second step.

Stir in the beaten eggs and the unflavored yogurt. Then add the sweetened dried cranberries and mix everything up together.

Add the milk and stir until everything is combined.

Drop the scones by soup spoonfuls onto a greased *(or sprayed with Pam or another nonstick baking spray)* baking sheet, 12 large scones to a sheet. You can also drop these scones on parchment paper if you prefer.

Once the scones are on the baking sheet, you can wet your fingers and shape them into more perfect rounds. *(If you do this and there are any leftovers, you can slice them in half and toast them for breakfast the next morning.)*

Bake the scones at 425 degrees F. for 12 to 14 minutes, or until they're golden brown on top.

Cool the scones for at least five minutes on the cookie sheet, and then remove them with a spatula. Serve them in a towel-lined basket so they stay warm.

Yield: Makes 12 large and delicious scones.

PETITE PEA BOATS

One small orange for every 2 guests
Package of frozen petite peas *(or 2 packages,*
    depending on how many guests)
Butter
Salt
Pepper
Crumbled bacon

Small triangles of colored paper for flags
Toothpicks

Cut the oranges in half and scoop out the fruit, leaving two half shells for the boats. You can cut a little off the bottoms of the boats with a sharp knife so that they won't roll on the serving platter. These "boats" can be made a day ahead and stored in a plastic bag in the refrigerator.

Cook the frozen peas according to package directions. Drain them, and then toss them with butter, salt, and pepper.

Arrange the "boats" on a serving platter. Attach the paper flags to the toothpicks and stick the end of the toothpick into the white part of the orange peel so that it will stand straight up.

Fill the Petite Pea Boats with peas, sprinkle them with crumbled bacon, and serve.

HANNAH SWENSEN'S CHRISTMAS EVE DINNER

Christmas Cheese Rounds
Shrimp Louie Spread
Holiday Squash Soup
Pineapple Cranberry Jell-O Salad
Christmas Bell Salad
Jeweled Pork Roast
Lingonberry Gravy
Scandinavian Spuds
Cranberry Scones
Petite Green Pea Boats
Minnesota Plum Pudding Flambé

PLUM PUDDING
MURDER RECIPE INDEX

Baking Conversion Chart

These conversions are approximate, but they'll work just fine for Hannah Swensen's recipes.

VOLUME:

U.S.	Metric
½ teaspoon	2 milliliters
1 teaspoon	5 milliliters
1 tablespoon	15 milliliters
¼ cup	50 milliliters
⅓ cup	75 milliliters
½ cup	125 milliliters
¾ cup	175 milliliters
1 cup	¼ liter

WEIGHT:

U.S.	Metric
1 ounce	28 grams
1 pound	454 grams

OVEN TEMPERATURE:

Degrees Fahrenheit	Degrees Centigrade	British (Regulo) Gas Mark
325 degrees F.	165 degrees C.	3
350 degrees F.	175 degrees C.	4
375 degrees F.	190 degrees C.	5

Note: Hannah's rectangular sheet cake pan, 9 inches by 13 inches, is approximately 23 centimeters by 32.5 centimeters.